"Do you rea   confess a conspiracy against your father?"

"Yes." Jeff struggled against the police drugs.

"Do you expect the court to put him under truthall?"

"I want to see him questioned as rigorously as you are questioning me. I want him to reveal how he forged my father's signature and prints on the incriminating papers. I want him to confess how he spacejetted my father into exile and death on Alpha IV. George McKissic has to testify. He has to be shot full of the same drug I am under."

"That," said the judge, "is impossible. A man of Mr. McKissic's stature need not subject himself to interrogation—his unimpeachable record as a leading citizen speaks for him. The ends of justice are better served by stopping criminals, not harassing reputable patrons.

"And you—not George McKissic—are the enemy to society."

THE RING

Tor Books by Piers Anthony

Anthonology
Dragon's Gold (with Robert E. Margroff)
The E.S.P. Worm (with Robert E. Margroff)
Ghost
Hasan
Pretender (with Frances Hall)
Prostho Plus
Race Against Time
The Ring (with Robert E. Margroff)
Shade of the Tree
Steppe
Triple Detente

PIERS ANTHONY AND
ROBERT E. MARGROFF

THE RING

A TOM DOHERTY ASSOCIATES BOOK

This is a work of fiction. All the characters and events portrayed in this book are fictitious, and any resemblance to real people or events is purely coincidental.

THE RING

Copyright © 1968 by Piers Anthony and Robert E. Margroff

A TOR Book
Published by Tom Doherty Associates, Inc.
49 West 24 Street
New York, NY 10010

Cover art by Don Maitz

ISBN: 0-812-50104-7   Can. ISBN: 0-812-50103-9

First edition: August 1986

Printed in the United States of America

0 9 8 7 6 5 4 3 2

CONTENTS

I. 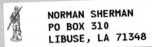 A Twist in Crime

1

THE wall was high, the night chill. Mutant crickets sang, unafraid of the intruder, providing a cover of sound that masked the inevitable noises of his ascent. Glossy foliage swayed against the wall in intermittent gusts, throwing speckled moon-shadows that camouflaged the climber's motions. Nature was cooperative—but the mechanisms of man that lay ahead would not be kind.

Jeff Font heaved his body to the top and lay flat against the lingering warmth of the stone. His chest labored, but he forced air through his nostrils steadily, smoothly, allowing his body to recover from the exertion. The wind cut into his eyes, bringing tears—for a moment carrying him to a time he had cried as a child for another reason, not so very far from this spot.

But this was not the time for such memories! He had to slash away the hypocrisy that had destroyed three lives and elevated a usurper.

The moon faded. Jeff's hand slid across the inner edge of the wall, finding the rope and its adhesive plastoid terminus. He worked it free, coiled it, and dropped it into the darkness ahead. He listened for the muffled impact and shivered in Earth's exterior climate.

The moon returned, flooding the enclosed grounds and the mansion beyond with its radiance. Jeff gathered his black fiber cloak, checked the four bulbs nestled in its fastened pockets, rolled over and dropped the shorter distance to the inner garden. The wind whipped up his cloak as he fell and fingered his naked body. He hit the lawn and tumbled behind shaped shrubbery. The damp green odor of cut grass rose about him as he found the rope in the dark and set it against the wall; then he began running.

The incredibly opulent home of George McKissic loomed before him, in this light a psychedelic skeleton of translucent timbers. Jeff dodged around the nude statuary, the woman-shaped pool, the suggestively curvaceous pathways and hedges, resenting the wasteful space they occupied in an overcrowded world, and the impact the symbols were having upon him. He tried to concentrate on the heat-perceptor units he was sure were there, the subsonic emplacements, the nightbeams. One miscalculation, one distraction would expose him, and that would be his exit.

He reached the house, again restraining his urgent breathing, and stood within its shadow. He had made it! Unless McKissic had converted to silent alarms. . . . But no; his informant had been positive on that score. Jeff had to assume that his precautions had been effective. There was no metal on his body, not even in his teeth, and he had studied the estate defenses intimately.

A sound? He listened, far more anxious now that he was stationary than while he moved. A routine noise, carried by a freak of the wind; a sniffing, shuffling. . . .

The hounds!

He had almost forgotten the hounds! The giant synthetics with bulblike noses, steelbone fangs, supercanine speed . . . watchdogs, partly flesh, partly metal, mostly savagery. Electronic circuitry for nerves, computer cells for brains and a taste for blood.

Prickling uncomfortably, Jeff felt in a pocket for one of the soft bulbs. His thumb touched the circular cavity in its base; his fingers closed about its small mass. Moving as though there were no hurry, he nipped the spout with his teeth. A few drops squirted into his mouth: the quintessence of machine oil, mansweat and fermented animal urine.

He suppressed the gag reflex and spat the stuff out gently. It was intended for the caninedroids, not humanoids. He aimed the nozzle at the ground and sprayed a tight little circle. He moved over and squirted a second, larger circle intersecting the first; then, as the bulb gave out, he dropped it in the center. There was no certain technique to foil the hounds, but this was his best hope. He stepped back spitting again.

A shimmering above betrayed a balcony rail of glastic. He leaped for it, caught hold and swung his body astride. He had performed similar maneuvers many times on Alpha IV, and the poor light was hardly a handicap. Glastic was transparent in varying degrees so that plants could grow beneath it, but it withstood stress as well as steel. McKissic's entire house seemed to be made of it.

Eight feet above the ground, he shuffled along what appeared to be midair. How easy it would be to omit a single panel, and thus dump the intruder into the house! But no—not with the exotic ornamentals he could see growing beneath, black-leafed in the filtered moonglow. McKissic might not care whether a visitor fell, but he would hardly permit his valuable plantings to be crushed!

Jeff walked beside the opaque second-story wall, matching the architecture to the floor-plan he had memorized. He stopped. This was the room—the one she should be sleeping in. The panel was secure, and he knew better than to try to break it physically. A full blow with a sledgehammer would make a very small scratch—and a very high-decibel noise.

He reached for the second bulb. He knew which pocket it occupied, but his fingers quested over the surface again, reading the pattern of indentations in its base. Two circular depressions, this time. Check. He brought it out, handling it with greater care than he had the first, though he knew it was quite sturdy until the seal was broken.

He paused. The hounds had come up; he could hear their distinctive snuffling within fifty feet. They could not reach him here—they were too stupid to desert the trail long enough to come at him by way of the stairs farther along the wall. If they were not entirely deceived, they would bay—and he would be finished.

He could make out the gross hulks of them, noses swelling and shrinking like breathing balloons, occasional glints from their metallic haunches. *And what rough beast*, he thought, knowing the words for a quotation but unable to place it, *its hour come round at last . . .* The rest was lost. He reprimanded himself once more for delaying unnecessarily; why he remembered such fragments he could not say.

The hounds trotted aimlessly, sniffing the spray-pattern: they had not bayed. The scent was working.

He unwound the tape and depressed the special tap to break the interior seal, pointing the nozzle away from his body. He touched the tip to the glastic surface and squeezed. The potent acid welled out and dribbled thickly down; he could trace its descending shadow.

His hand moved unsteadily. He was afraid now, and he suspected that the dangerous fluid he employed was a flimsy pretext. It was what lay beyond this entry that set his pulses pounding. *Who* lay beyond. . . .

Two tiny tri-pronged suction clasps to hold the pane; five minutes for the acid to eat through. He set the empty container aside, knowing that it too would disintegrate before morning, now that air had activated its content.

Three minutes. His muscles tightened. Fourteen years—and now a wait of a few more minutes was tearing him apart!

Time. He pushed against the panel, and it broke loose easily. Holding tight to the suction handles, he tilted it endwise and maneuvered it out. It would not be safe to touch for several minutes, until the acid neutralized itself on the overdose of glastic. He set the panel flat, pried off the handles, listened momentarily for some possible alarm, and stepped into the room.

Except for the opaque floor and the interior furnishings, it was as though he were still on the balcony. He glanced back through walls that were completely transparent from inside, and wondered what kind of person would revel in the illusion of exhibition. He had been plainly visible all this time, had anyone watched. . . .

There was a breathing. The hounds? No—it was gentle and even. It was the whispering respiration of her he had come for, audible in the utter stillness of the bedroom.

Pamela.

He had made his entry quietly, but not without some unintentional noises. Either Pamela was a sound sleeper, or she had taken a depressant. No matter—if it was sleepnol, a second dose would not harm her; if something else, there was unlikely to be any adverse reaction.

He found the bulb with three dents and a hard glastic cap. He uncovered the needle and aimed it, weaponlike. He trod silently to the bed.

A beam of moonlight descended slantwise through the ceiling and haloed the enormous full-circle mattress. Jeff stared at the form outlined by the clinging, static-charged sheet. God, she was a woman! He had not seen her since she was a child of eight, and hardly knew what she looked like now, but the sight of that body was reassurance enough. He could imagine the curves and valleys and the secret shadow places—and had done so, until this moment.

He leaned over her, his shoulder intercepting the beam and throwing her head into a delicate penumbra. He studied the fair curve of her cheek, the sleek diaphane of her hair spread out upon the pillow, the tilt of her face up and a little to the side. Even so might a girl sleep in the arms of her lover. Even so—but not tonight.

He brought the needle to her exposed neck, an inch away, and held his other hand above her mouth in case she tried to scream. He squeezed the bulb; the spray shot across, a jet so fine he couldn't see it in the shadow. Her breathing paused, then she sighed faintly and relaxed again. She had not really struggled against the drug. She hadn't tried to scream.

He looked about. Her robe was hanging neatly beside the bed. He fetched it and laid it out upon the sheet. His fingers pinched the edge of the covering and tugged it back.

She was wearing a sheer nightgown. He was relieved not to have to dress her. As it was, he had to concentrate to keep his mind on his mission. . . .

He slid his arms under her knees and shoulders and lifted her to the robe. He drew it about her, not bothering with the sleeves, and picked her up again. She was light, as he had expected. The long hair brushed his arm, the glossy black tresses that had fascinated him from childhood . . . Again he had to cut off his thoughts.

He carried her through the hole in the wall and onto the balcony. The dusky forms still ranged below, perplexed by the pattern of scents; if they did not hear him, there would be no pursuit.

He was not supporting his burden properly. He had no hand free to explore the brush and branches of the garden below, or to hold the fourth bulb—the weapon—in case he should be discovered before reaching the wall. He had let his infatuation blind him to business.

He maneuvered Pamela's body into an unceremonious drape over his right shoulder, her slim legs dangling down his front. He walked to the end of the balcony and descended the curving steps there. This was the reason he had taken the more dangerous direct route in: to leave the easier one free for the burdened return. By this time the noses of the hounds should be saturated with the concentrated decoy scent, so that even an upwind passage would not betray him.

He made it without event. He deposited her against the base of the wall and found the coiled rope. He unclamped it, held the end and flung the coil up over the wall; it unwound in air until only the adhesive plastoid remained. This thunked against the far side.

He tested it, making sure the shock of contact had jellied the plastoid enough to adhere firmly to the stone before freezing in place. It had.

This was the most difficult part of the retreat, because he had to scale the wall while carrying the girl—and making no noise. He was ready: he had scaled the cliffs of Alpha IV with heavy loads of explosive, and done it hampered by the cumbersome airsuit. Earth's breathable atmosphere was not the least of its wonders.

This time he had only a few feet to cover and a jar or drop would not blast him across the landscape. Still, the burden was not properly harnessed, and he was out of condition; four years in space had sapped his endurance in gravity, though exercise had maintained the muscles. He had been surprised by his exhaustion when he scaled the wall coming in. Now he had a harder job to do.

He shifted her to lie facing him across his shoulders and biceps, so that he could grip the rope with both hands without worrying about her support. He could do it with a quick effort, then recover on top of the wall before going on. This time he did not hesitate. He hauled on the rope and walked up the wall, wedging his chin against the girl's hip to keep her from sliding off to the side.

He manhandled her to the top, rolling her roughly over his forearms to lie on the stone, and clambered up beside her. He had done it—but this time it was impossible to quell his tumultuous panting. The wind played over his body, refreshing now, although he knew it was colder than before.

A bright column of light stabbed through the foliage and splashed against the wall. One of the rolling mechanicals! Jeff pressed the girl flat and covered her as well as he could with his cloak, knowing that the patroller would not leave its runway unless it became suspicious. He had not won free yet. If it spotted him—

He fumbled into the last pocket, cursing mentally as the folds of the tunic bunched resistively, and worked out the bulb. He held it lightly, his fingers tensed and quivering as though eager to break the restraint of the mind and crush its flexible shell.

The robot halted, its searchlight steady. Jeff knew what that meant. He crushed the bulb and held it, waiting.

The shadows of the trees leaped along the wall as the beam moved—and the machine rolled on, silently. Incredibly it had missed them.

Jeff sighed. The worst was over, and he knew he would not get a break like that again. He remembered the grenade he held. He could not let go now, since it had been activated by the pressure of his hand against the key grooves. It would go off upon release.

Well, he no longer needed it. He flipped it back the way he had come and ducked his head. One, two, three seconds . . . then a whistling puff, silence.

He looked. Taffylike white strings were draped over several cubic yards of bushes, an eerie network. Had that bomb struck in the vicinity of man, animal or machine, that target would have been severely entangled. The plastoid strands would stretch but not break, and were exceedingly sticky and slightly corrosive.

Jeff smiled. It was said that robots never lost their tempers, but this stuff brought them marvelously close to it.

He adjusted the rope, made the descent, and carried her across the phosphalt pavement to his rented monocar. It had almost been too easy, apart from that one scare.

The car was standing at less than a fifteen degree angle, tilting west. Good—that meant he had been gone less than an hour, despite the time the adventure had seemed to consume. He had had to do without a watch, since some of its works were metallic and would have activated the estate sensors. But a gyrocar was both compass and clock. It held its position without regard to the motion of the planet, which meant that it leaned to the west—when parked—at a rate of fifteen degrees per hour, unless set on its side with the gyro oriented east-west. Let Earth spin, fashioning day and night—the gyro was indifferent.

He deposited the girl in the front seat, watched the safety harness clasp her firmly, and activated the drive motor. He turned up the gyro, allowing it a moment to accelerate from standby torque, then got out and trod on the south bumper. The vehicle resisted, but slowly responded by tilting east, righting itself. That was precession: the gyro converted the stress he put upon it to a force acting at right angles. Such correction of a gyro's attitude was elementary physics, and the average driver did it routinely without being aware of the complex theorems defining the action.

White light again, turning the road dark. One of the roving highway robots was coming. McKissic certainly was well guarded! Jeff could not hope to outrun the cruiser in this middle-aged vehicle.

Well, if he could not run, he could pretend. He jumped into the car and shoved the steering bar out of the way. The police mechanicals were notoriously stupid, and programmed to ignore certain types of activities. Theoretically the colossal Vicinc industry provided for all needs of the flesh—but the lads and ladies still parked in the country lanes.

The spotlight swung over the shrubbery, igniting it in jumping patches as though a will-o'-the-wisp were dancing. Jeff leaned over to kiss Pamela.

The beam cut between them, illuminating her face and blinding him with its dazzle. He shielded his eyes with one hand, seeing the black-haired afterimage as he recovered. The cop was coming in to investigate!

"Damn flattread!" he muttered. The machine should have swerved away once it picked up the embracing figures—unless it had other instructions. Unless McKissic had already discovered the abduction of his daughter.

He gunned the wheeldrive, grabbed the steering bar, and slapped the reverse button. Dry sticks crackled under the single tire as it bounced over the side embankment, and the gyro vibrated against the stress of uneven terrain.

He braked and leaned back to allow his own seat harness to secure him, while the cop pulled up at the side of the road. He could discern its outline now: one of the large monorobots, equipped to clamp on to a speeder and bring it to terms in a hurry. Already the antennae were extended, tracking his car precisely, and the grapple-arms were unfolding.

Jeff's hands played over the controls. His car shot forward. He braced himself for the crunch of metal against assorted other materials as his vehicle careened into the side of the police robot and spun off, upright but out of control. The gyro could not protect against motion aligned with its own plane. He accelerated again, letting the wheel catch at the road and steady the car; then he was off, down the lane and away from the cop.

It did not follow. Its headlight shone aimlessly in the opposite direction, and Jeff could see by the reflected light that its antennae were bent. Between them, in the dark, the purple night-glow of the phosphalt surfacing reappeared. He had succeeded in putting the cop out of commission!

His own car seemed to he virtually undamaged. Had he struck the robot at any other time, it would have been a different story; only when its arms were extending was it vulnerable—if caught by surprise and from the proper angle.

His own headlamp picked out the winding drive ahead. Soon he would intersect the main highway, where he could lose himself in the traffic congestion, and be safe. Then he could take Pamela to his—

Pamela? Suddenly he remembered the blackness of her hair, in his eye's afterimage, as the robot's beam played over them.

That image should have been the opposite color, since it was a reaction to eyestrain.

The girl beside him had short blonde hair.

A siren wailed behind him, and lights flashed in his rear vision screen. The cop had summoned help—and this time there would be no element of surprise based on his off-planet driving experience to jog him loose. Not from several policebots, forewarned. They were not *that* stupid. And there would be others waiting to head him off at the highway.

He was committed now. Without further hesitation he swerved off the road, maintaining sufficient speed to crash over the underbrush. The car's headlamp picked out the small tree-trunks looming ahead, and he navigated desperately. The gyro would keep him upright, but guaranteed nothing else, cross-country. One had to be aware of the limitations of modern technology as well as the advantages, in such a situation.

He hated to think of the path of destruction he was carving through this valuable wilderness preserve.

The pursuers had not followed. They would be afraid to do even more damage to officially protected countryside— that was one advantage a lawbreaker had. The relief would be transitory, however—they would keep him under radar observation and be on hand to arrest him when he hit the highway again, unless he acted rapidly and unexpectedly. If he dallied too long, they would send a floater in after him.

He gave them no time. He had memorized a map of the area when he set this up, and he knew where he was going. He wrestled the car out the other side of the woods, hoping the tire would stand up to the punishment, and charged up a steep embankment. He landed on an abandoned freight road, overgrown but retaining a hard underlying bed, and followed it two miles into a current freight artery.

This would take him all the way into the city—but it was dangerous. He did not know with what frequency or velocity the monster trucks came by at this hour of the night. He had not had time for research in depth.

He learned. Ahead he saw a band of light the size of a historic football field, and knew that one of the house-sized vehicles was already bearing down on him. The trucks were so massive they did not use gyros; they had clusters of wheels at every extremity.

He cursed under his breath. This was no good. Nothing to do but take to the wilds again. He drove up the opposite embankment, over, and down into a rocky stream-bed. Behind him, the truck roared by, traveling at a hundred and seventy-five miles per hour, a juggernaut in the night.

Top speed for his car was hardly over a hundred. He could not even merge with that traffic!

The vehicle bounced out of the stream and struck an ancient stone wall. It caromed off, dislodging several of the irregular rocks, and the wheel began to slide back down into the stream. The uneven support exerted stress on the gyro, and precession nudged the car to the side. He steered it to level ground and shifted his body as far as he could to counter the effect; the seat harness and the girl's inert weight made the task awkward.

The gyrocar was a magnificent development, and it had revolutionized transportation—but a driver with the wrong reflexes could kill himself in a hurry. Jeff's reflexes were good. He had been brought up on gyro theory, and this was Alpha IV driving at its suicidal best.

Now he was at the edge of a cultivated field. Hydro-ponics and related projects took care of the great majority of Earthly dietary needs. Only the very rich could afford the conspicuously wasteful consumption of organic pro-duce. The land alone would be worth millions—

He had little sympathy for the ostentatious rich. He steered for the field. Two wire fences were strung between him and the next road, and no policebots were in sight yet. He could make a clean escape if the wire was flimsy enough—if it was electrical or barbed. If the fences were of the acid-coat variety—

He accelerated and crashed through the first. The strands stretched and snapped, making an almost musical jangle. He churned through low foliage, wincing in spite of himself at the damage he was doing to someone's phenomenally valuable crop, hurdled a narrow ditch and struck the second fence.

The wire broke again—but fine lines of color spread across his windshield. Acid: it would eat through both glastic and metal in a few minutes, but if it hadn't touched the tire he could make it into the city before the car gave out. At least he was going to try.

Such wire would never have been used had there been animals about. Probably robots tended the crop, programmed to stay well clear. What, then, was this deadly fence guarding against? Surely drivers did not make a habit of . . . unless people who could not afford such luxuries liked to make raids. Yes. . . .

The threat to his car was exaggerated, as it turned out. The farmer had been careless, and the acid was evidently too weak to do more than etch. There would be wholesale firings tomorrow.

He drove on down the highway, now an anonymous part of the traffic, thinking about the significance of the countryside he had traversed. Earth's population problems had been solved: that is, the rate of increase had been stabilized at an acceptably small percentage. Regular programs eliminated the original, random housing and substituted domiciles capable of servicing a hundred times the population on the same land area. In this manner, the schooltexts claimed, the cities maintained their original boundaries—that is, those existing at the arbitrary year 2000—while population continued to grow. Countryside remained—in moderation.

He reached the city-proper without further trouble and guided the car down into the parking levels under his hotel, hardly aware of what he was doing. All he had to worry about was the girl. The girl he had gone to such pains to kidnap. The wrong girl.

He knew he ought to leave her in the car and take the next flight to parts uncharted. He had no power over McKissic any more, not with this girl instead of Pamela. He had been outsmarted, and he had lost. It would take them only a few hours to run down his identity, and he had to be far away by then. She was a liability.

He walked around the parked car, released the harness and lifted the girl out. She was beginning to regain consciousness; that meant that there had been no prior dose of sleepnol before the one he had given her. He would have to watch her carefully—but before he let her go, he would know why she had taken Pamela's place. It was an obvious set-up, no mistake about that: she had had dark hair when he'd taken her from her bed. A wig, obviously; it must have been shaken loose and fallen during the escape, probably when he'd lifted her over the wall.

But he might still be able to salvage something from this episode. How had McKissic known his plan in advance? Could this girl tell him?

(Or was he simply that hungry for female companionship? She had cheated him of his mission. What did she owe him in return?)

Her feet were bare. He held her upright while he reached

inside the car for the slippers he had bought. He had thought to put them on Pamela's dancer's feet. . . .

As an afterthought, he touched the disconnect stud, so that the gyro would not fight the props. He did not expect to use this car again soon, if ever; someone else could align the gyro properly when the time came. Tonight it would rotate with the motion of the planet, unconnected to the chassis.

He got the girl's feet covered and walked her down the street—more properly, hallway. One parking lot connected to the next, under the city buildings, so that it was possible to travel quite a distance without coming up for air. If one cared to keep under the twelve mph limit, at any rate. The timing machines reacted in a hurry against speeders.

She was coming out of it, but her responses were those of an automaton; her mind was still under. He kept a good hold on her arm, in case she was pretending. Susceptibility differed.

His hotel presented no problem. It catered largely to Vicinc habituees, and would not pry into the affairs of clients. Vicinc: *Vice, Incorporated,* now legitimate business. Once industry had gained the right to police itself, vice had not been far behind. (That wasn't quite the way his schooltexts had put it, however.) Anything at all was legal, so long as all parties concerned were willing and of age. Willing, anyway. Since the victims were generally presumed to be *un*willing in cases of robbery and murder and, rarely, rape, crime as a legal concept still existed; but Vicinc had mushroomed into the world's most prosperous enterprise.

A Vicinc contact had provided Jeff with the devices he required to neutralize the McKissic estate defenses, as well as the map and house layout. The merchandise had been good—excellent, in fact. He had not been cheated there.

Now he wondered: had Vicinc also sold its services to the other party? That would have been good business—and a timely warning for McKissic. Yes, that must have been the way of it; it explained everything. The warning to Jeff Font was even more timely. He would work alone henceforth.

The girl was coming alert. Sleepnol usually freed the physical resources before the mental ones—a fact every man knew well and most women purported not to know. He had to get her to his private cell before she made a scene.

He marched her into the archaic elevator and punched for the tenth floor. The battered doors closed; the intermittent light came on, and the lift shuddered tediously upward.

Jeff studied the girl closely for the first time. Her blue eyes flickered at him, not coquettishly, and her close-cropped blonde head nodded. Now, given time to grasp the whole of it, he was appalled.

He had planned to kidnap Pamela McKissic—but not to harm her. He had hoped to persuade her of the justice of his cause, so that she would remain with him willingly—and thus technically exonerate him of any crime. Without her he had nothing. McKissic was too powerful to be brought down by ordinary means.

Instead, he had a stranger. She had worn a black wig, and in the haste and dark he had never seen it fall away. Probably the house defenses had been turned off, because there was nothing for him to steal. No wonder it had seemed so easy!

He scrutinized her face. Yes, she was older than Pamela would be. This woman was pretty, and more than pretty; she could have done well enough at Vicinc—as perhaps she had. Perhaps she had been supplied, a physical double to Pamela, to bait the trap. . . .

The elevator jerked to a halt. He led her out, hoping that no one would see them. It was not that there was any impropriety in bringing a woman to his room, or that anyone in this Vicinc subsidiary would care if there were— but she was obviously drugged. A drugged female was not, by common-law definition, "consenting." The derelicts that dwelt in cells all around his own would notice, probably with approval and envy, and he could not afford the attention.

Some, unable to afford the luxury of young, clean flesh, might attempt to ambush him. He could handle that. The man who could not defend his acquisition had no business bringing it here, and he knew the hotel ground rules: proprietary disputes had to be settled with natural weapons. Fists, elbows, knees, heels, teeth. Even spittle—the mixtures that some men chewed were deadly when hoisted at the eyes. Any gangup of more than two to one was frowned upon unless the prize was particularly rich. All this was prepared for—but not the official notice a scuffle could attract.

The hall was empty. Praise the lateness of the hour for that! He guided the girl along the passage, keeping her moving by repeated nudges in the back. She was on the verge of complete consciousness, and it would be wise to have her securely locked in his room when it happened. The moment she realized where she was—

They rounded the corner. His door was only a few feet farther down. If she screamed now, he could—

Too late he saw the man. A big man with a monstrous paunch and face discolored by cheap depilitant. Clothes old-fashioned and shaggy. A typical slum citizen standing directly outside Jeff's room.

He halted, considering the best way to handle the intruder quietly. The girl, unnudged, coasted to a stop.

Money—or a quick karate chop?

"Flont," the man said, spotting him. His voice was like the motors of an accelerating truck. "Been waiting for you. Have to tell you something."

Then Jeff placed him: the proprietor of the junkyard from which he had rented the car. "What are you doing here?" he demanded, nervous because of the girl's incipient awakening. "I paid cash in advance, and my time's not up."

The man—"Big Ed," the sign had said—advanced a step and focused unbecoming brown eyes upon him. "Have to tell you—that car's a fake. Can't drive it. I brought another for you, same price." His breath resembled that of a truck, too—the exhaust from the drivemotor vents.

"You're mistaken. I've already driven it, and it's in fair condition with a good gyro and sturdy tire." The girl's eyelids were flickering again, as though she were trying to make up her mind about something confusing. She was. "If that's all—"

"I mean it's a fake registry. Cops get one look at the plates—"

His meaning penetrated. "You rented me a stolen vehicle?"

"I didn't mean to. Honest, Flont. I didn't know until I checked the new listing. Soon's I found out, I spun right over here to—"

As though he weren't in enough trouble already! Driving a stolen car! It was a good thing he had eluded the police—and no wonder they had closed with him so rapidly. The robot scanner would have reacted instantly to the proscribed number. What irony it would have been—picked up for an inadvertent crime before anything was known of his real one.

Actually, it had been quite thoughtful of Big Ed to search him out, to warn him. Jeff had gone to Gunnartown to equip himself because that was where the law was loosest and Vicinc best established, and he had noticed Ed's sign on the way in. The man had a well-placed lot almost under the skyway. A simple business deal: a renovated unicar for a modest rental, no questions asked. Ed owed him nothing more.

"They'll haul us all into court," Ed said. "Truthall—"

Truthall! The savage interrogatory drug. Naturally they would question closely the possessor of a stolen vehicle. Naturally, too, a Gunnartown junkyard operator would have many secrets to conceal. Truthall would ruin him. Ed acted out of stark need, not generosity.

"A policebot did see me. I lost it, but—"

Ed sagged somewhat. "Then I have to flatten the car. So they can't trace it to me. Where—"

"Third parking mezzanine, left wing, about a hundred yards down," Jeff said, locating the parking spot. He handed over the magnetic key. Without that disk of flux, the drive motor could not run. Ed grabbed it and lumbered down the hall.

That had worked out nicely. In covering his own traces, Ed would also be covering Jeff's. The problem was self-canceling. *That* problem.

The girl was standing beside him, confused. He caught her arm and led her into his room. It occurred to him that she was just as dangerous to him as the stolen car. More dangerous, in fact. She would be able to identify him positively. It might be best to lock her in and run for it now. Before she really saw him.

But no—that kind of retreat was not his way, however

wise it might be. And—she was still a woman. Though he knew things were different on Earth, he could not rid himself of the attitudes engendered by frontier upbringing. A woman—any woman—was a precious thing.

He closed the door and turned on the light, an antique incandescent globe. His eyes moved over the shabby furnishings, the dresser, the bunk, the open closet. He had left the messiness in a particular pattern, and it was undisturbed: he had not been invaded while he was gone. Not, at any rate, by any clumsy neighbor.

He led the girl to the bed and let her sit naturally. He leaned against the wall, facing her, hesitant to begin the interrogation.

She did not look like a Vicinc creature. Her face was smudged and her robe creased, but apart from similar tokens of the rough journey over the McKissic wall and the cross-country drive, she appeared to be an innocent person. Still, McKissic must have known what he was doing, using her; Jeff hoped the girl herself did.

Her eyes focused upon him. Yes, she was almost classically beautiful, in the bones of her face and the complexion of her skin—or had been, a few years past. Now age or possibly emotional strain was beginning to perform its less delightful sculpturing. Perhaps she was one of the housemaids; McKissic had always selected his employees for both decorative and functional intent. Did he use them hard?

"Mmmmm, mmmmm, mmmmm," she said, speaking with the typical sleepnol cotton.

Jeff stepped into the bathroom alcove and drew on a pair of tights underneath his cloak. He had had to make his raid without them because of their inseparable metallic threads; only the cloak was guaranteed free of such.

The girl was conscious when he returned. "You, my

lady, are in trouble,'' he said, staring into her gradually animating face.

But she was better off than he.

2

> *We mortals cross the ocean of this world*
> *Each in his average cabin of a life;*
> *The best's not big, the worst yields elbow-room.*

Judge Samuel Crater reluctantly closed his genuine 1892 volume of the *Poetical Works of Robert Browning*, savored the enduring wisdom of that Victorian metaphor, and peered over his bench at the assembled citizens.

They sat respectfully in the jury box, seven nervous people distinct as individuals yet indistinct as a panel. He had seen so many similar collections that it was nearly impossible to remember them beyond a day and pointless to try.

His eye lingered momentarily upon the erect bosom of the brunette young woman on the right. Feminine fashion, during the past century or so, had ranged from voluminous coverage to almost total nudity, and today it was possible to glimpse anything. Literally, he thought. He fathomed intellectually that the two deliciously bulge-conical breasts were actually shaped from lesser flesh by opaque padded supportive stretch fibermolding tinted nude. Certainly—but half-hidden as the items were by the glastic chain-mail overjacket, the effect was realistic enough to stir even those who had long known better.

His gaze wandered beyond to the empty, plush-cushioned benches tiered at the rear of the courtroom. *The best's not big, the worst yields elbow-room,* he thought, and smiled. Marvelous how relevant Browning could be!

Later in the morning these seats would begin to fill. There would be tourists to gawk in wonder at the perfectly standard proceedings, classes of six-year-olds to make notes for their upcoming quiz on "Contemporary Judicial Systems," retirees playing "Second Guess the Computer" . . . none of them really concerned with the significance of what transpired. Attendance would be spotty, unless a ringing matter came up; then the hall would overflow and the 3V pickup would cut in so that every frustrated citizen could enjoy vicariously the mercilessly penetrating rape of a personality.

He brought his attention back to the immediate concern. "Citizens of the jury, I am sure you understand that the service you are performing today is not an onerous duty but a privilege of our democratic society. I am aware that it is inconvenient for most of you to devote a full day of your valuable time to what may at first appear to be an unnecessary task, and that the hundred dollars you are paid for this sacrifice is a nominal amount long overdue for improvement, but I assure you that . . ."

He droned on, repeating the speech he had committed to memory a decade ago and delivered three mornings a week ever since. The computer was fully capable of handling his job and that of the jury, but the law as usual lagged behind technology.

Perhaps it was just as well. It was good to have some aspect of this febrile society still reflecting conservative values. As it was, all too often situations arose that would have driven the logical machine to distraction . . . and there were times when human irrationality produced a more fitting verdict than the unimaginative jurybot could.

What was he saying now? He paid attention:

". . . which means that although your names were drawn by computer-lottery, certain guidelines remain. You will notice that the six of you empaneled as the formal jury are three male and three female, five white and one nonwhite, ranging in age from youth to senior status. You are, collectively, a valid cross-section of the functioning makeup of this region, and come as close to a typical peer-group as is compatible with random selection. In this manner we are able to . . ."

In this manner, he thought, the corpulent old judge was able to view regularly what the culture considered normal. Sterile, prepackaged peekaboo breasts flaunted on a woman who would probably go into hysterics if a square inch of natural torso were ever to show. Men whose independent mien and creative spirit were supposedly demonstrated by their dress: with one exception, uniformly somber cloaks. And that exception was a uniform.

". . . so please do not be offended by certain routine questions the law requires me to put to you. Should a defendant insist upon a jury trial today, this verification would be most important, since an improperly empaneled jury would invalidate the proceedings."

He turned to the bosom-flaunting woman. "Juror-designate number one, please state your name and occupation."

"Helia Johnson, housewife," she replied primly. That explained it—the few women who elected not to work had considerable surplus time. She would spend an hour or more every day viewing the 3V fashions, trying to compete with Vicinc models in the privacy of her well-appointed bedroom. "White, female, Protestant, middle class, introvert."

"I see you have served before," Crater said, smiling dutifully. He could have had the information from the police computer at the touch of a finger, but preferred to handle his court as far as possible without mechanical aids. "That does simplify things. Criminal court?"

"Civil court, Your Honor."

"Do you understand that in this criminal court, more than a preponderance of the evidence is required? That you must be certain beyond a reasonable doubt of the guilt of the defendant, whomever he may be, in order to convict?"

"I understand, Your Honor."

"You are heterosexually inclined?"

"Your Honor?"

"A number of the cases coming before this court involve morals charges. Custom dictates that—"

"Oh. Heterosexual, yes," she said with a moue of distaste. Doubtless her husband would have had a word to add to that—a sarcastic one. People seldom realized how much of themselves they gave away by hesitations and facial expression.

"Do you have any scruple against ringing, should this question come up? You would not hesitate to convict if—"

"Certainly not, Your Honor!"

No—she was in fact eager to specify a ringing. It figured. Make the culprits *pay* for their lasciviousness. . . .

He turned to the next, an elderly gentleman with a stylishly white hairpiece. "Designate number two?"

"John Bindlestiff, Auto Sales, retired," he said, somewhat faintly. "White, male, Roman Catholic, middle class, extrovert, heterosexual, and I served twice before in criminal court. I approve of ringing."

"Were either of your juries invoked?"

"No, Your Honor. Standby only. But third time does it, eh?"

"Perhaps." The man evidently assumed the judge remembered him. Crater did not. He turned to the next, a woman of indeterminate age, conservatively dressed. "Designate number three?"

"Sara Seniger, registered prostitute, Vicinc. White, female, Protestant, middle class, introvert, heterosexual."

"You have served in court before?"

"No, Your Honor."

"Do you approve of ringing?"

"No."

"Is this a strong disapproval? That is, would you refuse to convict solely for that reason, assuming that it was a ringing offense?"

"Well, if he was really guilty, I suppose I'd have to go along. But I certainly wish there was a better way."

"Miss Seniger, should such a case come up today, I will have to excuse you. Please understand that this is not a personal reflection in any respect. We can not afford to have a person on the panel whose judgment might be affected by a bias against the probable sentence for conviction, however fair-minded that person might consciously be."

"Yes, Your Honor."

The fourth one, a slightly heavy young man with pink cheeks, spoke without being called. "Bo Czechlich, executive, Androids, Inc."

Andinc. Crater frowned. Last week he had found his blushing pink nude dead in her bed, and roses of that quality were difficult to raise. He suspected some insect offshoot from the supposedly harmless mutants Andinc produced so recklessly. If only the company had stayed with the pseudo-men of its namesake, instead of diversifying into caninedroids, equinedroids, ornithoids, arachnoids . . . only such a grub would be invulnerable to the chemical treatments he employed to protect his flowers.

On the other hand, pollution could be starting up again. There *had* been some other wilting foliage. . . .

He had finished the interrogation of Czechlich. The man was upper class and homosexual, which helped balance this panel in a couple of respects. Things were falling into place fairly nicely, so far. Contrary to theory, the computer did not always manage to balance a jury suitably.

"Janet Hworp, maid," number five was saying. "White, female, Nova-Taoist, lower class—what was the rest of it?"

Crater prompted her on the remaining terms.

"I like men."

"Extrovert, heterosexual," he translated, smiling tiredly.

"But not ringers. They're no good."

He contemplated her, concerned that a second abdication would force him to summon a replacement juror. "Would you refuse to convict for that reason?"

"No. Criminals deserve it. But I don't have to like criminals, do I?"

He passed on to number six, disgusted and relieved. Lower class attitudes were merely balder statements of middle class attitudes, generally.

"Robert Smith, space service," the man said. His uniform had made that obvious long since. "Nonwhite, male, atheist, middle class, extrovert, heterosexual."

Crater glanced askance at him. "How is it that you are on the local jury list?" He inquired only to set the speculations of the other panelists at rest.

"I'm a citizen, and this is where I live. Haven't been home much. I hit 35 last week, and they retired me from ET duty. Guess I'll get a desk assignment once I'm reoriented. My number must have come up soon."

"It happens," Crater agreed. "Some go decades, others get called successive weeks. What was your position aboard ship?"

"Captain. It was a small complement."

"Do you object to ringing?"

"I'm not sure, sir. Don't know much about it. I guess I don't."

"It is not this court's intent to keep you in ignorance, but I must caution you not to seek information from your fellow-panelists. That could lead to prejudicial discussion. For now, I can tell you that ringing is a form of disciplinary probation that insures that a convicted criminal will not repeat the offense during the term of his sentence."

"No, I don't object to that, sir."

Judge Crater came at last to the alternate, a young nonwhite girl of demure aspect. "Mary White, clerical," she said, and there were some smiles. Her credentials were in order, however, and he reminded her that she would serve in lieu of Miss Seniger if a case came up involving a ringing offense.

"Are there any questions?" he finished.

Czechlich, the homosexual Andinc exec, stood up. "Is that the defendant?"

Naivete knew no class distinctions! "There are no defendants yet, Mr. Czechlich," Crater said with a pleasurable shade of condescension, remembering his dead rose. "The police computer will schedule cases as they manifest themselves during the course of the day. I myself am not privileged to have advance information; I only know that there will certainly be a full docket, a portion of which may require the attendance of the jury."

He swiveled to cover the remaining occupant of the room. "The gentleman seated at my left is Harry Webster, the court psychologist." The panel's several heads turned in unison to face the dour man. "Should you serve, you will see much of him." But they rapidly lost interest, knowing a functionary when they saw one.

Janet Hworp, the Taoist maid, rose. "Doesn't truthall hurt?"

Judge Crater refrained from pointing out the irrelevancy of the question. The lower class was particularly leery of truthall, probably for good reason; the poor, it was pertinently said, could seldom afford honesty. "I assure you that truthall, properly administered, is harmless and painless. It merely relaxes the controlling centers of the brain and prompts the subject to answer any questions accurately. There are no side effects and no residual effects. Our Mr. Webster is an expert. Any interrogation he handles in this court will be quite humane."

"You mean it doesn't hurt?" she asked uncertainly.

"It doesn't hurt in the way you mean. It resembles sleepnol more than anything else."

"Oh," she said, satisfied. There were no further questions.

"Meanwhile, should you have any personal needs, you may summon the robailiff."

The jury for the day had been empaneled, and it had taken less than an hour. Crater glanced once more around the pseudowood-paneled court and adjourned the citizens to the common-room. The odds were four to one against official action for this particular group, but one could never be certain when the call would come. Once in a while a defendant *did* demand a human verdict.

After the court was clear—he did not like to exit first himself, which might be considered his personal idiosyncrasy—he picked up his Browning and retired to his chambers. He had a good half hour to relax before his first case was presented. With luck, it would be routine, so that most of the detail could be left to the machine.

Slowly she lifted her arm to her face as the faint rays of the sun lightened the hotel room's dingy window. This was a strange place in which she found herself, a Vicinc outlet by the look of it, and she did not remember how she had arrived.

"You, my lady, are in trouble," he had said, and that was all she knew for sure. Now that man leaned against the greasy wall, staring at her. He was tall, and the long black cloak he wore could not conceal the muscularity, the masculinity of his body. The face under the close brown hair was young and rather handsome, but the lines about his eyes and mouth, even more than the distinctive spacetan, gave him an animal alertness. A man who lived in space long enough to gain such a tan . . . and the way those muscles moved under the cloak, in sudden jumps, as though he were overcompensating for gravity. She remembered that people who spent their formative years on worlds of high gravity developed big muscles, even the women.

The way he looked at her, as though he had not seen a woman in a long time. It had been too long since any real man had aimed that gaze at her. She found herself attracted to him, to his alien vitality, even to his ferocity, though he also frightened her.

He was waiting, silent, grim.

She looked away from him, knowing her eyes were glassy yet and that he could not be sure of the extent of her recovery. The fact that he did not force her to show him was significant. He had brought her here for some reason other than the obvious. He must have drugged her somehow—sleepnol, by the feel of it—but he could have gone to Vicinc if all he wanted was a woman.

Her hand moved to find her robe. It was uncomfortably bunched and twisted about, and the nightgown under it. Her body was bruised in several places, as though she had struggled—yet she remembered none of it. She had gone to sleep—without drugs—in McKissic's—

"Answer my questions," he said harshly. He was under some kind of pressure, and the accent was foreign. The tone was heavy, yet perhaps normal for him. Again: different air, different gravity.

"Your name, miss?"

How quaint, and how polite. He was like the city parks: pleasant on the surface, savage underneath.

"Your name!" Now his voice was imperative.

"Alice Lang," she said quickly. Then, because it had come out shrilly, she repeated it in calmer, more womanly tones, watching him, trying to evaluate him accurately, because her life might very well depend on it. "Alice Lang."

"Why were you impersonating Pamela McKissic?"

"Mr. McKissic requested it. He was afraid someone was trying to harass his daughter."

The man scowled. "You didn't know you were a sacrifice?"

"I knew there might be some disturbance. All I had to do was wear the wig and sleep in Miss McKissic's room for a few days, so that anyone watching from a distance—"

"So you're police."

She had to laugh. "Do I look like a robot?"

"Why did you take this job?"

"Mr. McKissic needed someone resembling his daughter, and I—I was available. I work for him."

"I can imagine," he said darkly, and she realized that he had mistaken her meaning.

"I work for G&G," she said. She moved her foot, but he didn't look at the ring she wore. "Do you mind telling me who you are?"

"Oh." He was suddenly boyish in his embarrassment, and she realized that the savagery she had observed in him before was a surface thing. Now the gentler aspect was beginning to emerge. "Jeff Font. Son of Geoffrey and Ronda Font. Sole survivor of the family destroyed by George McKissic." And he was harsh again.

"Font!" She recognized the name: the former partner of the firm, convicted for some kind of embezzlement. This was that man's son—no wonder McKissic had been afraid for his family! "But you're from off-Earth."

"Alpha IV for ten years and space service for four. Now I'm back on Earth."

"But I thought exiles were forbidden to come back."

"I'm the *son* of an exile. I did good service and won reinstatement."

She looked at him with new respect. He must have done very good service, because it normally took potent influence to bring a man back. "Who spoke for you?"

He was embarrassed again, and she liked him better for it. "I don't know."

She was no longer afraid of him. "So now that you have everything to live for, you're going to throw it away by harassing the family of your father's partner?"

He clenched both fists, turning his back on her—but she could still see the flush of his neck just above the cloak. "Do you know what it was like on Alpha IV?"

"Hot?" she hazarded.

"Damned hot, girl. But heat is something you get used to, and high gravity, too, if you're young enough. You don't need green grass or blue skies, either. All you need are pressurized tunnels and vehicles, so you can breathe and get your rations. I drove ore cars when I was sixteen— down the crumbling mountainside to the transmitters. You know how often some fool convict jumped into one of those transmitters, knowing that living flesh could not be shipped that way? How often I thought about it myself? Just park the gyro and—but I knew I had to get back to

Earth, to settle the score with the man who framed my father. That's what kept my feet careful when I hauled explosive, too. That's what kept me alive. That's all.''

Alice shook her head. He was so sure of himself—and so wrong! He hadn't learned that criminal action was no solution. "So you'll just drug yourself with ignorance, out of spite.''

He whirled to face her, his hand raised to deliver a killing blow. He was capable of it, she was sure; there was something professional about his stance. His face was distorted by rage and loathing.

But he did not attack. After a moment he dropped his hand, somewhat awkwardly. "It was a figure of speech, wasn't it,'' he said.

Why had it affected him so powerfully? "Of course. But it is still wrong to break the law. Kidnapping people— well, you see what happened to me.'' She drew her left foot from the slipper, exposing the wide copper band on the big toe.

He glanced at it. "A homing device!''

He didn't recognize it! He really *had* been isolated. "No. It's what they do to us—now,'' she said.

He squatted before her to study the ring, catching her foot at the heel with one powerful hand. She saw his gaze go past it to the expanse of thigh she knew the posture displayed, and knew right then that his responses in this respect were normal, however strangely he might react in other ways. Of course, *everything* was normal now, but she would have been disappointed if he had turned out to be normal-homo rather than normal-hetero. Suddenly she hoped he would forget about the ring—but no, that thought was dangerous. She had to tell him first.

He was reaching for the metal. "Don't touch it!'' she exclaimed.

He ignored her. She tried to jerk her foot away as his fingers closed on the ring, but she was too late. He took it roughly and twisted.

Pain lanced from her toe and shot up her leg, stunning her. She screamed, knowing it would do no good. How stupid of him, how stupid, stupid—

—But she knew it was worse for him.

His whole magnificent body stiffened, his face a mask of pain. His fingers crushed her foot spasmodically. The cords of his neck stood out as he forced his face around; his eyes strained, trying to fix on her face. Great drops of sweat oozed from his forehead and ran down drum-taut cheeks, mingling with the saliva at his twisted mouth.

With an effort so great it stilled even her scream of agony, he fought for control of his jaw and said:

"I'm sorry."

Then his fingers loosened slightly, and she was able to jerk her foot away. The pain ceased for them both. He fell to the side, unconscious, while she marveled as much at his words as at his astonishing strength of will.

She tried to stand up, but found herself too weak. Already she heard the hum of a steelhead in the corridor.

The cops had come.

II.   Brave New Man

1

THE Assyrians delighted in impaling men upon sharpened stakes and leaving them to die in public display. The Romans modified the technique slightly and called it crucifixion, the principal advantage being the extended duration of misery before expiration. The Christians improved it further as squassation: the suspension of the body with great weights attached to the feet, hoisted and dropped almost to the floor so that the jerk dislocated the joints. It was said that a man could sometimes be disciplined several times in this fashion before his divine soul finally freed itself from his sinful body.

Today's inquisitors achieved the ultimate: they ravished the soul itself.

They crowded in about the door of his self, those two-handed engines, those expressionless and emotionless ones. Close. Too close.

"I demand a jury trial!" he screamed, clutching at as much as he remembered of Earthly custom. "A human court! No machines!"

The reply was lost in sleepnol haze, but the metal specters seemed to retreat for a period. He became aware of a human torture chamber.

The overseer advanced with white-hot sword, sadism twitching in the narrow gray lips, the tapered beard. The hands were long-fingered, womanish. The blade drew near, thin and evil, shriveling the hairs of the captive's body with its ambient energy. It touched—

And left his body whole, while it sank into his being: a jet of spray from a hypodermic, permeating his physical system, reaching for his mind. Truthall!

He tried to scream but could not. The drug had saturated his defenses, leaving him excruciatingly tense—and silent. Vaguely he wondered, in the sane portion of his brain, whether those going under truthall didn't sometimes bite their tongues off or clench their jaws so hard the enamel on their teeth cracked. It did not seem farfetched.

"What is your name?"

Jeff Font! the drug shouted, but he locked his jaw and quelled the uprising. If action was denied him, inaction was not. Stalemate.

"I've never seen anyone fight it like this," someone said, a minute or a century ago.

"Give him a booster shot. It can't hurt him."

Six people were sitting on a shelf, looking down at him. A bare-breasted woman, a white-haired oldster, a young Negro girl, a flabby executive-type man, a Goontown woman—*Gunnar*town, he corrected himself fleetingly, or the drug corrected him, from the hero of Norse legend, husband of Brunhild—and a spacer. A jury! His demand hadn't stopped this demon court after all.

A spacer—at least there would be somebody on his side. No. On the side of justice, the drug corrected him, prying open his confessional mouth.

"Name?"

"Geoffrey Font Junior, commonly called Jeff or Jeffrey."

"Occupation?"

"Formerly, able-bodied spaceman."

The judge's fatherly face and black robes drifted into focus. "There, now that didn't hurt at all, did it, Mr. Font?"

"It did not hurt, Your Honor."

"That's correct, Mr. Font," the judge smiled. "The truth cannot hurt. Truthall cannot hurt."

"Physically," the forensic prosecutor amended.

Their faces swam around him—real faces, human faces mixed with the unliving and the illusionary. No, it would not hurt. Not at all. "There will not be a mark on you," the Turk had promised, and then the pistol shot had exploded deep, deep in the victim's intestines.

He sat, listening to his body spilling out the guts of his ruptured mind. Emotional vivisection was being done and he was forced to witness it and to participate. He was the victim. It was his personality being leadenly raped and splattered. Better a hot pistol ball than this—far better.

The gut had burst. Webster stood before him and tightened the ropes. He was being pulled further and further out of himself.

"Mr. Font, what had you in mind when you raided the McKissic residence?"

"I"—glowing tongs on tongue, eyeballs exploding—"wanted to carry off Pamela."

"You wanted to *kidnap* her. But then why did you kidnap instead the girl who was clearly not Miss McKissic?"

"I—did not know she was not Pamela. She wore a wig."

"But after you discovered your mistake—what then did you intend to do with her?"

"I—I—"

Webster extended the tongs. "What might you have done to this girl, given the opportunity?"

Oh God, he thought. *Is there no council for the defense? No one to halt this maiming of the self, this total and unwilling erosion of my privacy?*

"I would have gone to bed with her. I would have slept with her."

There were no shouts of "Objection!" No horror expressed over the way he was being forced to incriminate himself. No polemics in *this* trial. Only truth. Merciless, all-convicting truth.

His persecutor pressed on.

"You knew Miss McKissic previously?"

"Yes."

"When had you known her?"

"Fifteen years ago. When we were children."

"How had you known her?"

Oh God, not that!

"How, I asked!"

It all came out. Like blood-flecked froth from the mouth of the tortured: the dream, the urge, the phallic thrust.

"We were in a closet. The door was shut. She—she touched me. I had never been touched that way before. She took my hand. She—"

"You misunderstood the question, Mr. Font. Although I believe your answer does have its relevance. You developed what is referred to as a fixation as a result of early and normally meaningless experimentation. What I had meant to ask was: How did it happen that you and Miss McKissic were acquainted?"

Purgatory. Unintentionally.

"Our fathers were business partners. . . ."

"Understandable. And so you and Miss McKissic were—playmates. It would have been almost unnatural if one or the other of you had not become curious about the other's body. And when you were on Alpha IV, you remembered and you fantasied from that?"

"Yes." Dully, woodenly. There could be no further horror.

"If you had kidnapped Miss McKissic instead of this other girl, what do you think you might have done with her?"

"I—I was going to hold her for ransom. Not money, but a confession from her father made to a police official and destined to be carried before a court of law. It was to clear my own father's name that I—"

"Your motives were, I'm sure, commendable. But what would you have done to Miss McKissic? Pamela? Your Pammie?"

He shuddered. Alice Lang was only a few feet away, her pale features set like a coin of platinum in the midst of the dull specters. How could she bear this? How could any woman?

"I—wanted to marry her. I hoped that I could convince her . . ."

"You would have forced her to have had relations with you?"

He strove to deny it. Force? *He*—force? But there had been all those fantasies. . . .

"I . . ." He hesitated, bit his tongue and finally said, "Only if she wanted me to."

"*Only if she wanted you to!* And you would have seen her as wanting you to. What about Miss Lang? Wouldn't she have done as well? Wouldn't you have imagined her as 'wanting you to'?"

The sarcasm was like an acid bath. Yet he had to respond to the questions. There was no way that his squeezed mind could avoid them, seek to evade as he might.

"Miss Lang . . . is very attractive."

"And you wouldn't have raped her?"

"No."

"No?" Webster's echo sounded disappointed. "Not even if she 'wanted you to'?"

"No, not Miss Lang. Miss McKissic."

And Miss McKissic, too, was sitting only a few feet away. Perfect face in repose, beautiful eyes downcast, hands folded modestly in lap. How could she sit still for this? How could she?

Webster cleared his throat. His features underwent some sort of change that left them stern and professional. His voice was all inquisitor.

"What of your exile with your family to Alpha IV? Don't you realize that that was for your father's own good? Can't you accept that he deserved execution? Don't you comprehend that exile was merciful for a man who had embezzled his way through funds and obtained fraudulent patent rights? That your father *stole* the gyrobrake from his trusting partner? Can't you accept all that, at least?"

Jeff strained at his arm-clamps. "NO! NO, NO, NO, NO, NO, NO!"

Webster stepped back and smiled. "Thank you," he said. "Thank you for pronouncing your own incorrigibility."

Jeff slowly relaxed. He had done the worst now, the very worst to himself. He felt as Geoffrey Font Senior must have felt when he stood in a courtroom similar to this one and faced a computer. Like Jeff, his father had given away the worst that was in him because of a skinful of truthdrugs. Truthdrugs—what a deceiving misnomer!

"Your mother," Webster went on relentlessly, "bought her ticket to exile with a vial of acid she attempted to hurl into George McKissic's face. And because the law is just, not repressive, you were allowed to stay with your parents until of legal age to enter the space service. You owe everything to Earth justice and to the generosity of your father's former business partner."

Yes, I owe, Jeff thought. *I owe—but not for generosity. Not while I know that George McKissic bought the verdict.*

George McKissic was there, beside his daughter, listening stolidly. Was there a secret exultation in him? Was he enjoying seeing the son where the father had been?

The truthall slowly faded, taking with it unreality and substituting dullness.

"Did you really intend for George McKissic to confess a conspiracy against your father?"

"Yes." *Yes, a thousand times yes.*

"Did you expect the court to put him under truthall?"

"I anticipated it."

"Why?"

"I wished to see him questioned as rigorously as you are questioning me. I wanted him to reveal how he forged my father's signature and prints and applied them to the incriminating papers. I wanted him to confess how he had spacejetted my father out of the company and into exile. I wanted to tell you how Geoffrey Font died in a mining implosion and how George McKissic was indirectly responsible. I wanted—"

"If you were so eager to testify, why didn't you come in yourself? Why turn criminal?"

"Because the testimony of what is true is inadmissable evidence. It isn't enough for me to say what is true now— George McKissic will have to testify. He will have to be shot full of the same drug I am under."

"That," Webster said, "is impossible. You have opinion, not proof, and expressions of opinion are not evidence. A man may believe himself conspired against without foundation. Mr. McKissic is not a well man and it would be foolish of him to undergo truthall questioning when there is no evidence linking him to any crime. George McKissic is not on trial. George McKissic is not accused of anything."

Except by me, Jeff thought. *And it's plain to see what my accusation is worth.*

"You were, after all, apprehended during the commission of a felony."

Apprehended, apprehended, his internal demons sang.

"Now you have told us of your motive, but what was your *real* motive? Didn't you want to spoil the thing George McKissic held dearest? Wasn't that your motive?"

"No, I—I loved her."

"Loved her? Lusted for her, you mean. You would have held her captive, forced her to have been intimate with you. You would have told yourself she wanted it. That it was for love you were doing this. For love, and for your dear dead and innocent father's sake."

Webster shot a needle into his arm. The injection solidified reality, vanquished fantasy and restored his tongue's volition. He could speak now—speak as he wanted to. For all the good it would do him.

Webster held a glass of water to his lips. Jeff swallowed, spluttered, and watched the empty glass moving away. Webster brought out a cottonite swab and wiped the perspiration from Jeff's face. The interrogation was over.

Jeff was free to look at Alice, at Pamela, at George McKissic, at the silent jury. His mouth seemed dry despite the drink.

"Stand and face the bench," Webster instructed him, no longer seeming so evil now that the ordeal was done.

Jeff obeyed. His legs felt wobbly.

The judge cleared his throat, banged his gavel and grimaced judicially. "So you believe, Jeff Font, that you were justified, though you know your conduct was in violation of the law. Is that correct?"

"Yes, sir," Jeff said. There seemed to be little point in amplifying what he had already said under the drug. He had broken the law because he had seen no legal way to right the greater wrong. What choice was there?

"Ah, but your need for self-justification was never in question. Never for a moment." Hands that showed the stigma of advancing age moved back from the bench and clasped over the front of the judge's robe. "You must realize that *all* criminals feel they are justified, by their own perverted standards. All criminals. Mr. Webster has brought this out many times before this court. You wanted to relive a childhood experience, with certain, ah, embellishments. To that extent you were well within the law. You could easily have patronized Vicinc in a manner far more suitable than you did. They would have provided an extremely realistic replica of the girl of your desire who would have begun where your imagination left off, and for a very nominal fee."

The judge frowned again. It was apparent that he had had occasion to deliver a similar lecture many times before. Jeff had the feeling that Crater did not entirely approve of Vicinc, and disliked dignifying it in court. "But instead you sought to justify your fantasy by adding to it the notion of your father's innocence. Mr. Font, *all* sons of criminals will try to believe their fathers innocent, no matter how preponderant the evidence to the contrary. Your supposition that one imagined injustice to your parent fourteen years ago could justify your present crime is absurd. Felonies cannot and will not be permitted."

All was lost anyway. "Except when your name is McKissic."

"Another intemperate outburst and I will have the medic administer paralysol to your vocal mechanism," Judge Crater said. His eyes, like his voice, were steely now—an expression Jeff was sure he cultivated assiduously. "You are advised to remember that you are no longer on Alpha IV. No doubt you feel that the assignment of a ringed employee to impersonate George McKissic's daughter was in some way unfair. You feel the police should not have acquiesced in such a ploy. Yet the alternative, in the face of the danger which threatened, was to activate the estate defenses—expensive for the owner, and dangerous for the intruder. Mr. McKissic generously decided to provide every opportunity for you to revoke your intent, since he bears you no malice for your father's crime, as his disposition explains. Even when the perimeter guard identified you on the wall with your captive, no action was taken, out of concern for your welfare and hers. Yet you persisted in your malicious plan, damaging the police unit that was sent to apprehend you and wantonly destroying protected property. Finally you attempted to torture your captive physically, though you knew she was helpless. We could hardly permit—''

''Correction, Your Honor,'' Webster murmured. ''It appears he is not cognizant of the nature of the ring.''

Judge Crater paused, surprised. ''Thank you, Counselor,'' he said. He reorganized his discourse. ''At any rate, this action hastened our location of you since it activated the ring's alarm. Now you also feel we should have put the head of General Gyromotors under truthall, like a common miscreant.'' Some of the members of the jury smirked, but not, Jeff noticed gratefully, the space captain. *He* knew how far this differed from the forthright justice of space.

''Well, Mr. Font, the law is intended to protect the innocent, not the guilty. It might have been best to put you under truthall earlier, to determine your exact intent, but of course until you committed a crime you were inviolate. You were protected by this same policy you wish now to abridge. It was George McKissic's right to protect himself and his daughter through available legal means, suspecting that illegal means were about to be employed against him.

He did not resort to unethical coercion, and is to be commended for his delicacy.''

Jeff was certain now that no protest he could make would be effective. But he had to try. ''I would like to know why Mr. McKissic does not voluntarily submit to truthall here and now, if he is . . . innocent. My testimony at least implicates him.''

Judge Crater turned slowly to face McKissic. ''Do you wish to rise to the defendant's challenge, George?''

McKissic stood. He was a large man, fifty but still near his prime, the power of his frame barely concealed by his conservative cloak. His bearing compelled respect, even from one like Jeff who knew him for what he was. ''No, Samuel,'' he said.

Crater returned to Jeff. ''You have your answer. It is not required that a man of Mr. McKissic's stature either subject himself to such interrogation or justify himself for declining to do so. His unimpeachable record as a leading citizen speaks for him. The ends of justice are better served by preventing crime and restraining the criminally inclined, not by harassing the reputable patron. Mr. McKissic's actions have been open. He was concerned only for the protection of his family, and for your own welfare. Why, he even—''

McKissic was standing again, and the judge broke off. He pointed a gnarled finger at Jeff. ''Contrast *your* actions. You did not contact the police or even attempt to communicate with Mr. McKissic. You did not seek legal counseling or utilize any of the numerous channels available to the honest citizen with a grievance. You presented no evidence to the authorities who might have reopened your father's case had there been the slightest reason to do so. Instead you planned and executed the grossest kidnapping. You hardly seem to be in a position to question the motives of your intended victims or the validity of your sentence, whatever it may be. You require elementary instruction in the principles of good citizenship.''

Jeff made no reply. The horror of it was that though he knew the judge was biased, the lecture made sense. He *was* a criminal, and *had* been acting in an irrational manner.

''Jury will now retire to debate the verdict,'' Judge Crater said. ''Ladies and gentlemen, you have already been advised of the criteria upon which to base your decision. You must now agree whether or not the defendant is a present menace to society, and signify your conclusion officially. You will return to your places in the jury box in thirty minutes with a unanimous recommendation, on pain of contempt of court. Dismissed.''

They filed out, six uneasy citizens. Jeff could see that they had received the message as readily as he had. What had he thought to gain by demanding a human hearing? The verdict had been fixed since the time of his arrest; only the paraphernalia was variable.

McKissic and his daughter stood up and moved to the aisle. Evidently even the formalities were over.

Crater spoke to the retreating figures. ''Thank you for attending, George.'' McKissic waved backhanded in reply while Pamela clung silently to his other arm. Even in retreat she was very proper and astonishingly beautiful.

''Geoffrey Font Junior,'' the judge said after they were gone, ''conviction as a menace to society will require an automatic sentence of five to ten years of unqualified good citizenship in the custody of the ring. In view of your evident unfamiliarity with the system, I will give you the minimum. I suggest you meditate upon that, and prepare yourself.''

Jeff decided it would be useless to inquire just what the

ring was. He hardly paid attention as the jury returned to deliver the expected verdict and be dismissed.

"Take your seat," Judge Crater said. Jeff reluctantly returned to the torture chair. Whatever the court planned for him was bound to occur, whether he tried to resist or not. He sat down—and was immediately bound by clamps popping out from portions of the chair.

They meant business, all right.

"Mr. Webster," the judge said.

Webster came, carrying an ornate box. He set it on the table beside the chair and opened it. He stepped back. "Medic," he said.

One of the bulky red and white surgical robots rolled in, equipped with four arms and innumerable supplementary attachments. Jeff had never seen one this close before, and did not relish the meeting.

The med stopped before the counselor/interrogator/psychologist. "Place the ring on this man," Webster said.

The machine rolled to Jeff's chair, extruded two sterile hand-units and proceeded without hesitation. It slid a glastic panel under Jeff's anchored right hand and played a sterilizing beam over it. It aimed a needle at the base of the middle finger and discharged a single jot. Sensation faded almost immediately.

"Forensic medicine has drawn on mythology," Judge Crater said while the med worked, and Jeff listened, fascinated in spite of himself by the operation. The words and the robot's motions melded into one, as though functions of one equation—as perhaps they were. "Roughly: a young prince of the days of yore—a youth very like yourself—misbehaved so persistently that it became necessary to keep him under constant surveillance. At length the court magician"—the judge paused to chuckle at his own pun, while Webster looked wry—"the court magician placed an enchanted ring upon his finger."

The med extruded a scalpel. Jeff flinched as it cut into the joint of his finger, but there was no pain. He did not like to see his own flesh violated like this. Probably he would have been a better bet for torture than he had supposed.

The judge's voice continued: "It was a very special ring. Its property was that it punished the prince every time he did wrong—punished him by pricking his finger." The flesh peeled away from the finger, but no blood flowed. Evidently the coagulant anesthetic took care of that detail. "Of course, our 'ring' is less esoteric, but quite sufficient for our purpose. It is not, as you see, precisely a ring at all." Jeff saw a small ridged disk seated in the box Webster had brought and opened, and began to understand. "It will replace a section of your finger, anchored to the bone and perforated only to permit the penetration of tendons and natural conduits." The surgical instruments worked busily, stripping back the flesh and clamping it. A tiny laser saw cut rapidly through the living bone, avoiding the clumped tendons and vessels. Or was he exaggerating the situation, in his morbid attention? More cuts and clamps, and the med lifted out the disk of bone.

"A small electrical or neural shock that stimulates the pain centers of the area stands in lieu of the fabled pinprick," the judge continued, while the metal disk was inserted where the bone had been and miniature triads of spikes pressed into the marrow on either side to secure it. "It will not disturb you so long as you obey the dictates of good citizenship—the first of which is never to remove the ring or even contemplate its removal by any means except the lawful expiration of your sentence. Should it be severed from your hand or thrown out of commission for any reason, you will have one hour to report to this court for re-ringing, on penalty of being placed upon the robotic 'dead or alive' list. Lateness will prompt an inquest; exoneration of complicity will permit a mere re-ringing on another finger.''

The robot threaded tendons, nerves, blood vessels and lymphatics neatly through slots in the edge of the disk and fixed them in place. The severed ends of the bone were drawn together, riding the spikes, and fitted into the side pockets, where they were sealed by a bed of some thick plasmoid. Flesh was impaled upon the disk's hairlike interior barbs and shaped flush with the rim. Fixation held it in place, so that there was no break between the skin and the gently bulging edge of the disk, which now resembled a true "ring."

The emplacement was complete.

The medic applied a neutralizer, and in moments sensation returned to the entire finger. It stung, but there was no severe pain, and the finger seemed as strong as before. Jeff studied the band, which looked as though set upon the outside of a healthy finger—a trifle tightly, perhaps—and realized that it was very similar to the one he had seen on Alice Lang's toe.

He looked at Alice, who had not left. Silent tears were streaming down her face. She was suffering for him—yet he still hardly understood why. The ring was supposed to shock him if he did wrong—but how would it know? Why was everyone so certain it would change his life? What was the real secret of its operation?

He had a feeling he would soon be finding out—the hard way.

2

"Goddamn the ringin' mess," Ed Bladderwart said,

advancing on his erstwhile assistant. "One lousy, stinking night away from this place and you're acting like you own the whole ringin' yard. Who the hell told you to make a deal with Sam? Who, Flathead?"

Flathead Looey looked up from the motor he was disassembling: the heavy wire coils massed around the axle of a monocar. His thin, ferretlike face looked scarcely human with the good-sized wedge-shaped dent in the forehead. Flathead was not smart, but Flathead survived; he did so by learning who was smarter and stronger than he was.

"Gee, Eddie," he whined, "I didn't mean to do nothin' you didn't want. It looked like a good deal was all. Sam said all he wanted was for you to sell him parts for his cars and forget to put it down in the book. You know. I thought—"

"You're not supposed to think, Flathead. Don't you know Sam works for Slim? The crook who sold me this hot gyro? You tell Sam he's got to see me. Me, not you. You only work here. You get me?"

Flathead was not so stupid that he missed the tone. He straightened up. He looked at Ed's paunch. He looked at the wrench Ed held. It was a very big wrench. "You're the boss, Eddie."

"Don't you forget it," Ed agreed. "I'm the boss, not you. You're nothing." He had to express his frustration and anger at something. He glared at the snakeskin belt on his assistant with the Finnish filleting knife pulled around to the front. Ed knew that the knife was razor sharp and had never been used on the flesh the manufacturer intended. "And get that damned thing out of sight. I'm a respectable businessman, see. You want to show off to them punks in the park, okay, but not while you're working here."

"But Eddie, you wouldn't want me getting cut, would

you? Some of them guys don't like me much. They come 'round, I gotta show 'em ol' Fin.''

"You keep ol' Fin the hell out of sight! Any of them pals of yours wanta fight, you tell 'em the time an place.''

"Gee, Ed, that park ain't Vicinc. Hell, you oughta know what it's like—the guys all say you was tough once.''

"I'm tough *now*!" Ed said, nettled. He sucked in his paunch a little.

"Sure, Eddie, but—''

"You moron! Strap it under your arm like I showed you. Here, I'll fix it.'' He fixed it. "And keep it that way. Maybe some respectable customers come around, I don't want 'em scared away. Now get in this gyro I brought back and drive it into the crusher. I don't want anything left but a wad of metal, get me?''

"Gee, Eddie . . . Okay, Eddie.'' Flathead climbed into the vehicle, not thinking to inquire why a car in good condition should be destroyed in its entirety. That helped, at least.

Ed paused to puff up his last Nonic, inhaling the aromatic smoke while he cooled off. Finally he ambled back to the shack he had to call a home. God, what a night!

As he entered the door he heard Annie puking in the halfmoon. "Goddamn it," he said, and went to the refrigerator. He grabbed a quart bottle of beer—at least he still had some of *that*—from the top shelf, opened it at the sink and gurgled it noisily. The fluid ran over his heavy jowls and onto his dirty T-shirt.

After a long pull he lowered the empty bottle, belched, and dropped it into a crate of trash. The flies buzzed up angrily, then settled greedily upon it. "Annie!" he yelled.

Annie's face appeared around the jamb of the door. She

was exceptionally pale, and she had washed off her usual makeup. "What's up?" he asked her.

"My breakfast, damn you. Also dinner."

Ed sobered. "You really sick, Annie?" He moved over to her clumsily, his big hands seeking her shoulders.

"Damn it, Ed," she said, but she let him take hold of her and even pressed her ample front close. It had been that queenly bosom that first attracted him, too many years ago. His mother had had many babies, all of them sucklings.

"You really sick, Annie?" he repeated, sounding stupid to himself. "You need a doc?"

"I *saw* a doc," she snapped.

Ed had a horrible suspicion. "You mean Blucket?"

She nodded.

"Damn. I thought we—why'd you have to—?"

"Not without that three thou. I skipped the pill last month, 'cause we almost had enough money. But I can't get knocked if we're broke. So I had to get sick."

"Damn," Ed said futilely. "Why didn't you tell me? I thought—"

"None of your business, until I was sure. Figured I'd surprise you." Then she looked at him and softened. "Wasn't your fault you lost the car, Ed. You didn't know."

That damned car, he thought. Three thousand dollars he'd had to send into the crusher, to keep the cops off his tail. Three thou Slim had cheated him. And Annie—

Ed put his hands down and let them clench spasmodically. "That's why you was so hot to get married legal-like." So they could have a baby. He hadn't known that either.

He shoved her away, not harshly, and averted his face. He made it to his old armchair and dropped into it. He hadn't felt like this since that time when he was a kid and the bigger punks cut apart the little soft kitten he had found. Or maybe since the time he had stood back, afraid, and watched his oldest sister get forcibly initiated into a happy-club. He hadn't cried, not one trickle, since the age of ten.

By and by Annie came and sat on the arm of the chair. Her ample hip rested against his shoulder. Her chapped but gentle hand slid over his forehead and began smoothing it the way he liked it. "Poor Eddie, you really wanted a kid, didn't you. Well, maybe we can save up again. Make a good deal—"

He sat there, gathering his forces. Then: "This teaches me a lesson, Annie. A good one."

She waited.

"If I'd had the money I'd've married you and taken you out of here years ago. Nobody who's got money worries much."

"Ed—" Annie said, alarmed. He was speaking too quietly, with too much intensity.

"I'm going to get money, Annie. Any way I can. Try to run an honest business and this's what happens. Maybe Flathead's got the answer after all. Be tough and get yourself somebody smart to do your thinking. Somebody real smart, like that bastard Slim. Make a wad so big—"

"Ed! Don't talk like that. You go messing into that kind of stuff and you'll get—"

"*Not* Slim. Just somebody that smart, get me."

". . . ringed," she finished.

There was that. "Like BettySue," he agreed. "Sometimes I figure it's worth the risk, Annie."

"You don't know, Eddie!" she exclaimed. "BettySue— God, you forgotten what she was like? A zombie, that's what. All her friends quit her cold, 'cause they knew anything they let drop went straight to the cops. Just as soon's she could squeal. She got her own mother arrested, and there went the family income. She couldn't keep a job herself. Vicinc wouldn't touch her. Some loaded Uptowner would paw at her a little bit and she'd holler cop—couldn't help herself. You know what you'd be like as a ringer? A eunuch, that's what. No, worse than a eunuch. A zombie. Like her. And the first thing you'd do is turn me in for—''

"I'd never—" But he knew that it was true. Ringers weren't human anymore. Ed tightened his hands into rocklike fists. He thought of all the fights he'd had and all the smart boys he had known who had made it. And smart gals, too, though not like Annie. Annie was a woman, while they were—pros. But some *had* gotten ringed. . . .

"I'm going to make it," he said. "I'm going to find me some smart guy who can make it and keep clear of the ring. Set something up that—"

"No, Ed, no," she protested.

"Yes, Annie, yes!" Ed set his chin hard and repeated it. "Yes, a hun times yes, a thou times yes—for both of us. This damned town—it owes it to us, Annie. We've been on the bottom too long."

The new ringer stared at his finger, looking dazed.

Judge Crater had seen it many times before. Each one thought it couldn't happen to *him*—but it could and it did, and perhaps in time every criminal in the area would have his ring and be a perfect citizen.

The girl ringer still sat there crying. Well, her job was over, and she could go home to a nice bonus for this, though she probably hadn't been told what she was doing. It was sometimes best not to tell ringers; they were apt to blurt everything to the wrong parties at the wrong time. Maybe some day Forensics, Inc. would develop a variety of ring that permitted better cooperation with special projects. Compulsory honesty was fine in its place, but occasionally it got in everyone's way. Yet how could one define degrees of honesty?

"You will wear that ring for five years," the judge said, his mind returning to his dead rose bush. If only this unexpectedly burdensome day were over! "You may then go to the shop and have a new finger put on, or simply have your ring deactivated. It will not be any more painful than the placement."

"But what does it *do*?" young Jeff Font asked plaintively. The boy still didn't really comprehend.

"We are about to activate it," the judge said. "I believe its nature will become clear enough in a moment."

Webster placed an instrument over the ringed hand and pressed it down into contact. There was a brief hum. "It's working now," he said, removing the box.

"*What's* working?" Jeff demanded in frustration. "Ouch!"

"Just sit at ease and be careful what you say," the judge warned him. "What you felt was your first mild reprimand. You are now connected with what some like to call Ultra Conscience. He's the conscience that will always be with you, for five years at any rate, after which you probably won't need him. Do you know why your ring shocked you just now?"

The young man looked at his hand, perplexed. "I suppose it was because I used a disrespectful tone," he said, and winced.

"You are learning quickly. The ring, or rather the conscience it signifies, requires that you use the proper tone to the proper person—and the proper form of address. Actually, it is what is within you that activates the circuit; the ring merely gives it teeth."

Jeff looked again at his hand. "I don't understand, Your Honor. How can a bit of metal read my thoughts?"

Crater smiled. "This is a common misconception. The ring itself is not Ultra Conscience, as I explained; it is merely its terminal manifestation. You were thoroughly interrogated under drugs—subtler ones than truthall—before this trial commenced. This was not to elicit specific objective information, since that is the province of due process, but to determine your moral posture. Morality differs from man to man, you see—some have exacting standards while others have virtually no concept of propriety, and some have grossly distorted values, like the insane. Were the ring simply applied to the unprepared individual, it would hardly be effective. Not everyone, for example, believes that stealing is *wrong*."

He watched the man, ready to suspend his discourse, but Font appeared to be genuinely interested. That was a good sign. "I don't remember—"

"You were unconscious," Crater said. "The computer dealt directly with your subconscious, requiring no overt responses. It ascertained your fundamental ethical complexion and charted it against the presumptive ideal for current society. It then acquainted you with the deviations—*your* deviations—from this ideal. That is, if you believed that kidnapping is justified in certain cases, it told you that no such cases are recognized contemporaneously. It made sure your mind grasped the distinction, whether or not you were ready to agree with the ideal even theoretically. It did *not* require your adherence to that ideal."

The ringer was still perplexed. "Then the ring doesn't—"

"The ring does not set the standards, no. It merely enforces adherence—to that imprinted ideal. The ring is the least of the factors involved, but because it represents enforcement, you are most saliently aware of it. A superior moral code is valueless without effective enforcement—but the *code* is far more important than the reminder."

Font nodded.

"Your recent petulance was a minor matter, so the warning was mild. Try it again."

"Yes, Your Honor."

"You see, there was no shock that time. That's all there is to it. Obey the law in all respects, behave ethically, keep a civil tongue, and you will have little trouble. The ring is triggered by the same kind of bodily reactions men have utilized for decades to determine the truth of a given response—variations in blood pressure, muscular tension, other neural functions. You might call it a miniaturized lie-detector. The potency of its delivered shock varies directly with the disparity between your attempted action and the dictates of ideal behavior. Of course at first it will be quite easy for you to trigger warnings. Old habit patterns have to be altered, and that does take time. But in a few days the new patterns will form, and you will find that the ring reminds you less and less. You will adapt to citizenship.

"Consider yourself fortunate that you were adjudged a suitable subject for the ring—otherwise lobotomy or exile would have been necessary. How do you feel, Font?"

The man thought carefully before answering, and the judge knew what was going on in his mind. Crater had tried the ring himself, many years ago, because he made it a point to prescribe no punishment—correction: therapy—he didn't fully comprehend. He had thought himself an honest man, but the ring had made of his mind a screaming cauldron of everything he had ever known and thought and felt. Even a judge, he discovered, possessed integrity only in degree, not in kind.

He had blasphemed when a thorny rose trailer caught him across the arm, and the ring had shocked him. He had erred unconsciously, automatically, not even thinking of it as wrong, just as a Gunnartowner might steal a case of beer from a shop and think himself justified. Ultra Conscience had let him know. It had been a lesson in humility—and he had learned in a hurry to watch his tongue, and had been a better man for it long after the temporary trial of the ring.

It was good control, though stern, and he endorsed it wholeheartedly. The ring was far better than prison. Far better, he thought, watching the facial expressions of the man before him. The law had faced cumbersome alternatives, before the ring. In the case of murder or rape or other capital crime, the choice had been between execution and life imprisonment. Too often subsequent evidence proved that an executed man had been innocent after all, far too late for redress. Too often, on the other hand, a pervert was set free within a decade to rape and strangle another child, because parole made "life imprisonment" a misnomer in practice. The commendatory spirit of forgiveness was disastrous when applied to the incorrigible malefactor.

How could a judge be completely fair in all cases, when he had to risk either an unjust execution or the eventual freedom of a compulsive menace to society? The ring had at last provided the answer. It was hard initially on the criminal—but it was by far the best solution to the problem in the history of penology.

The young man had answered the question, and he had not heard. It was bad to let his thoughts drift while he sat on the bench. "You are wise, Mr. Font," he said, sure that this covered the situation. "And have you completely abandoned the vengeful plot you had conceived against Mr. McKissic? Do you understand that your way was wrong, no matter what you thought happened fourteen years ago?"

The ringer hesitated again. He would be discovering that

he could not answer until he *had* given up his illegal notions. The ring would not permit him to express an intent to violate the law, or to lie about the matter. Only by consciously giving up all thought of such action could he make a reply—and he had to reply.

"Yes, Your Honor," Jeff Font said, sweating.

"Very good. And how do you feel about George McKissic?"

"Your Honor, I don't think I can answer that."

"Try it and see."

The man struggled visibly, as well he might. "I believe . . . that he has wronged my father, but . . . I am aware that I have no proof of this. I'm—my attitude is therefore . . . unreasonable." He stopped to work it out some more, evidently unsatisfied. "Yet the ring permits me to believe in a God whose existence I cannot prove, and so I am allowed my opinion in other things . . . on faith."

He was learning with remarkable rapidity. A very neat parallel, though misapplied. Still, it was not yet appropriate to tell him the rest of it. He would have to become thoroughly familiar with the restrictions the ring imposed. Perhaps McKissic was right; perhaps there was real hope for this person.

Now that sentence had been passed, the judge could afford to dwell upon the things he knew about Jeff Font. The boy had completed the full six intensive educative years on Alpha IV with honor, which in itself was an indication of extreme determination and ability. He had developed phenomenal reflexes in the space service, and could have had an ambitious career there, had he chosen to remain. He had been betrayed by his upbringing into unsocial thinking and behavior, but he might become a really useful member of society if he didn't kill himself fighting Ultra Conscience.

It was unfortunate that the strong-willed individuals did not always survive the ring. They found ways to commit suicide that it could not circumvent. Many of the most promising were lost. Still, those who did adapt were worth all the trouble and effort. It was natural selection of the elementary variety.

"Personal opinions are permitted," Judge Crater agreed. "The ring is not a tyrant, Jeff Font. Perhaps in time you will decide that you have misjudged Mr. McKissic." And also his daughter, he added to himself. "You are free to go. Feel at liberty to return to this court for any additional help you may require."

"Yes, Your Honor," Jeff Font said. He turned with elaborate care and walked quietly out of the courtroom.

The woman, Alice Lang, started to follow him, but the judge gestured her back to her place. "Young lady, you know he must find out for himself, as you did," he said to her. She nodded sadly, mopping her face.

It was time for the next case.

III. 🔲 To Hell Descendeth

1

JEFF stood on the street with the too-cold wind of Earth blowing against his face, and his hands concealed beneath his cloak so that his new ring would not show. He had almost expected Alice to follow him from the court-room, but she hadn't. He waited several minutes, but she did not come. He wanted to question her about the ring—and perhaps, he added to himself as his finger twinged, he just wanted the companionship of someone he knew was in the same situation. It was amazing how his viewpoint had shifted in a few hours.

He was on his own, in society, against society, as always. But of course, he reflected with the second warning tingle, not really against society any more. No, he was now *with* Earth's society—with it against crime and injustice. Thus spake Ultra Conscience.

The pavement was a restful black in this full daylight, and the tall buildings were in excellent repair. He was at ground level, but in the distance he could make out multi-ple transport and pedestrian levels, and see the people crowding before the elevated shopping centers. He knew that there were similar complexes below the surface; the underground was not entirely taken up by parking. He could walk or ride anywhere he chose, in this elegant segment of the city, this "Uptown" district. He felt most secure, however, right here on the ground, where things were least hectic.

He forced himself to stroll down the street and not to look back at the mechanical policeman he suspected was following him. He paused before a store window displaying a wealth of toy weapons, bombs, torture kits and other kiddy delights that reflected the good old days. Was this the way Earth prepared its juveniles for citizenship? Perhaps a truthall hypo and a ring should also be included.

He waited for the stab at his finger, but it did not come. Evidently Ultra Conscience agreed with him here.

He glanced sidelong the way he had come, but saw no cop. And why should one follow him, anyway? He was guaranteed pure.

The street ahead was empty except for people, odd as that thought was. Apparently vehicles were not permitted here—but no, there was a gyrobus coming toward him, and taxis cruised softly. There were men in cloaks of conservative cut and women in gaily colored dresses severed just below the knee . . . except for a few that became transparent from mid-thigh up. He watched one girl walk away from him, her remarkable bottom flexing under translucence . . . and still the ring did not protest. Girl-watching was healthy entertainment too, fortunately . . . or was it that he knew he was seeing nothing? It would be nice to know whether any fashionable ladies were well-enough naturally endowed to present *real* flesh and pass it off as costume padding . . . and at last the ring reproved him for that lascivious speculation, but mildly. Yes.

He shivered, and wondered again how native-born Earthmen could tolerate this climate. What was it out here—sixty-five Fahrenheit? And in Northern Canada where his father had lived and G&G had had its first crude factory, the temperature had been known to drop a hundred and thirty degrees below that! Dimly he remembered a snowball fight he had had somewhere with Pammie, throwing the caked crystallized water at each other. It seemed incredible that he could have enjoyed such cold, and he wondered, shivering more decisively, whether he would ever manage to readjust to it.

He walked vigorously, trying to heat himself. Pamela. Should he try to contact her legally, as the judge had suggested? Certainly he had that right, and no motives to be concealed. She had heard him under the truth drug. It was keenly embarrassing, but at least it had brought the matter into the open. He could call her, and if she refused to talk with him—well, he would at least have tried. He could attempt to apologize for his sewerlike dreams. He knew she was far above such things. He had always known that, consciously. He felt guilty for mentally taking advantage of her. He had no right.

He looked around for a vidphone booth. There was one on the corner, occupied by a heavyset man in a silver cloak. Well, he could wait. He had plenty of time. Five years of it.

He ambled toward the phone, getting cold as he slowed. The man came out. Jeff entered. He checked the book— but Pamela's number was not listed, nor her father's.

How could he get in touch? Through her former school? That too was private. The G&G plant, or its local publicity office? No, probably no one there would give out her number—especially to Jeff Font, who had tried to kidnap her. But damn it (ouch! mustn't subvocalize like that!), there had to be some way of contacting her.

He left the booth, disheartened. He could not phone.

There was practically no way he could do it. Even if there were some way to obtain the unlisted number, the ring might react to his base anxiety and forbid it. And why should she even accept the call?

How far had that computer-interrogation really extended? he wondered as he moved on toward the more congested end of the street. He could have spilled all he knew . . . it could all be on file, waiting for routine investigation. The identity of his Vicinc contact, for example. They could pick the man up any time, subject him to truthall, and ring him in turn. From that they could gain the names and deeds of others . . . it was a miracle that criminals still managed to operate.

Or was there a loophole? Vicinc was a recognized business. Probably it was legal for it to sell special equipment, on the legal supposition that it would never be used. If it *were* used for unlawful purpose, the supplier could not be held culpable. . . .

Then why had that Gunnartowner, Big Ed, been so worried about his car? Because he was *not* Vicinc? Would the police be looking him up . . . or were they simply too busy to care, knowing that if every small time accidental contact were arrested, business would come to a standstill?

Only the fool got ringed. Probably there was some graft too. He had not missed that first-name basis between McKissic and the judge. The big boys hired the little boys, and the little boys were discouraged from being too curious.

Odd—the ring was permitting this line of thought, too. Perhaps it was because he was making realistic conjectures about the problems of society, not contemplating any action of his own. He was granted freedom of thought, so long as it didn't get too personal. It was dangerous to think about Pamela, but not about general matters.

Or else the ring had been overrated as a preventive.

Ultra Conscience surely hadn't abolished crime; it had merely made the criminals more careful. Truthall made it beneficial to function in ignorance—which encouraged machine organization. Blanked-out vidphones and go-between robots and all the other blessings of modern science were probably still ahead of truthall and the ring. Look at McKissic—not, he qualified his thoughts carefully, that the man was necessarily guilty. But he had the resources to accomplish certain things, and to protect himself from the consequences. He had no fear of truthall, because he knew the judge would never subject him to it.

If Jeff could find out why . . .

But this wasn't solving anything. He still wanted to contact Pamela. But how, how, how? His mind skipped back over the faxzine stories he had glimpsed during his hurried researches into the McKissic itineraries yesterday. Only yesterday? There had to be something. She remained the key to his . . . misunderstanding. If anyone knew the truth about McKissic, it should be Pamela.

His glance fell upon a display of footwear in another window. High-heeled rhinestoned affairs . . . of course!

Dancing class. Pamela had a ballet rehearsal in—he glanced at his watch—about an hour. He remembered that distinctly. And that, he understood, was not quite so exclusive. People came to watch the young women pirouette and twirl over closed-circuit 3V monitors. He had heard that some units broadcast from the stage floor, and anyone could watch . . . in the name of art. If he could get into the live audience section he might have a chance to speak to her. To explain . . . whatever he could explain, that might expunge the dismal taste of that court interrogation.

He was now in a general traffic section. He looked for a cab. He found one cruising near him as though anticipating his thought. He went to it and got in.

The human cabbie looked at him and revved up the wheel motor. "Where to, mister?"

Jeff swallowed, wondering whether the ring was going to sting him, but it was quiescent. "Ballet Academy."

The wheel engaged and the cab pulled into the stream of traveling gyros: cars, trucks, buses. The driver controlled his vehicle with one finger on the bar and scarcely seemed to look where he was going, but the maneuvering was sure. He drove, Jeff thought, as though he had a computer picking out the course. Jeff glanced over the back seat; there was no computer.

"You lookin' for somethin', mister?"

"Uh, no," Jeff said, and winced at the sting for the slight lie he had told. "I haven't been in the city long. As a matter of fact, this is the first human-operated cab I've taken." He didn't find it necessary to add that he had rented his own car, until this morning. The ring did not object.

"Oh, really from out of town, huh? I figured as much. Probably figure that ballet stuff is really something, hey? Well, I'll tell you." The driver squinted sidelong at him while veering dangerously around a lumbering duocar. His voice became confidential. "If I was you and I was just in town for a few days, I'd look for hotter action. More, uh, participation. Get what I mean?"

Jeff did, to his regret. The ring was twinging already, and he hadn't even spoken. He hoped the driver would shut up. "It's really because I know someone who's taking lessons there," he said.

"You know one of them rich bitches? Sure, and me mudder was the king of Europe," the cabbie said without rancor. It appeared that neither the manners nor the originality of the breed had improved in the last century or two. "Look, mister, you don't have to pretend with *me*. Watcha think cabbies are in business for?"

Jeff wondered. He could almost imagine a robot operated vehicle making a similar solicitation for an Andinc mockup . . . "All curves and no brain, just the way you like her . . ." Was that farfetched, here on Earth?

The narco-coated tongue licked lips. "So if you want somethin' maybe a little hotter—?"

"I'm just a fare," Jeff said. "Just a fare, that's all." But he had the feeling the cabbie wouldn't take a hint.

He was right. "One of *those*, huh," the man said, unaware of any incongruity. "What makes you so self-righteous all a sudden? You got the hots for one special gal? Hell, you know you can't reach her, not if you're in the take-a-cab class. You want action? I can get you action. Free-lance. No Vicinc regs. Real—"

"I'm not interested!" Jeff insisted, prompted forcefully by the ring. "Look, I'd rather you didn't tell me any more."

"Mac, you're listing to the north. *Why* ain't you int'rested?"

Jeff pondered the figure of speech. It was not the first time he had encountered one new to him in his brief stay on Earth. Listing to the north: as a gyro parked with props and not disconnected precessed to the north when left too long, moving at right angles to the force the turning of the globe exerted upon it. Obvious meaning: way behind the times. It was an apt expression, particularly for him.

"Because of this," he said, and held out his ring.

The cab's wheel skidded, halting at the curb with the squeal of protesting rubberite. The driver slammed his fist on the button that opened Jeff's door. "Okay, ringer. Out!"

"Why? You were the big-mouth." The ring warned him. "The one doing all the talking. If I have to report you, I have to report you. It wasn't any of my—"

He barely got his head out of the way in time to avoid the driver's fist. He got out.

The cabbie sat shaking. "Nobody gets in my cab after this without I check their hands first," he said. "The decent women, at least they wear them seethroughs on their feet so you know they're clean. But you, dammit, keeping your hand in your pocket like that! It ain't honest. I thought you was hot for it. Get outa my sight before I run you down!"

"I assure you I could protect myself."

"You and what army, ringer? You ain't had that band long, have you! If you had, you'd know better. You'd know to keep it out an' showin' so folks don't go blabbing men's business to you, you goddamn stoolie. And you'd know another thing—no damn ringer protects himself."

"That's ridiculous," Jeff said. "If people keep clean, they don't have to worry about what they say. As for protection"—he stirred inside uneasily—"there are police."

"Oh, ringer, have you got lessons comin'! You just go take a little stroll in th' park." The door slammed shut and the vehicle screeched off.

Jeff stared after it. Another figure of speech? Take a walk in the park: cool off? Think things out? He wasn't sure.

He shrugged it off and walked to the corner, ignoring the hostile stares of other pedestrians. There it was: the local Ballet Academy.

He crossed the street, noting the contrast here between the handsome modern buildings and the rather shabby people. The whole structure of Earth society, from what he had seen, was like this: high-minded theory, ugly reality. Most of the people here were males; no doubt the cabbie had reasons for his assumptions.

The ring gave him a twinge. *Think no evil.* This was too personal. He could not attribute base motives to every person watching the ballet on 3V or live.

"Hey, buddy, you going to the Underwears?"

Jeff held out his ringed finger without even looking at the man. The stranger cursed and moved off. The common citizen, it seemed, was not particularly anxious to help a convict rehabilitate.

The police were undoubtedly aware of the fringe audiences to these shows, yet did nothing. Would he have to report the driver and this other man? Or was a certain amount of voyeurism tolerated, as it was on the street? He had been away from Earth so long that he couldn't say. The suspicious manner in which both the cabbie and the other man had reacted to his ring—was that in itself enough?

Forget it; they were typical.

The ring reacted immediately. No, they must be reported, whether or not the report was ever acted upon. And his prior use of a stolen car.

He spied a rolling blue mechanical and walked up to it. "I want to report," he said clearly, "suspicions of soliciting, or whatever the current term is. And a stolen car. I don't like it, but"—he held out his ring-hand—"I understand that this is what a good citizen must do."

"Report," the cop boomed. Jeff was sure every person on the block could hear.

Jeff reported. He felt guilty doing it, and the ring stung him—for the guilt, he realized, which was a hangover from his prior uncitizenlike attitudes.

On either side the streaming pedestrians broke apart to give him a clear berth. He continued speaking until all the facts were out; whenever he hesitated, the ring prodded him.

"You will require protection from possible retaliation," the robot said.

"I made no such request," Jeff said. "I can—"

"Lawbreakers do not like to be fingered," the cop explained, surprising him with the colloquialism in its programmed vocabulary. Or was it standard usage, now? "You, Geoffrey Font Junior, are an honest citizen whose wellbeing will be endangered so long as you continue to make such reports. It is therefore recommended that you avoid situations which may lead to such activity."

"But a good citizen—"

"You are a *very* good citizen," the mechanical assured him. Was there a burr of irony in the voice? He looked closely at the faceted jewels of its dome, but there was no way to read facial expression in such a machine. "Unfortunately, good citizens are a minority in this section and are unpopular."

"But what about the *bad* citizens?"

"The men you designated will be arrested and questioned, provided they can be located. Since you do not know their names and addresses, this is unlikely. In future you will note the registration numbers of all vehicles operated by such individuals, and of any vehicle you believe to be stolen. We cannot proceed without this information."

"But that includes the entire human cabbie staff of the city, and maybe all the junkyards too!"

"Guilt cannot be presumed prior to solicitation, nor can an unverified statement be taken as evidence of theft. Unfortunately, truthall may not be employed except in formal court interrogation."

"You mean those men will get off, even if you catch them? They don't *have* court procedure for misdemeanors."

"This is the probability."

"But I still have to report such things?"

"Yes."

"Great!" Jeff said, and was stung for his tone. "So

every procurer and minor crook who has the foresight not to commit a felony goes free, while the ringer who is forced to report him gets in trouble. I guess things haven't changed much after all.'' And now that he thought about it, he realized that the soliciting itself was probably not illegal; it was the bootleg, non-Vicinc aspect, that avoided taxation, that made it wrong. ''Where do I get this protection you say I need?''

''I will be your protection,'' the cop assured him. The minions of the law were certainly pragmatic.

''For how long? My sentence is five years.''

''For as long as there appears to be a need.''

''I wish,'' Jeff said, deciding to drop the subject, ''to attend the immediately upcoming ballet practice. To watch it live and to speak to one of the participants I expect to see there.''

''You may attend and watch on monitor and I will accompany you. You may not see the participant in person or speak to her unless you have a clearance permit.''

''How do I get one?'' Discovering this robot was a stroke of good fortune—perhaps.

''From a member of the girl's immediate family responsible for her, or the head of the Academy.''

''And that, for a ringer, is damned—very nearly impossible.'' Every time he forgot the ring, he regretted it. Already it was ceasing to be a game and was becoming maddening. Five years of this nagging? ''Okay, forget about that for now. I know the family, but it wouldn't do any good. Let's watch the ballet.''

Admission, past a red-uniformed robot, was routine. The cop led him down the plush hall and up a plush escalator and onto a sparkling glastic balcony. The stage was far below. Apparently this distance didn't count as ''live'' viewing.

The separate 3V monitor brought it much closer, if one cared to look. Jeff did. 3V: Voice, Vision, Verisimilitude, which meant stereophonic sound, a three-dimensional image in color, and selected additional effects, such as odor and a tactile panel. Some termed it 3S: sound, sight and stink.

However described, it was effective. The screen was two feet square. It was like looking through an open window; he flinched as a slipper came at him and a perfumed breeze wafted by his face. He put his hand on the panel and felt the vibration of hard toes hitting the floor.

The girls did pirouettes and twirled in the light traditional tutus, outfits that had not changed materially in centuries. The monitor pickup was set at floor level, ostensibly to focus on the intricate leg maneuvers. Those who hoped for more were bound to be disappointed, he quickly saw; there was no angle from which a ballet dancer was indiscreet. Oh, he knew there had once been nude ballets, but these had been a passing and commercialized novelty, rather than the real thing. The somewhat modified gravity onstage enabled the girls to leap and drift gently to the floor.

Jeff watched, entranced, though this was a far cry from anything known as "entertainment" on Alpha IV. In time he saw Pamela.

At first he failed to recognize her. She had twirled away in the background while others flitted and fluttered as gamboling nymphs and naiads upstage. Then suddenly she was foremost, her long limbs flashing, her shining hair revolving about her cameo face, alive and luxuriant. He stroked the panel and felt it, the laquered tresses like rare silk, the stiff frills of the tutu. He smelled forest pine, heard the cadence of dainty tapping toes, saw in close-up the smooth dancer's muscles of thigh and calf.

This was a different creature from the demure girl who had sat beside her father at court. She had been a caged bird then; now she flew.

There was a muscular lad in tights acting out some chase scene with her, and she was floating to him, being caught and flung lightly away, twirling back, caught again, bent backwards over a level forearm, one leg pointing at the sky. Jeff watched and listened and smelled and felt and imagined the costumes dissolving and himself as the male participant. He expected the ring to object, but it did not.

The canned applause burst from the monitor, joined by real clapping on the balcony around him, and he realized that the number was over. The time had come for him. He moved to the railing and waved across the space between them.

Pamela did not look up. Then, miraculously, she did glance his way. She saw him, he was sure; did she recognize him from this distance?

He turned the monitor screen and looked at it. She was still on it. Yes—her lips were trembly, her face abruptly fearful. She knew him.

She gathered in her tutu with a quick flurry and hastened offstage and into the wings where neither man nor monitor could follow.

Jeff swore silently, clutching his throbbing hand but refusing to repress his mood. He had not meant to *frighten* her! He had hoped, even at this stage, for a glad smile, or at least a forgiving one. And he was a fool. A ringed fool. Her part in his life was over; how had he let himself be deluded otherwise? A lady like her . . .

"It is inadvisable for you to continue such behavior," the blue robot said. Jeff discovered that he had actually fallen to his knees with the pain, fighting the ring. "Many ringers are taken to the hospital with nervous disorders and functional breakdowns. Moderation is best."

"Thanks for the objective advice," Jeff said. "Where will she come out?"

"If you are referring to Miss McKissic, she will probably change and ascend to the roof, where she will return to her home via chauffeured helihopper."

Naturally, in an age when robots could perform miracles of surgery and law enforcement, human chauffeured vehicles would be in vogue among the wealthy. "Is there any way I can follow her—legally?"

The machine did not deign to reply.

"Let's get out of here."

On the street again, he turned to his protector. "I don't want to hurt your metal feelings, but I don't think I need you."

"You wish to terminate protective surveillance?"

Jeff watched the flashing, flexing blades of a gaudy pink heli leaving the roof before he spoke. "Is there any sensible reason I should retain it?"

The robot hummed, evidently communicating with its boss, the main police computer. "It would be unwise for Geoffrey Font Junior to terminate at this point."

"How am I to make a living, with a ring on and a cop overseeing me? My bankroll won't last forever. It may not last more than a day, as a matter of fact. I have less than a thousand dollars on me."

More humming. "You may return to the justice building for leads on ringer employment, Jeff Font. There you may also obtain additional instruction on behavior among unringed citizens."

"Thanks. I'm picking up plenty of practical experience

in that line now. Is there any place to walk and think, away from the crowd? Any countryside nearby?''

"The main city park is three blocks from this spot. The trees and shrubs are genuine, and there is a fountain with marble nymphs bathing. It is unwise to go there alone, however, if you lack experience.''

"Sounds great,'' Jeff said with irony enhanced by a jolt from the ring. "Especially those nymphs. Marble ones aren't fickle. Where did you say—''

"Three blocks in that direction.'' A stubby arrow pointed.

"Dismissed.'' Obediently the cop turned and rolled away. Jeff watched its knobbed dome riding above the human heads for a short while, then lost sight of it amid the vehicular mass. It had been an interesting experience, but he did not care for company, animate or inanimate, right now.

The park. He walked. Now and then some stranger edged near, male or female, but a flash of his ring gave him immediate privacy.

It was strange, he thought, that the exclusive Ballet Academy he had just left had been built in so obviously an uncultural neighborhood. It must have been part of some foredoomed master plan to move parks and playgrounds and aesthetic enterprises into disadvantaged regions, and so spread culture to the masses via propinquity. Great idea—in theory.

In practice, the masses simply ignored culture, once they discovered they couldn't drink it or inhale it or sleep with it, except for the jaded oldsters and inexperienced youngsters who came to ogle the unaesthetics they imagined they could glimpse. Apart from these groups, such things as the ballet were the exclusive property of the rich, who never even set foot on the street outside.

Well, this failure was in accord with the general pattern

of this world. Earth was prettier than Alpha IV, but the gulf between basic values was not as great as he had thought.

Ahead some distance he could make out the elevated throughway that traversed the city, with the upright, space-saving little gyrocars bobbing up and over the rise like one-wheeled eggs. The locals paid no attention to the astonishing congestion of traffic, but it continued to awe him. Vehicles were not used for pleasure or even straight transportation on Alpha IV; they were used for the rescue service and for serious liaison between the bases along the poisonous surface. He had had to train savagely and pass a stiff practical examination before obtaining his driving job; a poor driver was shortly a dead one, and the community could not afford the loss of a car. Here—well, it was just something he had to get used to.

The park should be just ahead. He had come to Earth expecting to find trees freely growing, but apart from the scrub surrounding the McKissic estate he had seen few. He was sorry he had not been able to halt his nocturnal careen through the wilderness woods adjacent to the estate; to walk through the rising forests and dream of nature as it once might have been. Strange that Earth had so little now—when it was the only place man knew of where trees could grow naturally.

It would take generations to renovate the forests destroyed by avarice, construction and pollutants, even though few chemicals were being spewed into the atmosphere or waters now. Trees and grass and shrubs and flowers— didn't people realize how rare a privilege it was to have such things? How could they so callously blank out this essential backdrop to life on the planet, with concrete and metal and the omnipresent glastic?

Someday, perhaps, that tide would turn again.

He could see them now, the trees. Enormous ones, trunks gnarling up a hundred feet and more, foliage overhanging the pavement. Along the edge of the park were poles with lights for the night strollers, each bearing its little box. Call boxes? Who cared. He hurried over the rise in the walkway and stepped into the park premises. Trees—actual, living, adult trees!

Then he was among them, touching the mossy bark, and he could hear the tinkling of a fountain and breathe the freshness of nature. It was cooler here, too, but somehow more comfortable, and the air seemed softer.

He looked for the audible fountain but failed to spot it. The sound seemed to come from everywhere. It was delightful. He stepped off the sidewalk, wanting to hide himself from civilization, and started down one of the obscure winding paths, kicking up round colored pebbles as he walked.

A new sound alerted him: the beat of rushing feet. Old habits took over; he stepped to the side, whirled and fell into a karate stance. The ring shocked him for the warlike posture, and he realized that it would object to physical conflict. The law was supposed to handle affairs of violence.

His instincts had not been mistaken. Three pursuers appeared and closed in on him. They were teeners, he was sure, and juvenile gangsters. Already they bore the marks of their trade: one had a broken nose that had been improperly reset, another sported a scraggly adolescent beard, the third had a malformed left ear, probably slashed in a fight and never brought to a medic. All had that peculiar intensity associated with certain drugs. He had seen similar on Alpha IV. Jackals, berserkers, intent on helpless prey.

"Now, Ringee, don't you wish you hadn't been a bad boy? Don't you wish you could really hit and kick and slice like us honest folk do? Don't you, hey?"

He watched them silently. Word must have spread rapidly that a ringer had entered the park alone; any of the hostile pedestrians he had met could have dropped a hint. The police mechanical must have suspected something like this. But what none of them knew about was his particular training. He had not come here to fight, but he could do it.

"Aw, don't fun with the poor slob. Make him a regular guy. Take off his ring for him."

"Break all his fingers an' toes, so's they can't band him again. Do him a favor, see."

"Yeah? You know where they got to put it *then*!"

They laughed cruelly, the drug in them dominant, infusing them with courage. They circled him, played with him, taunted him. Jeff remembered, now, the cabbie's crack about walking in the park. The man hadn't been using any figure of speech that time!

But these *were* jackals: had they not been cowards, they would not have needed the drug. Even so they hung back. Weren't they quite sure the ring would prevent him from pulverizing one of them?

The one with the broken nose charged. Jeff crossed his arms in front of his face just in time, making the karate X-defense and warding off the blow. But the youth had concealed a cupped razor. The blade sliced down. Jeff sickened to the punishment, not of the blade but of the ring, as he dropped and kicked out in defense. All the shocks before had been minor, compared to this. It was a terrible crime, it seemed, to hurt anybody—even in pure self-defense.

The boy groaned and fell back, while Jeff writhed against the ring's savagery. "It's fake!" the one with the deformed ear cried. "He hit back!"

"No fake, ya stupe!" the third shouted. "Look at 'im."

"Yeah!" They moved in again. The bearded one kicked

at his groin. Jeff blocked, got to his feet. The two still on their feet charged, one holding a knife.

"Now you're going to get it, gyrobrain!" the broken nose said from the ground. "We're really going to ring your bell!"

Jeff threw a sweep block with his left arm, narrowly deflecting a kick. If only he could use a scoop defense—something to throw his attackers down and keep them down while he got to one of those call boxes. But the kid just might know how to use that knife—in which case he would need great luck even if not ring-hampered. As it was—

The knifer made his play. In and down, overhand, going awkwardly for the gut. Jeff threw himself back and stuck out a leg, getting the groin.

Pain exploded in him, from his ring-hand, more than he had imagined one limb could generate, and he knew then that the ring's discipline was no bluff. He could not overcome it. He was finished. There was no way to convince Ultra Conscience that his kick was only established blocking technique. Not when his mind knew better.

"Now you're really going to get it, Ringee! We was only going to tease you, before. There won't be *no* place to put the next ring. Now, Ringee!"

If only he could defend himself . . .

Flop! Flop! Flop!

"Scatter, men!" one cried. "Cop-ter!"

Jeff looked up and sagged in relief as the idling helihopper dipped close overhead. He could see the soft blades flapping. But it was not a blue police hopper. It was garish pink.

Then it was gone, rising over the trees.

The jackals were probably still running—but there might be others. Jeff got up stiffly and felt the cut on his arm. His cape had sustained similar damage—a long rip. He had also twisted a leg slightly in that last fall, as though Ultra Conscience weren't handicap enough. He still wasn't quite used to Earth gravity.

At least his automatic fighting reflexes had enabled him to survive. The ring had not been able to prevent the motions he made without thinking, though it had punished him cruelly immediately afterward. But now he knew more of its power, and did not think he would be able to fight again, that way.

He limped back to the sidewalk.

2

Ed Bladderwart raised muddy eyes to look out his shack window across the junkyard to the distant skyway and its bobbling cars. Sometimes he hated those cars and the snooty people who rode in them, and he hated the overall view all the time. His eyes traveled in leisurely fashion down the exit ramp that made a steep climb from Gunnartown to the skyway and back again. That he hated worst of all—the cars skimming insolently down here from the mainway, right past his yard, each carrying within its upright body its load of upright citizenry bent on a little upright hell-raising.

Oh, he had seen them, the smug smart-alecky kids, the happily scared brats, the sly older men, the fat furred women, the amateur psychologists who claimed they were—ha-ha—just looking. Sometimes he had almost wished that one of the little bubbles would fly from the steep incline to land smack in his yard. He could visualize the faces of the occupants as they stepped out, or as he dragged them out half-conscious, and they realized that this time they were not going to get what they were after—that feeling of complete superiority over the rotting carcass that was "Goontown," and over the human maggots that inhabited it.

"Ed," Annie said from across the table, concern in her voice. "You've been sitting there just staring for an awful long time. Don't you think—"

"I *am* thinking, woman. That's the trouble. Shut your face."

Annie poured some caffeine. Her eye was a little swollen yet from the last time he had blacked it, he noticed. She was a good woman to take so much from him. She didn't have to. They'd never been married or even made a formal common-law declaration. He hated to think what life would be like if she should ever walk out on him. Probably he would drown himself in stolen beer until there was nothing left but a sodden hulk. Then that demon court would put the ring on him. God.

That reminded him again of BettySue. Quite a gal she had been, quite a gal. Ed had been in a position to know. Probably she was a half-sister to Annie. She had been hot like Annie, and a little younger and a little prettier—before. But after the ring, what a difference! He had seen her move about her old haunts, not young and not pretty, with a look of unbearable disgust. Before the ring she had been a tough broad who knew how to handle men for fun and profit. After the ring she hollered cop if there was the least look on a man's face. Before, she had worked the joints; after, she had not been able to work anywhere. They claimed she had lost her mind, finally, and been picked up by the psychbots and carried away to some institution the Uptowners maintained. Ed hoped she was happy there.

That in turn reminded him of his own sister. She had

been sixteen when the gang initiated her, right in the house. Backed her into a corner and put the spray on her, all over. It had taken about five minutes for the stuff to get through her clothing and sink into her skin. After that—

Well, it had been quite a party, her and six men. They had booted him from the room, but he had heard it all. So she was an official member then, and hadn't even had a hangover next day. He decided it was all right after all; the bad things he had heard about the spray were just cop-talk.

Still, she had been smart to take the cure at the clinic right away. If she had waited a couple of weeks, even, she would have been hooked hard. And dead by now. As it was, a couple years later she got married, legal and all, and the happy-druggers were forgotten. . . .

"Ed," Annie said, "there's someone."

He blinked. She was right. No, she was wrong. His lower lip curled as he recognized the long, low duocar that hummed into the yard. Sam Selmik.

Ed grunted. "Sam. Flathead's new hero."

"You think?"

"He will be if Sam puts me down. But he won't. Sam's stupid. He's headed for a ring. Someday I'll land me a really smart operator who can beat the ring. Sam can't."

He waited until Sam, his flashy filigreed cloak whipping lightly in the breeze and showing all the animate orgy scenes imprinted upon it in flexmotion, was nearly to the doorstep. Then he got up, went to the door, opened it.

"Hi-ya, Sam," he said without enthusiasm.

"How are you, Eddie. Flathead tell you I wanted paks?"

"He told me, Sam. Come in, we'll talk about it— maybe." He held the door open. Sam entered daintily. Ed indicated chairs at the table. This was, after all, business— and there just might be money in it.

Sam sat, getting the chair with the split bottom. Ed

joined him, thankful that he had landed the reinforced-seat job. It gave him confidence.

"I'll explain how it is, Sam," Ed said. He studied the nymphs and satyrs on the other's cloak, appreciating the naked sexual acts that transpired every time the cloth bent. He contemplated the scrawny hand that protruded from the sleeve, the fingers covered with diamond rings. Sam was the only man he knew who would wear a ring of any type on his hands. He didn't seem to mind the snide remarks. Maybe he even liked them. Women would wear rings, because everyone knew they were ringed only on the toe, but men . . .

"The law makes me report every powerpak I take from a gyromotor," Ed said. "You know, those gyropaks are special, not like the wheel motors. They keep that gyro going all the time, so the car won't fall—"

"I know," Sam said shortly.

"I know you know. Now there's been talk about linking a bunch of those permanent units together, hitching 'em to the wheel, and making a motor that damn near takes off and flies. Great for getaway cars and racing—if the law didn't make G&G number 'em and keep track of where every last single gyropak is. The big computer's got it all stored away. I get a car with a good powerpak, I gotta report it; I sell that pak, I gotta report where it goes. There's no slipups. First time I even make a little mistake, they got me on a felony—selling a pak without reporting it. I get truthdrugged, maybe ringed. The customer gets arrested. The whole thing's one big ringin' proposition."

"Maybe not," Sam said meaningfully. He stabbed out with a diamond claw. "There's maybe some big fish behind this, get what I mean. How about, just for instance, if the pak's from a car the law doesn't know about?"

"Huh? I told you, every car is registered."

"Across the continent, yes—but some of those cars are not with the registered owners any more, maybe. Lift out the gyro, junk the body—presto! No registration."

Then Ed caught on. Stolen cars, shipped from thousands of miles away, so that no local suspicion developed. This *was* big. He kept talking, to cover up his confused emotions. "You know you can't cut into a gyro motor unless it's all the way out of the car, and taking it out is damned difficult and dangerous if you do it wrong. I can handle it; Flathead would get another dent in his skull if he tried it again. Punks who swipe a car get a faceful of flying gyro if they try to mess with the motor seals. Sometimes they bring me an old clunker and I tell 'em no, they can get the fixture out themselves, or wreck the car and let me work on the carcass, legal-like; but I ain't working on just anything. That gets 'em. They know it takes a first-rate crackup to bust up a motor seal. That gyro's protected, and it's going all the time. It's hard to wreck a gyrocar and wreck it right and do it without making a splash everybody knows about, and then the cops check it in. Fool that tries it usually gets killed, or caught."

"Yeah," Sam said, taking the objections seriously. "But suppose it could be done right, quietly, without drawing the cops?"

The picture loomed larger and more frightening. He knew he ought to kick Sam out before it became a ringing matter for sure—but there was still that smell of money. "Impossible in Goontown. Some other place, maybe. You can't have a bustup that size here and not have every loafer in the section know about it. And there's another little matter—" Now, he knew, was the time to bring up the subject of his own loss on the stolen car. Now, while they wanted something.

"How much you figure that car was worth?" Sam inquired bluntly, not even attempting to avoid the issue.

"Three thou I paid for it. Ten thou for what else it cost me," he said, thinking of Annie and what she had done, and feeling sick again. In his business, each car was a big investment, and it would take many sales to make up the total loss of one unit. Annie had known that.

Sam brought out a monstrous wallet and opened it. He laid a five-thousand dollar bill on the table. "Impossible is a big nasty word," he said. He laid three more bills of the same denomination on top of the first. "Friend of mine sends his apologies. It was a misunderstanding."

Ed stared. "That's bear'cash!"

"Negotiable anywhere," Sam agreed. He gestured toward the skyway. "You have an interesting layout here. Note the drop. Note that turn to Gunnartown and the ramp running by your place."

"I look at it every day. Sick of it," Ed said, eyes fixed on the money. He had an idea what was coming. He knew he was going to listen. "But I hear they're going to repair it. Bumpy as hell, the Uptowners claim. Jiggles their wigs. Hell of it is, you can't wreck gyrocars."

"Can't is another big nasty word." Sam put away his wallet, leaving the cash on the table between them.

Bladderwart looked at him. "What's on your mind?"

Sam smiled, knowing the bait had been taken. "They'll have a detour there, and they'll be making repairs."

"That's what I just—" He paused. "Oh. So you figure you can just change a detour sign and wreck yourself a car or two. Forget it, Sam. They'll start tearing this end first, not the other, and—oh, you mean one'll crash in *here*?"

"More than one, Eddie. They'll crash and blow their gyros all over and then you can just clip off the paks and hide the rest in with the rest of your junk. Maybe some won't be any good, but most—''

"And I'd have all those dead drivers to explain. Uh uh, not unless you want to take care of *that* detail. I ain't a killer, Sam.''

"Who said anything about people in those cars?''

Ed stared again. "I don't figure it.'' But he did.

Sam nodded. "These are not local cars, Eddie. They'll run 'em down the cutoff at night, while it's closed for construction, and smash 'em empty at this end. How's that sound? Yard full of junk, and a little more junk and nobody notices. No bodies. No stealing anywhere near here. You just do your job and make sure none of those serial numbers get loose.''

"Just one thing. How's it sound, you wanta know. At night, no regular traffic on the cutoff, most Goontowners sleeping . . . well, sounds loud to me. Real loud. Whole damn town'd be coming to—''

"We thought of that. Seems there will be some pretty noisy shows at the Easygo, running pretty late. Maybe some fireworks outside, boosting it. Big ones.''

Ed had heard some of the special effects before. There was one little box set off by an electric spark that sounded like a spaceship crashing into a skyscraper. A few of those in the vicinity, and no one would notice a real crackup. The tavern belonged to Sam's boss, and it was close.

Ed knew he was going to do it. "How much for me?''

"Thou per unit. Maybe ten units per night, if the highway's clear, long as the construction lasts.''

Ed gaped. Ten thousand dollars a night! For a week, possibly two weeks, if nothing went wrong. Enough to buy into a used gyro dealership and move into a decent house. Enough to marry Annie and raise a yardful of kids. All he had to do was extract the powerpaks from vehicles wrecked right on the premises, and keep his mouth shut. It was his big opportunity!

But dangerous. He'd have a ring on every finger, if the police caught him. "How about insurance?"

"The best!" Sam said. From an inner pocket he brought out a small pillbox and snapped it open. "Look, happy-pills, see. Only, strong ones. You take one—no talk, no ring for anybody, only sweet dreams. Anybody gets caught he takes one of these before he gets to the truthall."

"If he gets the chance."

"If he doesn't take it in time, somebody might give it to his wife instead," Sam said.

These boys weren't fooling, Ed realized. There was money enough in it to make his fortune—but once in, there was no backing out. He hoped Annie wasn't listening in from the bedroom. "Yeah," he said, picking up the bearercash notes.

Judge Crater was pleased. The new ringer had capitulated already. He had undoubtedly spent the past three days wandering aimlessly about, escaping antagonisms and being refused service. It was tough, the judge knew, but always best that a new ringer break himself in in his own fashion. Jeff Font was not just another criminal, of course, and there had been fear that he would get into real trouble before coming to terms, but he had survived the worst of it now. Crater waited.

Jeff cleared his throat. "Your Honor, a police robot suggested that I return here. I'm finding it difficult to obtain employment and to live like a good citizen. Even," he added with carefully subdued irony, "with Ultra Conscience's help."

"And you wish to request some leads and recommendations from this court," the judge said. "Commendable and practical, and we shall be pleased to accede to your request.''

''It isn't easy to be a good citizen. I'm broke.''

Crater rubbed the side of his nose with the handle of his gavel. ''The situation for parolees seeking employment is naturally arduous. The adjustment period is harsh. But this court never interferes unless requested to do so.''

''But you *can* help me, can't you, Your Honor?'' The lad was pathetically anxious. It would not be wise to divulge the next stage prematurely, however. As a matter of fact, he had some doubts about the entire procedure in this particular case; it could explode into most ugly trouble if not handled diplomatically.

''Hmmm, yes, I believe so.'' Crater shuffled some papers while the young man watched. Perhaps Font thought the delay in answering was a mere ploy to make him suffer more. If only it were! ''One of our leading citizens has taken an interest in your case and has made an offer of employment for you. It is an offer you would be well advised to accept.''

The ringer stood in silence. The judge could almost hear the thoughts running through the tired brain: sullen, impotent anger; suspicion that it was a very unpleasant job; the nagging question whether the judge had had this information before and deliberately withheld it, just to force complete surrender. And the irony was, he *had* had the information, and *had* withheld it—but not for any reason Jeff Font could be expected to comprehend. At times the processes of justice and rehabilitation were devious.

He sighed. ''Do you wish to consider the offer, Geoffrey Font Junior?''

''If you please, Your Honor.'' Well, at least the young man had learned a certain amount of control. Perhaps it would work out.

"I had better advise you again that this offer is a very generous one and that you are not likely to receive better terms. If you refuse it—as it is your privilege to do—you are in fact unlikely to obtain an equivalent offer for some months, though of course this court will do its best for you. There are other parolees who are trying hard to be good citizens, and who are eager to work."

"I'm prepared to accept it, Your Honor."

"Of course, if you *do* decline, there is the public subsistence program. I should warn you that most persons in your circumstance find the acceptance of state relief money or charity quite humiliating. Most would prefer to work almost anywhere, rather than—"

"That's the way I feel, Your Honor. What is my new position?"

"The offer is for factory work. Specific type not specified by the employer, but the assumption is that it is within your training and capability. The initial salary is generous. Living conditions will be adequate. You will not be associating with the kind of people who make existence awkward for a—good citizen. Middle class, mostly, and unprejudiced. You will find them understanding."

Now the young man was wondering where the catch was. It was so easy to read the expressions on the face of a new ringer!

Jeff spoke: "May I ask where I should report to this employment, Your Honor?"

"The place is the main manufacturing plant of McKissic General Gyromotors."

Jeff Font stared. Was this fish going to snap the line after all? Perhaps that would be best. There were so many dubious aspects to this whole business.

"Your Honor," Jeff said at last, "I can't think of anyone I'd rather work for than Mr. McKissic."

It had to be true, oddly, for the ring would not have permitted a false statement. Still, his motivation might differ substantially from that desired. The judge gave him the application form, dismissed him, and called a recess, ill at ease.

George McKissic was waiting in the judge's private chambers. "Did he accept?" he inquired, as eager in his fashion as the lad had been.

Crater sat down heavily. "He did, George."

McKissic smiled. "You do not look entirely satisfied, Samuel. I assure you, the position is legitimate. He will receive precisely fair treatment, and will be promoted exactly as his demonstrated merit deserves."

"He is not an ordinary ringer, George. I don't like it. You cannot be certain you comprehend his incentives."

"Samuel, *you* are the one who insisted that he be ringed before I—before this. It appears you were right; he *did* make an attempt upon my daughter's welfare. But surely he is safe now."

"Surely," the judge echoed. "But I did not anticipate that the computer would assign the case to my court. It was a grievous breach of—"

"You handled it exactly as any other competent judge would have, Samuel. There was no conflict of interest. And you know how much this means to me. I'm glad it happened this way."

"George, I have a gun at home. As a public servant, I am not in a position to afford the elaborate mechanisms you might place about your estate, but I do feel the need of some minimal security against the criminal element with which I deal. Some blame the law for their mistakes. . . . At any rate, I keep this weapon in a vintage leather holster hidden on an upper shelf in an inconspicuous closet. It is an exact replica of a late nineteenth-century six-shooter. I used to practice with it, as a hobby, in the little woods I maintain. I could draw it and fire it in one quick motion and generally strike the target. But once I used it on a wild pseudo woodchuck that appeared unexpectedly. I wanted to know whether I could actually hit an animate, moving thing—but when the creature fell with half its head blasted away I knew I had done wrong. It was only a product of Andinc, but I had destroyed it unnecessarily. I put the gun away and did not practice any more.''

He paused to marshal his point. ''A gun is a deadly thing, George. The man who plays with one carelessly, thinking it harmless because obsolete, is too apt to do great damage to himself or to another. Somehow I feel that this young man, this Jeff Font, is in fact a gun, and that you are making yourself the target. He could destroy you; you know that. Why are you so eager to tempt him?''

McKissic contemplated the elegant fibroid rug. ''Geoffrey Font Senior *was* framed, just as the boy believes,'' he said slowly.

''That's such an oversimplification it is meaningless!'' the judge exclaimed. ''I know the boy was not to blame for the . . . situation of the Fonts—but neither are you, George. He will be given every chance. You do not need to take any further personal hand in the matter. You have already done more than enough.''

''Because I spoke for him, to bring him back to Earth? That is hardly—''

''Because you secretly took over his entire training and welfare, after the Fonts died. You arranged to provide him with the best education and care available on Alpha IV, letting him believe it was financed by the savings of the Fonts. You secured an opening for him into the local branch of the space service. Surely you realize what a dangerous man that made of him! He is physically capable of killing a man in an instant of time, barehanded—and you know he was raised to hate you intensely. You know the intelligence he possesses. Look at the way he broke out of that police trap outside your estate, and got that girl into the city unobserved.''

''I knew before he was born,'' McKissic said sadly. ''He can certainly handle a gyro. But I cannot afford to wait until he adjusts on his own. I must act now.''

''Why, George? It's not like you to imperil everything by such urgency.''

McKissic was grave. ''You must admit that I owe the boy something more than anonymous schooling, or passage to Earth, or even a decent position in my company. I don't expect it to be easy, but I must at least try to—''

''You are evading my question. Is five years so much, now? You were not rushed before.''

''Samuel, you know too much.'' McKissic smiled tiredly. ''Call it doctor's orders.''

Crater looked at him, assembling certain factors into an uncomfortable framework. ''That nervous . . . disorder?''

''That nervous disorder.''

''I understood that to be a genetic factor that would ameliorate with time.''

''With dilution by new blood, Samuel. My progeny benefit, not me. Age and strain intensify the effect.''

''And your medics say culmination is imminent?''

McKissic nodded. ''Any severe physical or emotional shock. That's the reason I must act now, while—''

''I see. Well, I cannot tell you 'no,' George. But at least keep him away from your daughter. That would be—''

McKissic flinched as though he wore a ring.

IV. Companions in Hades

1

THE man who met Jeff as he stepped out of the police helihopper had wide shoulders and big hands and dark hair. He was not nearly as large as he appeared from a distance, however. His back was bent, and it occurred to Jeff that part of his vertibral column was artificial. He had been seriously injured at some time.

"Hello," the broken-backed giant said. "I'm Ralph Blois. The factory foreman here. You're the new—employee."

"Glad to meet you," Jeff said, taking his hand. He realized uncomfortably that even such a greeting was out of the question for him unless literally true. He *was* glad to meet someone who treated him like a man.

God, but that was a big hand, he thought, and stiffened momentarily because he still got shocked for inadvertent blasphemy. Some incredibly Puritanical mind must have programmed the original Ultra Conscience. When even thoughts were subject to control—but that wasn't the case. He could think as he chose; he merely had to do it in formal language.

Blois led him into the factory through a door in the roof.

93

He heard the police heli flopping off behind them, as though marooning him. They descended.

In the cathedral-sized room below robots were busily working over metal bodies and parts of bodies, attaching bubble-shaped canopies, steering assemblages, and all the other paraphernalia necessary to the finished product. The robots—actually automatic machines, since they were anchored in place and had no random-selection circuits or humanoid traits—worked with built-in wrenches and welders and other tools. The din was terrific.

"You know how it is," Blois said, his voice audible above the factory roar though he did not seem to be shouting. He handed Jeff a pair of ear filters. These cut down on the extraneous noise while permitting vocal sounds to pass unhampered—a neat trick, he thought. "The machines do practically all the manual labor and the clerical work. Human beings squeeze in here and there where there's room. The robots assemble the cars from bubble to wheel, including the powerpaks. You know about them?"

Jeff knew, but didn't want to answer immediately. He had made it a point to learn as much as he could about gyromotors, since, if his plan had worked out, he would eventually have had to run the business. The ring stung him.

"They are enormously efficient capacitors that can take a charge suffcent for a decade's normal use," Blois said, taking his hesitation for ignorance. Now Jeff could not speak without embarrassing the man. But he realized that the question had been largely rhetorical; Blois was making a point, and wanted to be sure the background was clear. No replies were necessary, and there might be practical information Jeff really didn't have. The ring stopped bothering him.

"Because of that charge, these powerpaks are dangerous to handle. That's why we seal them into an immobile metal case built into the car's frame. Only the shaft of the gyro enters the motor. It's a common misconception that the gyro is booby-trapped; actually, any interference with the system is apt to short the charge and blast the entire motor apart. Voltage of that magnitude is a booby-trap in itself, but efficiency demands it. The gyro is dangerous too, since it's always going, and it's a good, solid, high-revolution mass. Has to be, to keep a half-ton vehicle steady. The entire unit is vacuum-sealed for greater efficiency, and that's a third danger: implosion."

Implosion. Jeff certainly knew about that. His parents had—but he had to pay attention to this.

". . . can miscalculate the precession and break it open—and then the fun begins." Blois smiled grimly, unaware of Jeff's brief lapse of attention. "Amateurs don't usually survive. That's why the robots handle it all. We send them to accidents to deactivate or remove the assembly, which means destroying the car, and we keep all units registered. But people are sure it's because we have some terrible secret to protect."

"I've, ah, heard that story," Jeff agreed.

"There's no secret. The average Joe simply isn't capable of comprehending gyro theory. The basic patent is available to anyone. No tricks—every gyro we install has counterclockwise rotation variable up to—"

"I understand," Jeff said gently. "They think that just because the car is parked, the gyro is inactive. Actually it retains very high angular momentum, because the powerpak is designed to deliver a steady flow within a specified range and is never cut off entirely. Both electrically and physically, a General gyro is always dangerously 'live.' "

Blois looked at him. "You seem to have done your homework, Font. Know how to calculate precession?"

"Yes." The formula was complex, but he had been thoroughly grounded in both the theory and the mathematics of gyroscopy. It was, after all, his business—or would have been, but for—

The ring warned him.

"If you know as much as you seem to," Blois observed, "you'll advance rapidly here. But we have to start you out on the routine end. You'll be outside man the first month. All you have to do is keep the line clear. Just start the auxiliary motor, check the gyro to make sure the axis is vertical, and drive the buggy out to the lot. Now and then you'll have to ask some tourist to move, or explain to him why we can't make factory sales to anyone other than our authorized dealers. Another thing you'll have to explain is that we don't sell powerpaks for private quote experiments unquote. You'd be amazed at the number of hotrodders who try that line. Rest of the time you'll be on your own."

"Clear enough," Jeff said. He well understood why the company did not place new employees in positions of trust or delicacy. It was exactly the way he would have set it up himself. Whatever decay McKissic harbored in his soul, he remained a first-class businessman.

He looked at the mechanical arms overhead swinging newly molded or hammered parts down to the assembly line. There were catwalks and two other men. People to check the machines which checked the machines, he thought. Big fleas have smaller fleas that have still smaller fleas *ad nauseam*. All of it organized into a magnificently functioning unit, like society itself—which was rotten at the core.

"You are wondering, of course, about your fellow employees," Blois said. "Well, they all wear rings. There is no ringer prejudice here. Mr. McKissic has been exceptionally far-sighted in this respect. I am the only employee in this department who isn't ringed."

Curious. McKissic would sound like a good man, if Jeff didn't know otherwise. *Suspect* otherwise, he corrected himself as the ring reacted. Or did the man do this to compensate for a guilty conscience? "How long has this policy been in force?"

"Since the rings were first instituted. That was, oh, a dozen years ago. G&G isn't the only big industry to cooperate, though. Glastics, Andinc, Spaceways and even Vicinc maintain staffs of ringers. A ringer can move up fast, if he's capable, because the employer knows he can't cheat. He—"

"*Vicinc?*"

"You know—prostitution, gambling, dope—"

"But how can a ringer—?" He discovered he didn't like to pronounce that word. "I mean, at that kind of place—?"

"Why not? It's all legal now, so long as the tax is paid. Put a ringer in charge of accounting and records—"

"Oh." Probably the ringers weren't allowed to participate in the earthier aspects of the business. But it seemed one *could* patronize the Vicinc outlets in a moderate way. Gambling within reasonable limits was not a crime, but the ring would call a halt long before he went into debt. "Normal" pleasures were permitted, abnormal prohibited.

"But Mr. McKissic was the first to hire them in a big way," Blois said, picking up on the earlier question. "And it has paid off. The ringers get a good break, and there is no industrial sabotage or theft or betrayal of company privacies."

"That I can appreciate." What baffled him was how McKissic could live with such honesty. If just one of those conditioned informers learned anything of any possible interest to the police . . .

Either McKissic kept exceedingly close watch on what information was available to his employees, which would handicap his operations somewhat—or the man had no secrets to hide.

Time would tell. "I understand my shift is from ten to fifteen," he said to the foreman. "That's all—only five hours?"

"Five hours a day, four days a week. Standard contract. Where have you been—off-planet?"

Jeff nodded. Evidently Blois didn't keep up much with things outside his department.

"Well, just don't rock the gyro. Five hours may seem like a lot to you, but you get good pay for it."

The man had taken his question as facetious! After twelve hours a day, no days off, at Alpha IV, and the full-time duty in the space service, this hardly seemed real. No wonder there were so many people on the streets— most of their time was spare-time.

"Put your thumbprint on the time clock over there and get started. You can come to me about any problems. When the shift ends, I'll introduce you to some of the fellows; every couple weeks we have a little company frat party. You'll fit in, don't worry." The foreman walked away, leaving Jeff wondering, for the first time seriously, whether he had judged McKissic correctly. Surely the man had not fashioned such liberal company policy a dozen years ago just to impress the son of a cheated—*alleged* cheated—partner.

Or was his ring already making him rationalize to avoid pain? McKissic-Honest Businessman now brought no shock. . . .

Earth was after all a wondrous place, with free art

galleries and ballet shows and beautiful parks and tremendous leisure time. How easy it would be to forget his purpose and accept things as they stood. Why torture himself with memories he could not change and dreams he could no longer achieve?

He was still thinking it over at the end of his first shift. Blois showed him around as promised, and the other men seemed perfectly decent, and certainly none of them looked down upon him for being a ringer—not with the decorations on their own hands. If there was a catch in all this, it was well hidden.

They had fixed him up with a comfortable room in a privately-run rooming house, and it had a homey atmosphere in spite of the thousand-odd other apartments there. Its appointments were cheap by Earthly standards and luxurious by those of Alpha IV. It lay beyond the park— the same park he had learned to be leery of. Earth was *not* paradise; he could not afford to misjudge it either way.

The walk was nice, however, so long as he was careful to stay on the pavement and near the call boxes.

"Hey, buddy—how's about a bill?"

Startled and defensive, Jeff looked up to see a wizened man standing in his path with a hand out. A panhandler—on modern Earth?

"I, uh, haven't been paid yet," Jeff said apologetically. Would Ultra Conscience encourage a donation to such a person? Let's see—a bill was slang for ten dollars—one of the lesser notes of Earth, long out of use elsewhere, which was the reason the term surprised him. Actually, the theoretic units called dollars were seldom seen; credit covered routine expenses. An average paycheck would be about three thousand, for him—three thous. According to the history books, single dollar bills and even lesser coins had once existed as meaningful currency, but had soon degenerated into virtual worthlessness.

"That's okay, buddy," the wrinkled face replied. "You can owe it to me. You'll be seeing me again. Maybe here, maybe at a G&G party. Somewhere, for sure. M' name's Dave Paxton."

Owe it—to a panhandler? Earth had surprises yet.

The man began to move away. "Wait, uh, Dave—" Jeff was embarrassed, but he wanted to know more. This encounter was so unlike what he had already come to expect in the park, and there was something about this man. "What, uh, why the—I mean, I'm a ringer." He showed his hand.

Dave immediately returned the gesture, thrusting out a liver-spotted extremity. He pointed to a section of a finger that was not freckled. It glowed with artificial health—in that isolated ring-sized band. "That's why, buddy. That's why you. Any other questions?"

"A great number." This was a *former* ringer!

"Yeah. Thought you'd say that. 'Cause you ain't had yours long, right?" The oldster smiled, and Jeff noticed that he had excellent teeth. "Sure it is. Well, let me tell you. Ten years of ring is a lot of straight and narrow. A hell of a lot of heavenly behavior, right?"

"I'm sure it—"

"Right! And I served all of it. Every damned day, and now I can swear again. For an act the foulness thereof you wouldn't want to hear. I deserved it. So I paid. I still pay."

"Still—?"

"I ain't free yet, am I? You can see that. I tried to prove something by learning to cuss again, but that's as far as I ever got. Buddy, don't you know what the ring does to you? A year would do it to anybody. Ten years—"

"I'm sorry to hear that," Jeff said. He wondered whether Paxton ever got violent. He could break the relic in half—or could have, before the ring. Now he was lucky to defend himself against teen punks.

"Yeah, you got it, don't you, buddy? You got it like everyone else. That urge to beat the crazy ol' coot in the mouth. In his big mouth where all the truth spills out. Sure. Don't blame you. Felt the same myself. Only now I'm educated. I *know*."

"I'm afraid I *don't* know, Dave," Jeff said, embarrassed again by the old man's bluntness. "You've served your time. Can't you make a living now? Is that it? You have to beg?"

"Living—hah! I got a living. Pension for honest work. Honest. *Honest*—you hear that? All my life honest after I put on the ring, after a life of—I couldn't be anything *but* honest. That's why it don't count. I'd ask myself, then I'd ask the ring. Now there's nothing but ring answers left. Not mine. I can't lie or cheat. Can't even spit. Can't say Boo to a cop. Truth is, buddy, it's harder to put off the ring than to put it on. What I wouldn't give for a little prick for a cussword—but I'm alone now. All I can do is annoy people in a cause my ring-devil would've approved of, while it was alive. Have to do it because I don't *have* to do it; that's why it counts."

"A cause? People like me?"

"You? Naw, not you, buddy. Not anyone like you. Not entirely. Someday I'll tell you. If I figure you're a pal of mine. I don't know you yet. Other pals of mine, they give me a bill, maybe two bills, every week. Ain't much. Not when they really need it, of course. Only when they've heard and they start to catch on. So long, buddy. See you again in a couple days."

Jeff walked on, wondering about Paxton. Crazy, but

maybe smart-crazy. The old con must have been one of the very first ringers—but he almost seemed to regret the exemplary life he had led. Regret, yet somehow rejoice in it, too. Had the ring really unhinged him, or was it just a difference in values? Was he as old as he looked, or was that too a manifestation of the strain of the ring? It was a distressing thought, at the opening of a five-year term.

If a hardened criminal—as he presumed Dave had been— could have been changed so much, what would happen to the ordinary man? Would Jeff himself wind up, after five years, a helpless derelict? Would he beg in the park?

At the end of his third day's work (he had missed the first day of the pay-period) Jeff was feeling like a veteran McKissic employee as he waited in line at the window. He watched the ringers ahead take their envelopes and go. They did not look demented, nor were the ones he knew already at all strange. They talked, they joked, they punched each other on the shoulder, they treated him courteously. He had already visited for an evening with one, chatting about Earth and space and women and the usual run of things.

Idly he thought of Dave Paxton, wondering whether he really would meet the strange old man today, now that he had money to offer, or whether the whole thing had been some weird Earth-joke.

"Geoffrey Font Junior."

Jeff was startled out of his reverie. The voice that had called his name sounded familiar. He looked up to discover the face of Alice Lang behind the pay window. She held out his voucher, smiling.

"You're the last one, Jeff."

He accepted the card. He had not expected to see her again, though the sight of her gladdened him. "Why— why—?"

"Why am I here? Jeff, that really isn't very smart. You saw the ring on my toe. You knew I had to work somewhere, and for McKissic. Didn't it occur to you it might be . . . in the daytime?"

The ring shocked him, retroactively, for what he had assumed.

"I'm sorry. I shouldn't have said that," she said. "Of course you had no way of knowing. You thought Vicinc hired me out, I'll bet. I should take that as a compliment. No, this is where I work—not that the machines need me. When they told me that the boss's daughter was in danger—"

"It's just that—I mean, after the trial—"

"Because of the truthall hearing? We've all been through that, Jeff. We all have similar motivations, believe me, and if you think it hurts for a man to have his exposed, just consider what it's like for a *woman*. Anyway, now we meet again, and no kidnapping. Isn't that better?"

"Much better."

"So that's settled," she said brightly. "Care to drive me to my hotel in my bouncy on-installment car?"

He looked at her in surprise. "You really—"

"Of course I have a car. A ringer can't lie, you know. We get a good discount and good terms, as employees."

"I mean . . . well, do you really want to be that friendly? After what—"

"New start," she said. "We are two people who never happened to meet properly. Does it matter what we were? We're both good citizens *now*."

He swallowed like a bashful adolescent. She *was* rather pretty. But he wasn't used to women. On Alpha IV one either kept his mind very busy on other things, or tried a drug . . . but he'd always known he would return to Earth someday. He had, thought . . . dreamed . . . that it would be to Pamela. No—

"You haven't answered my question," she said. "The car, remember?"

"I—there's someone I should see."

"Oh. A—woman? I know you can't hide it."

He smiled at her apparent naivete. "A man. An old man."

"Dave Paxton?"

He nodded. "I want his . . . story, I suppose."

"It's a good one," she said. "You'd better change your voucher for some small bills, though. Why don't we both go see Paxton. Talk to him."

He placed his card in the change machine and obtained several printed bearercash notes. "You are a persistent woman. But sure, why not?" Then he stopped to consider. "That is, if we can locate him."

"I know where to find him," she said. "If we go immediately, we can get there before there's a mob around. Some of the guys pay their respects to old Dave with their families. It can take several hours."

"Several hours! To pay off a panhandler?"

"That's not exactly it. Dave is something of an institution around here. You'll see."

Wondering, he drove her car to the spot she indicated in the park. They got out, following a winding path to a secluded spot. Jeff worried about lurking punks, but Alice seemed to know where she was going.

Dave Paxton sat alone on a park bench, out of sight of the drive. They went to him.

"Here, Dave," Alice said, and handed him a bill.

"Thank you, Alice. You're the third this afternoon."

So the man really did know the ringers. How could he look like an inebriated bum, yet be treated like a patriarch?

Jeff looked at the box Dave slipped the money into. It was square, secure, and had a handle and slit. Evidently he was geared for regular collections.

"What's it for, Dave? Do I get the story now—or don't you get my contribution?" The ring protested, and he handed the bill over. It was not right to hold back money for information, in such a case.

"I want it, buddy," Dave said. "Or rather, somebody does. You see, I use the money I bum for what you might call charity. Yeah, charity. Children's things, mainly. Don't ask me why. That's the way it is, is all."

"But aren't children taken care of by—"

He became evasive. "Children. A party for under-privileged kids, and the ones who don't have much happiness. If you look hard, you can find something written about it."

Alice took his arm. "It's a good cause, Jeff. Better than you know."

"I'll want to learn the whole story someday, Dave. There must be some reason ringers contribute to you. I'm not sure that I can just—"

"Come, Jeff," Alice said, urging him away. "Others are coming." Reluctantly he went with her, back to the car.

"Why?" he demanded as they drove on through the park. "He isn't compelled, is he? Not by the ring or the police. And that park is a bad place to hang out. Doesn't he think he's paid enough for whatever crime he committed? Why—"

"He was indirectly responsible for the death of three children," Alice said. "Three innocents that just happened to be in the line of his flasher. He didn't know it at the time, but he wouldn't have cared, then. Now he knows he can never make it up, never bring back those lives, never remove the anguish—yet the ring made him the kind of person who has to try. It's a gesture for him. Why not? All of us will make similar gestures eventually. That's why the ring is good, even though there are bad features of it.''

Jeff shook his head. ''I don't understand. I always thought myself good, or at least right. But this? To build up such a thing about something long in the past?'' But he remembered the structure of desire he had built up himself, from one unimportant adventure with eight-year-old Pammie.

''You'll learn to appreciate it eventually, Jeff. The ring never comes off, inside. When you discover what it is you must make up for, and know that you never can—then you'll appreciate.''

Jeff frowned as he steered the car and compensated for trace precession by shifting his balance. ''Every ringer has his monkey—is that it?''

''That's right.''

''Even you?''

''Maybe sometime I'll tell you, Jeff.''

He drove on thoughtfully. Alice showed him the way through the cliffs and canyons of an unfamiliar section of the city to the gigantic corncob that was her hotel, and he tooled the vehicle into one of its several subterranean entrances. Inside was a splendid lobby for cars, with a drive-in registration desk and a wide, open-to-the-sky parking lot. He marveled at the space available, until he realized that instead of being horizontal, the parking was vertical. Monocars and duocars found their individual paths up spiraling ramps that wound all the way to the top and down again, like the twisting streamers of a maypole. The faces of drivers and passengers peered down at the lobby through transparent barriers while their vehicles climbed or descended.

''Twelfth floor, please,'' Alice said.

He drove onto the nearest open "Up" ramp and followed close behind a dark blue monocar with custom silver spangles. "This must be very expensive, Alice."

"Not so very, Jeff. It's nice, more luxurious than economical, but still middle class. There are certainly more expensive places to stay. You should see the sort of hotel the McKissics patronize. They opened their suite to employees for the company Christmas party last year. That hotel didn't even have a street entrance. We had to show our G&G identifications before they let us land the helihopper. Over the phone, while we hovered. And inside, it was—"

Jeff looked into the busy whirlpool of the lobby as he pulled around the wide curve onto the first upper level. "Lot of guests. They seem to be driving in and out of all the entrances."

"It's a popular hotel. Tourists come here and there's a lot of partying and gaiety. I used to think that if I could only live in a place like this, I'd be happy. Now I can afford to—there's little else to spend my wages on—and I find it isn't as I imagined."

"Because of the ring?" Then he wished he hadn't asked.

She seemed not to hesitate. "That, and *my* changing values. You'll find out what I mean eventually. It's going to be hard for a while, though."

"It seems to me I've been warned about that before," he said, and smiled. He hoped nothing turned out to be harder than the park initiation of several days ago.

He was driving past rows of doors on the outside. There was a carport for every apartment and a parking space by every entrance. The floors were divided into sections and every quarter-spiral had an additional parking lot. He could see petite shopping sections on each floor, and even crowded cafes and junior Vicinc outlets. It was a town within a city, lacking only the extremes of McKissic estates and Gunnartown filth.

"You drive well, Jeff. Extremely well for someone who's never traveled a spiral before."

"The driving is easy. It's the looking that gets challenging."

"You mean you find the sights distracting. Don't you want to know how I know this is all new to you?"

"How?"

"Your eyes, Jeff. They're trying to drink in everything. I know the experience. You really don't remember such hotels from your boyhood?"

He shook his head. "I never stayed at one. I suppose if I had it would have been quite plain, though. Father didn't go much for flash. Mother did, though—the two of them were always arguing functionality versus decorativity." He continued talking, telling what he remembered of a life that was now so dim he might only have read about it.

He followed her guiding indications down the twelfth floor corridor. The apartments in the deeper section were not as fancy as those fronting the spiral, and many did not have individual carports. *Tough for them!* he thought.

"Jeff, my room!"

He slowed and pulled into the parking cubby before her door. He got out and walked around the car as she stepped onto the carpeting that served as a sidewalk. He wondered just what came next. He was certainly out of touch with this world.

"Jeff, would you like to see my apartment?"

"I *am* curious. . . ."

She touched a coded key to the recognition-panel and pushed the door open as it unlocked. As they entered, a shrill whistle started from the phone: the sound that came on when the normal blinker was not answered within a reasonable time and the caller was determined.

"Oh dear!" Alice said.

Jeff looked about the apartment as she answered the phone. The furniture was attractively curved and comfortable, and there were art reproductions on the walls. Compared to his simple room, this was the height of luxury.

He was thumbing through a book of poetry he had picked off a black glass table as he wandered back to Alice. She was still talking. On the screen was the face of a woman a few years older with peppermint-stick dyed hair and artificially heightened red eyebrows and blue lips. She looked past Alice, and he tried to step out of range.

Too late. With gleeful dismay the woman exclaimed: "So that's why you can't come. Alice, I'm surprised! And you a ringer!"

"Please, Darlene!" Alice said, but the woman went right on talking.

"That man with you—isn't that—yes, it *is* the one we saw on threevee last week! I'd know him anywhere. What a spectacle! Delightful! Yes, I think you *must* introduce him. And you know, Alice, I'm going to be *very* hurt if you don't . . . you wouldn't want that, would you, dear?"

Alice stepped aside. "Jeff Font, meet Darlene Wilson. Darlene has the apartment across the way, Jeff."

"I'm pleased to meet you, Mrs. Wilson." This time the ring responded negatively; he was not pleased. But he couldn't insult her, either. He was damned whatever he said.

"It's *Miss* Wilson," the woman said. "I've been divorced for ages! Only it's not Miss Wilson to you and Alice—it's Darlene."

She should know that his words were only a formality, not intended literally . . . yes, the pain faded. He moved his ring-hand out in front of the poetry book so that she could not miss it.

"Darlene," Alice said, completing the introduction, "this is Jeff Font. He works for McKissic Gyromotors, as I do."

"And that's how you met. Isn't that sweet. Delighted to meet you, Jeff."

Jeff nodded. He felt extremely foolish.

"Oh!" Darlene said. "I see you've discovered Alice's Tennyson."

Jeff felt himself reddening at this prying interest. "I'm afraid I just picked it up."

"Yes, of course. It was a gift to you, wasn't it, Alice? From Mr. McKissic? You must be very close."

Jeff decided as he listened to Alice's choked "Yes" that he didn't in the least like Miss Wilson. He put the book aside and tried to think some charitable thought.

"And now you *both* must come to my party," Darlene said. "There are guests here that have never seen a pair of ringers. Really, everyone will want to look at you. Now I simply *won't* take no for an answer. You must come."

Alice looked at him helplessly. The Wilson woman was taking calculated advantage of them, making it impossible to refuse without being discourteous. Such tactics might be the height of rudeness, but Ultra Conscience did not concede any justification for return rudeness.

"Right away; don't bother to change," Darlene persisted. "Things are just beginning to swing."

"You're a persistent woman, Darlene," Alice said with resignation. "All right, since it means so much to you. But only for a few minutes."

"Now don't you be too *sure* of that, Alice." Smiling a smile that had more than a hint of taunt about it, she faded from the screen.

"Well, Jeff," Alice said, turning to him in pretty frustration, "we're going to a party. Unless there's something else you have to do . . . ?"

Jeff thought of inventing something and decided against it. "No valid excuse," he confessed.

"I was afraid of that. I so wanted to avoid that woman this time, but I knew when I heard the phone . . ."

They left the apartment, crossed a rainbow bridge over the corridor while cars hummed below, and were at Darlene's residence. There was a bewildering number of people present and more furniture, but otherwise the two apartments were very similar. Darlene took them in hand before they had quite reached the door and ushered them inside and among the guests, making unnecessarily elaborate introductions.

Attending were a 3V engineer, a script writer, some nondescript neighbors and several presently-unattached females with gaudily colored hair; Darlene carefully explained they were in the process of obtaining divorces. Jeff marveled that these were normal middle class people of this age: obviously with the short working hours most of them enjoyed, the idea was to emulate the standards of the idle rich. High wages helped, undoubtedly, and the high fees of the professional men.

The last they met was a heavily tanned space captain. Jeff was appalled to recognize him as one of the members of the jury that had convicted him, but the man didn't seem to know him. Of all the embarrassing coincidences . . . !

"And now," Darlene said expansively, "both of you ringers will want cocktails."

Jeff shook his head, glad for the moment to get away from the captain. "I don't think my ring would approve."

"Dear boy! You certainly showed more imagination than that under truthall—"

Alice said: "Darlene, you know drinking is not permitted for us. It interferes with the—"

Darlene's reddish eyebrows lifted and her blue lips

quirked. "Now don't tell me tonight won't even be an exception! Two ringers don't match up every day, on or off the job."

"Darlene," Alice said with more than a hint of exasperation, "Mr. Font and I aren't—I was only showing him—"

"Your apartment. Yes, dear, I grasped as much." Turning a back whose covering plunged to the buttocks, with shoulderblades creamed to a disconcerting yellow, she wriggled like a Vicinc vamp across the room. She raised her hands and clapped them loudly for attention. The room quieted: some expressions were more annoyed than interested.

"Beloved Guests," Darlene said. "We are fortunate to have two ringers in our presence. Now you have all met Alice and Jeff and you know what charming people they are—would be, even without their jewelry. They can only stay a short while—a loving matter, I'm sure," she simpered, making the implication dirty. "And for that reason I think we should proceed immediately to the entertainment. I was saving this for a surprise later in the evening, but—Margo, please bring the can."

Margo, a svelte young woman with lemon colored hair decorated with bright green splashes, rose from her chair and brought over a distinctively shaped spraycan.

"Jeff, I don't like this," Alice whispered. "She's planning to—"

"Yes, Friends," Darlene said, silencing Alice with a glance, "we are going to play Sensuals. Oh, not as some of us would *like* to play it"—a teasing snicker—"but as we must in order to maintain proper decorum and to avoid shocking our latest arrivals." Jeff felt her eyes on him even though he was looking at the floor. His feelings were mixed, and he wondered whether the ring would really shock him if he permitted himself to think uncharitably of their hostess.

"Volunteers?" Darlene inquired lightly.

No hands shot up. She looked about the room, peering through a lorgnette she had suddenly found amidst the bulges in the top of her gown. She spied someone and pounced. A pale-faced woman with untinted brown hair came from a divan. Darlene pulled her to the center of the room and placed her hand over the victim's eyes. "Now don't peek, Opal."

Margo touched the cap of the can. A fine mist played about Opal's right ear. "This is your mouth," Darlene said. "Your mouth." She continued to cover the girl's eyes for a full two minutes, while the audience waited nervously.

At length Darlene removed her hand. "Now that wasn't so bad, was it, dear? You thought it would hurt or something, didn't you, never having played Sensuals before."

Opal was perplexed, as was Jeff, watching. "That's all? Nothing happened," she said.

"Nothing, dear?" Darlene's smile was cruel.

"All you did was cover my eyes and say 'this is your mouth.' What kind of a game is that?"

Darlene signaled to a robot waiter with a tray of drinks. The machine came forward and she lifted a concoction and handed it to Opal. "Try this and tell us what you think of it. It's a new formula."

The dark-haired girl took the slender glass, raised it hesitantly, conscious of the eyes upon her, and touched its rim to the ear that had been sprayed. She moved her head to the side and the drink slopped into her ear. She paused judicially. "I think, Darlene, that it's a little sweet."

Laughter exploded from three of the divorcees, while the men looked uncomfortable. Opal glanced at them in confusion, then at the drink, wondering what was so funny.

"Try it again, dear," Darlene said with a straight face. "You must be mistaken. This is a very special drink."

The girl poured the rest of it into her ear. The thick greenish liquor made long ribbons as it ran down the side of her face and into her undyed hair. Her face was very serious.

Even the men laughed now, somewhat shamefacedly. In moments the entire assemblage was convulsed with embarrassed mirth.

Suddenly Jeff realized what the stuff was. He had seen something similar on Alpha IV: a colorless fluid, contraband, that desperate men painted on their hands before fighting. Hands so treated appeared to be insensitive to pain. Once a man had painted it over his entire body and gone about in a continuous orgy of pleasure, laughing every time he touched anything. "He's dosed himself in ignorance," a cynical oldtimer had observed. "He'll be dead in a day." And he was.

A broad back interposed itself between them and the hostess. A dark head half-turned and Jeff saw that it was the space captain. "Get your ringer girl out of here, Spacer," the big man said. "This is not for you."

Jeff needed no urging. A moment later he stood with Alice outside the closed door while the laughter continued unabated within. He took her arm and walked her toward the corridor bridge. "What was that, Alice?" He wanted to know what Earth called it.

"It's—oh, Jeff, it's Instant Confusion, a hallucinogen. People spray it on a part of themselves and then someone tells them it's a different part. A foot becomes a hand, a leg an arm, and it's real for them even when they know what's happening. They think it's very funny—but it's a dangerous drug. If someone gets an overdose he can become addicted and gradually lose his sanity, and if he had children—"

"You mean it affects the—"

"The genes, yes. If the dose is bad enough."

He put his arm around her, feeling the shudder in her body and wondering at the devilment of the woman who had brought them to this unwholesome party. Darlene obviously enjoyed tormenting people in the same way that a drunk might enjoy tormenting a reformed alcoholic.

"Where are the *decent* people?" he asked her. "Isn't anyone on Earth—"

"They do exist, Jeff. Most aren't like these—" She hesitated, prevented from speaking evil. "You have to judge them by what's inside. Most of the ones at that party are all right; they just got dragged along. That captain—"

She didn't realize who the spacer was. Still, the man had acted to spare them further trouble.

"Alice, have you ever taken that stuff, before—"

"No!" she sobbed. "Not that—and some wanted me to. I was afraid of it, always. I've seen too much of what it does to people. I—don't ask me, Jeff."

Why did he care? Because of the possible genetic damage? He loved another girl. "Do you want to go back there?"

"No!"

"To your apartment?"

"No. Please, Jeff, let's go drive somewhere. To the park. Just to take a break. Later, if you want, I can leave you at your rooming house."

If you want . . . He considered the odd phrasing. This brief acquaintance had become quite serious quite soon. Strange how readily his life was meshing with hers.

He could ask her exactly what she meant, and she would have to tell him. The ring didn't permit much subtlety. But he shied away from such a question.

In the park, he found a place along the now empty curb next to a lightpost. He helped her out and they crossed the

lawn—one of the few grassy areas open to public feet—
and circled the robomower just finishing up. Beyond the
grove of trees was the bench where the sainted Paxton
conducted his service.

The sounds of blows and heavy breathing brought them
to a halt. It was not fast enough. Jeff had already taken a
step into the glade, with Alice's hand grasped in his. He
stood staring at the four pseudoleather-jacketed youths,
and at the sprawled form of the old man beside the broken
cashbox.

"Well lookee here, it's old glastic-finger!" the one with
the broken nose said. He opened his face in an ugly smile.
He raised a bloody chain. "And a doe ring-ding, too."

"Double feature tonight," the bearded one added,
gloating.

"Triple feature," the fourth tough, the unfamiliar one,
said, staring at Alice.

2

Ed Bladderwart stood in his junkyard and faced north.
The exit ramp of the Eastbound highway cut across his
northeast corner, and the pilings came down onto his land.
That was why he had been able to afford it; the land beside
the ugly uprights was cheap, provided the renter agreed
not to touch the supports and to report any trace damage he
might observe in them immediately. His entire property
was on the skyway right-of-way; some year they would
preempt all of it for an expanded artery. That was why it
had to remain undeveloped. Had it been possible to buy it

outright, the price would have been millions per square foot.

Actually, the massive ramp served as shelter for some of his equipment. He had to put up with alcopop containers and Nonik cartons and similar refuse thrown from the cars on their way to blowouts in Gunnartown, but it was worth it. He had a large lot, and its location brought him quite a bit of business he might not have had otherwise. The descending cars could see his sign as they made their turn, and when the time for junking came a significant number remembered him. Still, it was not enough. By the time he covered the rent and other operating expenses, there was little left for himself and Annie. Until recently.

But as he looked north in the evening he saw a brighter future. The surface of the Eastbound had become worn, and then engineers had posted plans to strip it down, reinforce the undergirders, and resurface it. Tonight the barricades had gone up, cutting off a three mile segment which included his exit ramp; traffic had been detoured across to the near lane of the Westbound for the week or so it would take them to do the work. For the first time since he had established his business, the highway was silent; no headlamps zoomed across the horizon, no tires screeched as careless drivers tried to upend their un-upendable gyros, no snotty Uptown brats yelled insults from the safety of their speeding vehicles. Tomorrow the construction would begin, and then there would be a week—more, if he was lucky—to implement Sam's plan. He did not like dealing with an operator like Slim, who he knew was behind the deal, but the money was just too much to pass up. A lot of cars could be wrecked in a week. . . .

As he stood there he remembered, oddly, his sister. Things had looked pretty good for her, too, when she married a storekeeper at age eighteen. Another year and she had had a baby—

The worst thing about it was that the creature had lived. He shuddered, seeing once more the hairy snout, the cloven skull; hearing the banshee wail of its crying. It had lived, and grown, and even developed a certain animal cunning. One night two years after its birth it had used those jagged, mismatched teeth to gnaw through the plastoid locking bar of its cage, those human hands to work the severed ends free.

Ed walked up to the pilings, shaking off the chain of thought. The ramp entered Gunnartown a couple of blocks to the east, but curved here to join the main span. The elevation was about twenty feet, from his lot to the surface of the road. Enough to crack open the motor compartment of a gyro, what with the fall and the forward motion. Sam had figured they'd have to push the cars off at forty miles per hour, to be sure. He'd have to clear his lot to make room; no sense having a car overshoot and ruin some of his good junk accidentally.

Yes, it could be done. The far barricade shunted the cars away a good two miles from here, leaving that long quiet stretch before the exit ramp. It would not be hard to sneak the darkened cars past in the night, then bring them down here. Until the construction actually got into the ramp, and beyond the turn, that section would be available. . . .

Ed turned and walked toward his shack. Give it a week and some hard work, and a little longer to fence the paks off to the agent and get the accounts straightened around, and Annie would not have to take any more "sick" pills. They could get married the way she wanted and have a kid. Several kids.

Yes, it looked good.

Renay, the pretty dark-haired girl with the tight spangled slacks, carried the tray of varicolored drinks and offered each guest a cocktail. The guests accepted, laughing in a way that caused her pink mouth to quirk and her normally smooth forehead to wrinkle. She was walking on her hands and presenting the tray with her calves and feet extended.

Darlene Wilson shook continually with laughter as she sat beside the sober-faced space captain on the divan. She wondered why of all the guests present he was the only one who was not enjoying himself. What was his name? Smith—Robert Smith. Would it be possible to trap *him* into a round of Sensuals . . . ?

Now the girl's plum-colored rump trembled. It had been a good five minutes and that was the most anyone could expect from a normal spraying. The girl was in good health, but her arms should be about ready to give out, too.

The climax came. Spectacularly.

Smith tried to move aside, tried to reach up and catch the descending tray. His reflexes were very good, but he misjudged—a typical failing of those unused to Earth-gravity—and slapped the girl's legs instead. The tray landed with a thump on his partially bald head. Bright drinks splashed.

Renay's legs and hips were not far behind. Liquor exploded over the spangles and soaked the plum fabric. She came to with a start, felt the cold liquor and the captain's fumbling hands, and reacted as though emerging from sleepnol. Her foot kicked out and Smith jerked back, the print of a high-heeled shoe visible upon his cheek.

Darlene hurried, towel and sympathy masking the glee she felt. "Renay, Renay—it's Sensuals! Don't you remember? Goodness, one never loses the memory, only her composure. You *shouldn't* even lose that. Now take your feet down and apologize to the captain."

Renay gave her a deliciously dirty look. Her legs came down, knocking an overturned glass almost into Darlene's lap. "I'm sorry, Captain. Truly sorry."

Smith stood up, brushing at the mess. "This—"

Darlene clapped her hands. The robot waiter rolled up. Its sensors took in the scene and digested it. From one of its many cubbyholes it took a basket, sucked up broken glass, deposited it and folded the basket back into the shiny carapace. Next it brought out a brush and cleaned debris off the guests and divan. Finally it extruded a hose at shoulder level and approached the captain with it.

Smith backed away from the machine, not trusting it. "Captain, it only wants to dry you off," Darlene said. "I don't know what you have in space, but *our* robots are tame."

He relaxed. The nozzle went over him and a hum sounded. Slowly the dampness disappeared. It then turned to Renay and gave her the same treatment, though it had to cover more intimate portions of her anatomy.

"Well, I suppose we've all had enough of Sensuals," Darlene said, laughing. "It's back to conversation. And dinner! Waiter, bring the buffet!"

"Wait, Miss Wilson," the captain protested. "I really can't—"

"Now you just sit down there like a good swab," Darlene said. "You are an interesting guest and you came here to make the party interesting. I'm sure there're many things you must be able to tell us."

"Not as many as you can tell me," he said. "Twelve years running the deeps and then service on a kangaroo panel—" He broke off, then quickly covered his slip. "Sent here at your invitation by the Spacer's Reorientation Committee to learn what life on Earth is really like, today—I find it all pretty confusing."

"Fine, Captain. We'll talk. You'll tell us things and we'll tell you. That's what you wanted, isn't it?"

Smith threw a glance at the retreating waiter. He seemed to hesitate.

"Isn't it, Captain?"

His large shoulders seemed to slump and then go back as though his body remembered his uniform. "I'm sorry, Miss Wilson, to be so—"

"Now you just relax. We'll forgive you." She hurried to supervise the waiter as it passed out the plates with its multiple hands and took orders from the various guests. She made the circuit of the room and met all her smiling and jabbering guests again. Three out of four had been collected through civic organizations specializing in a help of some kind; these were the guests that she and her regular guests summoned for their amusement. "Now, Captain," she said predaciously, returning to him.

Smith watched the tray's legs flip down and make solid contact with the carpet. He looked with dismay at her as she sat down beside him and had the waiter position a second tray. "Miss Wilson—"

"Darlene." She took up a fork from his tray, speared a bright morsel and held it to his lips. "We eat this way, Captain. I feed you and you feed me. It's considered an honor to a guest."

His smile was strained. "Things have changed . . . considerably in the past twelve years." His eyes went to the bit of red meat with its dripping orange colored sauce and the yellow seeds sticking to it. "That's Titan crab," he said, "with zoobie sauce and stickwick seeds. If you had ever seen those crabs in their natural habitat—"

"Now, now, Captain. Mustn't insult your hostess." She pushed the forkful to his unwilling lips.

He ate, slowly, stolidly, not enjoying it.

"Now you feed me," she said.

He fed her, not liking that either. His traveling eyes tried to avoid her partially exposed breasts.

She leaned forward deliberately. "Captain, what is it that interests you?" She well knew that space was conservative and woman-starved.

"I, ah—" He had been reduced to virtual adolescence, she thought with satisfaction. This tough spacer! "That stuff you used—the spray—"

"Instant Confusion? Captain, you haven't seen anything! Some people spray their whole bodies with it. It's a fine way to commit suicide." She stuffed his mouth with spiced bread. "Would you like to try it?"

"Madam, I know better. In space—"

"Do you?" What a challenge, to get him into a game of Sensuals! "Do you know what one suggestion comes to the body, to all of it, when all the senses are confused simultaneously?"

"I—"

"Sex," she said succinctly, wiggling her decolletage. "Every part of the body. All one living, pulsating experience."

"It—"

"The addicts last anywhere up to two years. Every part of the skin delivering the sensations of orgasm, no matter what stimulus is applied. There's even a demon cult that specializes in it. Of course, they have to rest a few days between jolts, or they die too soon."

"Sounds . . . great." His mouth twisted distastefully.

"It undoubtedly is. Especially for those who haven't long to live anyway. I wouldn't mind going that way, if I had to go. So long as I had the money to maintain the supply. An addict who runs out—"

He stopped her from feeding more of the crab. She

prepared to spoon-feed him the concluding hotcream confection. "Those rings," he said. "How do they—"

"You mean you don't know about the shocks?"

"That, yes. But what determines them? Science can't harness an individual's conscience, can it?"

"Why no, Captain. A conscience is a subjective thing, I think. Ringers know when they break a law, even a little one, and that's when their nervous systems react and trigger the punishment."

"Then it's law by machine, not by men?"

She spooned up a cherry and the bakefluff surrounding it. "If you look at it that way. But what's the difference?"

He pushed the spoon aside. "The difference is that the *individual* should decide what's right and what's wrong, not a machine."

"That's what we have laws for," she said. She forced the cherry on him and watched him chew disinterestedly.

"In space," Smith said, "we could never get by that way. In space a man must be free to go against the book sometimes. Do you think I always follow the rules that have been laid down for me?" The babble of conversation elsewhere died out; this guest was finally beginning to entertain. "If I did that I would have precipitated a new spacewar or two and gotten my crew killed or executed a score of times. Individual judgment is what counts, not the laws of Moses."

"Now Captain, don't get yourself all worked up. *You're* not a ringer."

"But for the grace of . . . " he muttered. He chewed, swallowed. "That boy and girl. What about them? They got ringed—but did they do anything worse than what anybody would have done, in the same situation? Or did someone have it in for them?"

"Who knows, Captain?"

"But they'll wear those things anyway, right?"

"Right, Captain." She fed him some more of the creamy dessert. It was a rich chartreuse beneath the crust and throughout the baked froth there were bits of blue ice crystals. She was pleased that they now had the attention of the entire group. If she kept the conversation going, it might develop into a real spectacle.

"Suppose there's a moral decision," he demanded. "One the ring can't handle. Suppose a child is drowning and it's forbidden for the ringer to swim there?"

"Then the poor child drowns, Captain. The silly brat shouldn't have been there in the first place."

"That's no answer." He wiped blue specks from his mouth. "The child might have fallen in—or been pushed."

"Then the good ringer will rush to the nearest call box. There's always one around."

"Suppose there isn't time?"

"More dessert, Captain?"

"No!"

"Then I'd like some."

"Oh." He began feeding her abstractedly. The stuff had a tangy, sweet flavor that was hot and chill at once and seemed constantly to change in both temperature and texture. It was a so-called psychedelic pastry—one of her favorites.

"But suppose there's no choice—really no choice," he continued. "I mean a child in front of a speeding car and the only chance to avoid hitting her is to violate a traffic law. Either way the ringer's damned. What's the answer, does the conflict short out the ring so that he can act for himself or—?"

"Captain, I really don't know," she said, savoring the

dessert. "But something like one percent of our population is ringed, now. I haven't heard of much trouble."

"That's no answer either. What do you *think* would happen? You must have some idea."

"I *think* the ring would shock him. That's the law, after all."

"And what about the child?"

"The child?"

"The child his car may hit while he's getting shocked?"

"Well, Captain, there's a tragedy every second." She finished her bite and realized that the next would be the last one. "You and I can't help it so why worry about it?"

"Don't you think it's unfair?"

"Captain, it's not for you or me to say what's unfair. We don't make the laws. We don't commit the crimes. We don't put the rings on the murderers and the rapists and the kidnappers. They make their beds and I don't cry for them. We don't have anything to do with it. We're not involved."

"But you don't feel particularly bad about it?"

"Captain, Earth is not a starship. If one feels bad for everyone who suffers a tragedy, there's no time left for gaiety."

He put the spoon down. "Get me a drink."

She signaled the waiter, hoping he hadn't given out already. He had been so delightfully intense. "Your pleasure, Captain."

"Triple Bombast."

She turned to the robot. "A triple Bombast for our guest, a mocker cocktail for me. And see what the others want."

It mixed, shook and handed. Darlene placed the Bombast before Smith and sipped delicately at her mocker while she studied him.

He drank it fast and hard, space fashion.

"My, Captain, you'll become intoxicated."

"Yes. Waiter, another triple, on the double."

The robot chucked disapprovingly but obeyed.

She watched him, amazed. "Captain, you really don't have to impress me with your capacity."

He stared thoughtfully at the empty glasses. "Darlene, I've been thinking. Those ringers are really better than us."

"Why, Captain! How can you say that?"

He nodded, the powerful drinks working rapidly on him. "It's true. You didn't mind bringing that girl here and embarrassing her, and I know I'm no better than the other."

She shrugged. "Captain, you seem to forget that the rings are for punishment. They're *criminals*."

"Punishment? Not for cure?"

"Well, that too. Cure through punishment, perhaps."

"You know, Darlene," he said, taking her hand, "out in space it's like being in prison. A captain there is a law unto himself, but all the time he's there he's separated along with his men from the society he comes from. He knows what it is to be punished. He knows, Darlene."

She patted his hand. "Now, Captain, you're just being silly. Too much cocktail. I'll get you a sobrol and—"

"No. No sobrol. I'll have my hangover in my own good time." He looked owlishly at her. "You don't mind punishment, do you, Darlene? You don't mind someone suffering if you know he deserves it?"

"Of course not. Not if they deserve it."

"Darlene—" He leaned close. "I haven't had a woman since I got back to Earth."

"Why, Captain! I'm sure—"

He leaned closer as she retreated. "Darlene, I want to play Sensuals with you."

Victory! "By all means."

"*With* you. Both of us take it."

"Together? I don't see how—"

"It isn't done publicly yet, is it?"

"Done? What isn't done?"

"Sex."

There was not a sound from the spectators.

"Captain, I think you need that sobrol!"

He stood up, tall, straight, commanding. "Listen, everybody," he said loudly. "Darlene and I are going to—"

"Captain!"

"—play Sensuals." He jerked her upright, his left hand clamped upon her right wrist. His jaw was set, his nostrils flared. "You shouldn't miss all the fun of participation. You with that can—toss it here!"

"Don't, Margo—" Darlene cried, but Margo pretended not to hear in time.

Smith plucked the can from the air, turned, and smiled a smile she did not like. What had he said about punishment?

"Close your eyes, Darlene," he said. "Close them, Woman-who-does-not-mind-giving-embarrassment, Wench-without-feelings, Society-female! Close them tight!"

She obeyed, embarrassed.

He hauled up her right hand. She felt him positioning her fingers into a fist, molding them around one of his fingers. "Hold them that way," he said, and withdrew the finger.

She heard the hiss, felt the slight wetness. "This is not your hand," Smith said. "It is an orifice. You know which one."

Another hiss. "This is not my finger. I'm making it stiff, see, but it is not my finger."

Her eyes popped open, but it was too late to escape. His

left hand still gripped her wrist with excruciating force while he held his straight right forefinger aloft. He counted off two minutes.

The script writer began to chuckle, first to catch on. "Wait'll I write *this* up for threevee!" he murmured.

Darlene suddenly felt shamefully naked. "No!" she cried, but she was helpless. She closed her eyes, but it only enhanced the effect.

His treated hand covered hers, setting off unmentionable reactions. His finger drove insistently at her fist, forcing it to loosen. It pushed inside. She felt pain, emotional and physical, and, as in a great wave, the comprehending laughter of all the rapt party-attenders.

Smith drew out the finger, then thrust it in again. She reacted in spite of herself with a corresponding rhythm. The contact became more violent.

The watching men slapped their knees, choking over their mirth. The women blushed furiously. Darlene fought it, but the sensation was too powerful. The captain made a final lunge.

She screamed.

Alice saw the four youths: one with knife, one with chain, one with bat, and the last, who was staring directly and lewdly at her, with no weapon in evidence. She heard Jeff, still clasping her hand, shout "Stop!" but it was a distant cry. All she could think about were Dave Paxton and the broken cashbox. They had—

Paxton moaned. The boys looked down and sneered.

Jeff dropped her hand and took up an odd spreadeagle stance. His legs were splayed, toes pointed outwards. She could not understand what he was doing, but he seemed determined. Some kind of defensive posture? She was sure he had forgotten the ring again.

"Jeff," she said. "We'd better run. You can't—"

"You run, Alice," he said, watching the group ahead. "To the call box. When you can do it without being spotted. Meanwhile, stay close."

Such foolish bravery! "You can't fight—can't win. Not with the—"

"I can try. I can't leave Dave in their hands. I may be able to divert them, and the ring should let me *try* to do something honorable. It's the only way."

"It doesn't work like that, believe me. They'll kill you. They'll—"

"They sure will, Ringee!" one of them called.

"Well, you run while they're doing it," Jeff whispered. "If you can get the police here before they finish—"

She saw him making little practice gestures, and knew he was trying to remember which moves were purely defensive and which were not. But she also knew it was useless—a ringer could run, but he could not fight. Yet if she ran now, the fourth punk would go after her, leaving three against Jeff.

What real difference did it make? He could not defend himself against *one*, let alone three or four.

The toughs closed in. They were strangely slow and careful, as though they held their opponent in respect, for all their wild talk. How could—but yes, they *had* recognized him from somewhere. Had he fought them before, when he wore no ring? Still, it could make no difference.

Suddenly they were rushing, the three at Jeff, the fourth circling toward her. Her only chance to reach the alarm would be if Jeff, somehow, impossibly, engaged them all, while she escaped. He would surely die—unless they took time to play with him. They might; punks were like that . . . at any rate there was no alternative.

Jeff's leg shot out in some kind of kick, held straight, and the leader ran against it with his kneecap. The chain went whistling, slicing air by Jeff's cheek and stirring her hair with the breeze of its passage. She saw the chain crash into Jeff's shoulder and glance off. He staggered to the left, shoving her to the side with a quick sweep of his arm, and chopped with the edge of his hand down upon a wrist that just happened to be there supporting a knife. She saw Jeff flinch, not from the knife blow but from the shock of the ring. She knew what that was like. She was amazed he had done as much as he had; a ringer could not ordinarily aim a blow intended to hurt any other person, for any reason.

If only she could do something! But even if she swung her purse at—

The ring warned her.

The fourth boy was suddenly upon her. His sweaty hands grappled at her waist. She put both hands up against his chest and shoved him away as hard as she could. The ring stung her, but not harshly; it did not require that a woman be raped for the sake of nonviolence. Indeed, it would have punished her for submitting without a struggle.

The youth stumbled back and fell against Jeff. Jeff grasped his sleeve without seeming to look and threw him into the three before him. All four went down in a heap.

"Now!" Jeff cried at her. He stood over the pile, unable to attack but ready to block whoever stood up first.

Alice ran. She dodged into the forest, hearing the sounds of renewed fighting behind her. It was astonishing—Jeff was actually managing to hold off the attackers, in spite of the ring. She had not believed such a thing was possible. He had to have incredible will-power—and somehow he had arranged it so that they had to attack him, then made purely defensive moves that kept them busy.

She looked back as she ran. They were all up now, and Jeff was staggering. There was a red splotch on the side of his face as though his ear had been smashed. Now he was on his knees, fists up, knuckles pointed outward, elbows down, as if he were hiding from—

She fell headlong as her foot caught on a vine. She scrambled up, leaving her purse behind. The call box was in sight, just a little way ahead, and she was going to make it.

"The girl!" someone cried. "The doe, you idiots!"

She fell against the post and slammed her hand against the police panel. It sprang open. She saw with dismay that it was not a regular alarm; it was a whistler.

She glanced apprehensively over her shoulder. Two of them were charging across the walk. That meant that two were still working on Jeff. She clutched at the call box ear-plugs, jamming them in frantically, but one fell to the ground as she pulled the whistle release.

There was no sound—but suddenly a terrible nausea built up in her. It was the infrasound recording: vibrations of seven cycles per second. They were below the level of hearing, but deadly to health and life. She could feel her internal organs vibrating—stomach, heart, lungs. The ear-plug, actually a ceramic resonator that interacted with the sonic waves to multiply their frequency, fed its counter-impulses into the bones of her head, protecting the brain; but its effect beyond her head was slight. She swept up the second plug and held it to her stomach, praying for relief.

The two punks were writhing on the ground, curled up and clutching at their bodies. Alice ran past them, toward the glade where the others were.

The whistle cut off after thirty seconds, and she straightened up with relief. The ones near the box did not get up;

they had been very close to the source without protection. Ahead, two figures raised themselves, vomiting and gasping, then staggered away. They would be sick for several hours.

Now she could see the carnage, the two bodies remaining. . . .

V. For Love or For Hate?

1

FOR Jeff, it was like waking from sleep into nightmare. Slowly the white blur above his head resolved into a ceiling. Slowly the pavement and dirt under him became a firm hospital bed. An asceptic, white-shrouded—

He *was* in a hospital!

He sat up, his innards hurting. He had been very sick, apart from the fighting; the ring must have done that to him, though it had never made him nauseous before.

"Jeff!" It was Alice, leaning toward him from a chair beside his bed. Ralph Blois, the G&G foreman, lounged beside her. Jeff felt a stiffness on his face and shoulder and discovered light bandaging. Yes—he had been hurt, and severely, too, if the mechanical medics had not been able to heal the wounds outright; but not knocked out. What had happened?

"A little matter of an overload," Alice said. "You can't fight Ultra Conscience. You should have realized that by this time, you stubborn hero." She smiled, thanking him for that stubbornness. "Also, the whistle. . . ."

"But—" Then it came back. He had gone mad. He must have. Seeing the old man dying, determined to save

133

him but blocked by the ring; knowing that Alice could only get help if he occupied the punks a little longer. . . .

He remembered using the peek-a-boo defense, good so long as his hands and arms held out. He had knocked away the chain but couldn't use it himself. The bent-eared one groaning on the ground, clutching his possibly broken kneecap—and the ring raging for that offense. He had *hurt* somebody . . . ! The broken-nosed one still with the knife but holding the wrist, cursing, kicking at Jeff ineffectively. The third, with the scraggly beard, on his feet again, the hand not holding the club cupped around his Adam's-apple— and the ring reacting to *that*, too. The fourth one, angry because he had been balked in his attack on Alice, an ice-pick suddenly in his hand—

The searing pain of that point slicing down the side of his face, the stab just missing the eye it had been aimed at—or *had* it missed? His own rage at the situation, where even four-to-one odds against him did not change the so-called morality of Ultra Conscience; the kill-rage, uncaring of pain—

And abominable nausea, as though an internal gyro were shaking all his organs. That would be the sonic pacifier, striking down everyone within its range. Unconsciousness.

Dave had died. He knew that. Dave had been victimized by a machine-morality that could not yield to human necessity.

"Jeff?" Alice asked, alarmed. "You're not . . . again? You've been under drugs for hours. If a policebot hadn't come right away and taken you to the hospital—"

Jeff tried to relax. Hate was no good. Hate was bad.

He lied.

Hate *was* good. Revenge *was* sweet. He was glad he had hurt those killers.

He felt his system tingle with the drugs he knew were supposed to deaden the effect of the ring. Its shock was muted, for the moment—but so was Jeff Font's respect for Earthly values.

He relaxed.

"Dave died," she said unhappily. "I'm afraid it was the whistle that . . ." He saw that her ring had spoken, for some reason. She felt guilty, though she had done what was needed. "They got two of the boys, Jeff. They were pretty sick. But they'll be ringers now. And the others will have to hide, because they'll be identified now, too. In time they'll be caught. So it wasn't all a—loss. The part of them that made them do this evil—that will be dead. The ring will kill it, Jeff. Maybe someday those boys will be collecting for children, or for old men—"

Jeff clenched his jaws in the worst of all impotence: the inability to think clearly.

"There's something you should know, Jeff, before you—" Alice hesitated again. "I think Ralph should tell you."

Blois cleared his throat. "I used to be a cop," he said gruffly. "A human cop, back in the days when it meant a copper badge instead of a copper man. Stopped a bullet once and—well, that's why the back's the way it is. Not worth the expense to fix it now. Now about this ring, Jeff—well, I'm not a ringer, but my experience—"

"I don't want to hear."

"This you *have* to hear. You're thinking right now about the injustice of being attacked and not being allowed to defend yourself effectively. That *is* unjust, but it's the lesser of evils. It is better to have the ringer be helpless, than a normal person. Do you know why?"

"You're going to tell me," Jeff said. "You'll spell it out, I'm sure, for my simple, primitive mind. Why the guaranteed law-abider has to be defenseless against the lawbreaker. But my admiration for scientifically administered quote justice unquote is at an unfortunate ebb. Don't you have things reversed?''

''No. Listen, if there has to be crime, it's better that the victims be selected from the ranks of the guilty, not the innocent. A ringer is guilty; he has committed a crime and been convicted. So he should be the one who—''

''What about his *present* life? Dave was good, wasn't he? He would have gone on being good, while the punks who killed him—''

''If any old man had to die that way, Dave would have wanted it to be him. Why do you think he stayed in the park so much? He knew that sooner or later some kids that were old enough to make trouble and not old enough to know better would mug someone. Most of the park's regulars stayed clear of him; but new ones are always moving in. Dave knew that the ring would catch them and cure them—but he didn't want an innocent person to be the instrument of their capture. So he made himself available, and he died the way he wanted to die—saving the life of some other person. Someone he never knew, but who *would* have been the next victim if the punks went free. To him, that was true justice. That's what the ring taught him. If you deny that, you are denying what he died for.''

''And now those kids will lead saintly lives, because of his sacrifice?''

''Yes!'' Ralph and Alice said together.

''Even the two who got away?''

''The ones they caught will be ringed, then they'll help run down the others. Within a week that bunch will be finished, Jeff. Perhaps they'll do more good, as ringers, than old Dave Paxton was able to do.''

"Sure."

"Jeff, Jeff," Alice said, "you don't know. Ringers are more protected than other citizens. They are watched because they are likely targets, and are given a police guard when they ask for it. How do you think the police got to you so quickly—or to me, before?"

"I couldn't care," Jeff said. "They were too slow. A faster reflex, unhampered by the ring, would have done better. Just a little more of Nature's natural survival instinct would have fixed those dirty little—" But the medicine was wearing off, and the shock got through this time for the unkind sentiment.

"You see," Ralph said. "But for the ring, you would have been the killer. That's what you have to overcome. Someday you'll see that you can't kill evil by practicing more evil."

"Maybe," Jeff said. He thought about the original reason he had come to Earth. "When I stop believing that proper justice should be served, I'll accept anything. Until then, I'll—"

"Jeff!" Alice cried. "You're only punishing yourself. Don't keep hating. Don't keep thinking that way. Control your thoughts. You can do it. You don't want revenge. You—"

"DAMN!" Jeff burst out, and the shock hit fiercely.

"Jeff," Ralph Blois said finally. "Jeff, you're so upset and so determined, you're likely to do some violence to yourself. Some new ringers just burn themselves out, fighting it. Alice and I have arranged to take turns watching you, until your crisis is over."

"Great," Jeff said, not pleased. "And who's going to watch this fouled-up society until *its* moral crisis is over?"

The two looked at each other. A doctor came in with another spray hypo.

"No," Jeff said. "Don't need it. Don't want another pacifier."

When he woke again, only Alice was there. "You're coming along fine, Jeff," she said. "We all go through something like this. I did myself, when—"

"Yeah," he said.

"You know I can't lie about it, Jeff. It's a natural reaction."

"Okay—tell me about it."

She sighed. "You won't like it, Jeff. I don't know what your impression of me has been, but—"

He waited.

"You know of course that I see you as a potential—husband. Ringers need other ringers, and I need you. Other people don't know our problems. Other people aren't as—moral."

He had not known. It was obvious in retrospect, but marriage had been far from his mind. They had had one formal evening together, and her frankness made him uneasy. How could this be a basis for permanent liaison, when he loved another girl?

Alice knew. She had heard all of the truthall testimony, and she had experienced some of it firsthand. Did she think that if he ever did get satisfaction from McKissic, she would share his share of G&G?

Shock.

"Oh, Jeff." He saw her bite her lip and look away. She must have seen his reaction to the pain and thought it was his reaction to her, personally. Perhaps it was.

Slowly she began talking. "Once there was a girl named Alice. Not this Alice, but the one who had this body before the ring. That Alice couldn't help herself any more than this one can now, about certain things. She had a mother but no father. All her childhood she paid for her birth. She paid her mother, her schoolmates, and the parents of the other children she knew. She knew somehow that an injustice had come about, and that she had to pay for it, though she was the victim and not the perpetrator. She grew up feeling that someday the accounts would have to be straightened, that she had to get back what she had been denied. So she went out to get it, Jeff, not certain what it was, but determined. Alice set out to get her own.''

Jeff listened, marveling. Was she consciously paralleling his own experience? His father had been disgraced; hers did not, practically speaking, exist. He had known that he had a score to settle; so had Alice. He had set out to correct the situation his own way; so had she.

Or was this simply the route all ringers took, the basic pattern, with only the names and dates modified to suit the individual?

"Alice became a call-girl, Jeff—but not a common one. Not a legal Vicinc businesswoman. She did not sell a few moments of imitation love twice a week instead of working for a living. Oh, no, Alice played it smart. Her agency was strictly herself, and she picked her clients carefully. She didn't give value, even so simple a value as the one expected of a call-girl. Instead she used the old trick of a knockout drop and a quick fadeout with the customer's money—the money she had decided belonged to her. She searched out men who carried large negotiable notes on them; sometimes it took several contacts to be sure. She remained a virgin and she made a nice income—during her teen-girl years.''

The other facet of the park punks! The boys prowled for solitary or helpless strangers, while the girls exerted their savagery in more subtle fashion. *That* didn't exactly match his experience. Her story was real, not allegorical.

"Only once it didn't work. Once—and only once—a mark caught me doping his drink. He laughed, Jeff—then he beat me, just as I'd seen a man beat my mother. Then he took me by force. When he was through with me he paused to go through my purse. A lot of money was there, since I couldn't risk any formal savings registration. It astonished him—and while he was counting it, I got up, slipped off my shoes and moved quietly behind him with a lamp. The small, heavy type that draws its power from broadcast. I hit him over the head with it, knocking him out. I should have taken his money and left him there—but he'd beaten me and raped me and I was blind with shame and fury. It seemed to me that that ugly man on the floor was all the ugly men who ever had hurt innocent women."

She took a breath and finished it. "When the police got there, I was spattered with blood and graystuff, and he was long dead. There wasn't enough left of his face to recognize."

"So you were ringed," Jeff said, not really accepting it. "Yet in a way you were innocent. You—"

"As innocent as anyone who commits a terrible crime can ever be. But is it innocence, really, when it pretends to one kind of wickedness in order to perpetrate a different crime? That avoids the proper solutions in favor of the seemingly expedient ones? Is it, Jeff?"

He was silent.

"You're confused, aren't you, Jeff? You're wondering about that purity of motive you thought you had. You're thinking that perhaps the abduction you planned wasn't quite as reasonable as you thought. You never tried to approach McKissic honestly."

"Do you really believe he would have handed over my share of G&G stock, after cheating my—" Again the ring. "Well, at that time my action seemed proper to me. I'm still not certain there is any honest way to straighten things out. I can't prove McKissic is guilty unless he goes under truthall, and they won't put him under unless I first prove his guilt. For me, reconciliation with the ring is acceptance of an injustice.''

"But what makes you so certain he *is* guilty?"

"They were partners. No one but McKissic was close enough to the business and to my father to have framed him like that."

"Are you absolutely certain your father *was* framed?"

"He went under truthall," Jeff said.

She looked troubled, but did not point out the obvious. Geoffrey Font had been interrogated under the drug, and had been found guilty. Not only McKissic, but the entire court of law would have had to be corrupt, if Font had actually been innocent. Such a situation was unlikely to go unremarked for so many years. "But can this excuse criminal action on your part?"

"I don't know," he said sullenly, and was punished.

She stood up. "I think you'll be all right now, Jeff. I'll leave you to your thoughts. You know how to get in touch with me." She smiled at him and closed the door.

Jeff lay back and closed his eyes. His bandages were gone and he was feeling better, physically; things had been happening during that period of blankness. It had been good to see Alice, however briefly they had known each other; she *did* understand . . . much . . . and she had been very pretty in her—in whatever she had been wearing. His memory refused to cooperate.

He did have thoughts. Her interest in him was flattering—but he had never imagined that Alice had such a sordid history. She had seemed so much the normal woman, polite and proper, yet she had been more criminal than he. If she now believed wholeheartedly in the ring, and if it had been so great and beneficial a change in her, could he doubt that the same would come to him in time? And she wanted to marry him.

He remembered his mother and father, killed in the accident on Alpha IV. There had been no doubt about the circumstances; such things were too common on the prison planet. But it had been McKissic's crime that put them there, and thus McKissic's final responsibility. Geoffrey Font had cheated no one, but he had taken the blame and the exile, and his family had gone with him. Jeff had sworn to see justice done. Not for his own sake, though he would certainly become a rich man. No, not for fifty percent of General Gyromotors; for the sake of those two distant graves.

Yet how pure had his motives been? He hated McKissic—but what about the man's beautiful daughter, Pamela? Was it possible for such an evil man to raise such an angel? Jeff saw now that the kidnapping of Pamela had occurred to him naturally, not because it was the best way to gain justice but because he wanted to have the girl in his possession. Heiress falls in love with kidnapper. . . .

No, the clearing of his father's name had not been the only imperative, and to that extent he had been in fact as well as in theory a criminal. Was it after all primarily wealth and lust that activated him?

He was not aware of sleeping until he woke again, a minute or an hour later. Someone was stealthily trying the door. Now who? A nurse with another unnecessary vitamin shot. He kept his eyes closed. The door opened and shut; someone tiptoed in.

"Jeff? Jeff Font?"

He let his eyes open. He looked up. Then he sat up, amazed. "Pamela!"

She blinked dark eyes at him. Her hair was brushed

back, rich and long, and her face was cameo. She wore a short translucent skirt and a remarkably tight blouse. He stared at it—at *her,* he hastily corrected himself.

"Yes, it's really me, Jeff, girl of your dreams," the innocent face said at last. He winced to remember that she too had attended the hearing. "And you wanted to carry me away with you!"

He felt his face burning. Did she *have* to bring that up? "You're a very pretty girl," he said lamely.

She sat down on the bed. "So I've been told—but never guaranteed before by truthall," she murmured, leaning toward him. "Did you really believe I'd do those things with you? Those things you imagined—"

The ring was stinging him, and he hadn't even spoken. "I'm sorry you had to hear all that. But men do dream about women."

Her delicate hand went to the front of her blouse. "But did you ever believe, deep down inside, that I was that kind of—"

"No!" he exclaimed, but the ring shocked him.

"You're lying. You just got pricked, didn't you?"

"Yes. But it's easy to believe what you want to believe, when you're alone. Now that I've met you again, I know those dreams were wrong."

"Surprise!" she said.

"I don't understand." But he felt the ring again.

"Don't try to lie to me. I get you all excited, don't I?"

"Yes." What game was she trying to play with him?

"The ring does allow a man to love, doesn't it?"

"Yes."

"Don't worry—I put a 'Do Not Disturb' sign on the door. No one will come in." Her body was exactly as he had imagined it. "Move over, lover," she said, stretching out beside him. Somehow he had not seen her undress.

"We never did finish that business in the closet," she continued. "Better late than never."

Was this the lovely innocent he had known would never be his? This voluptuous, breathtakingly available creature?

She slid her cool, lithe, vibrant nymph-form body against him, her lips seeking his. Her silk-smooth thigh came over his leg, her bare foot hooking behind his. Her tongue darted out between moving lips. "Oh Jeffy, love me!"

His free arm circled automatically around her body, his eager hand skimming over the slenderness of back and waist. His other hand was somehow trapped between part of the bedsheet and her breast; then her hand caught his hand and pressed it closely to her.

"Oh, Jeffy," she whispered, flexing against him again. "The other day I saw the strangest thing. It was a sabbat."

"A what?"

"A sabbat. An assembly of demons and witches for some big orgy. We all had to put on devil-suits and flesh masks and go to this Goontown tavern where the ceremony was. Satan gave a lecture on the way human beings used to have sexual relations with supernatural creatures. Actually, the demons were made from air and were neuter; they became succubi in order to sleep with men, then they saved the semen and used it again when they became incubi and slept with women."

"You—slept with—"

"Oh, no, Jeffy. There aren't any *real* demons, and it was all just fun. They had this girl who worked there, and Satan sprayed her all over with Instant Confusion and then we—"

There were some things the ring wouldn't even permit him to listen to. He cut her off before it spoke. "You mean this is a drug cult?"

"No. Nobody else took any of the stuff. Not all over, I

mean; that's dangerous. They must pay that girl a lot, or maybe she's an addict. We just lined up and—touched her.''

He could imagine it. Every touch would send the victim into a paroxysm of pleasure. It was the dose of ignorance again, as he had seen it on Alpha IV, except that the spray was probably much milder than the paint. The others would spray a hand or a finger and—touch her. So innocent, yet so morbid.

''She was the succubus, you see,'' Pamela said.

''Why are you telling me all this?'' He was acutely aware of her close against him, but this was a strange way to make love. Assuming that that was what she contemplated.

''I was coming to that. You see, your truthall visions— well, they excited me, too, Jeff. But I'm still technically a virgin, and—''

''What are you getting at?''

''I brought a can of that spray—''

SHOCK!

It ran from his finger up his arm. Normal love between consenting adults was one thing, but drug-perversion was forbidden.

Pamela released a low, shuddery breath and rolled away from him. His ring had been pinned between her breast and her hand; she had taken the external portion of the charge. The ring was designed to shock only the wearer, unless someone attempted to remove it, in which case it let fly on the external circuit. How it acted on an ungrounded subject he didn't know—but it did!

Perhaps she had inadvertently twisted the ring as she talked. At any rate, she had felt it on hand and breast.

She was crying. Jeff reached for her, but she bounced off the bed and grabbed for her clothing.

He found himself trying to apologize. "The ring—when you said—"

"So now it's *my* fault!" she flared. "What kind of girl do you think I am?"

The ring shocked him again before he could reply.

In a little while she regained her composure. "Do—do you have to go through that every time you—?"

"Maybe there was a misunderstanding. Did you really bring that spray?"

"I think you're right about my father," she said. "I'll have to get you out of that ring. I always knew there was something funny about that exile. But it isn't going to be easy. He's dying, you see. Leukemia, and not over a year or a year-and-a-half to go. Then he'll lie dead and it will all belong to me—all of it."

"Leukemia? They developed the cure for that years ago," he said, perplexed.

"It's a new strain, or something. I—I don't know how I can get you off, Jeff, but I'll try. I don't think I can wait until your five years are up, even if you do want your name to sustain the disgrace."

"Pam, don't do anything foolish," he said, hardly able to keep up with her. She was dressed and heading for the door.

"I'll try not to," she said. The cameo expression slipped just a bit; then she closed the door and he heard her footsteps retreating.

He shook himself. He had been dreaming, of course. A side effect of his medication. The "events" of the past half hour—Pamela, nudity, sabbat, leukemia—the ring and his injuries were really playing havoc with his imagination! None of it fit what he thought he knew. None of it.

It had been an entertaining fantasy, though!

2

The big, sleek duocar was waiting at the corner. Pamela looked at it without surprise and climbed in through the door the chauffeur held open. She had thought her visit to the hospital was secret, but secrecy was something no realistic person took for granted.

She relaxed against the seat cushions of the rear compartment, crossed her legs, and carefully hiked up her skirt. The hum of the gyro increased and the car nudged into traffic.

Now to find out what her father was up to. She switched on the communicator and eyed the acne-scarred face of the driver. "Well, Phil?"

His serious mouth thinned as he glanced at her. He knew what was coming. "Orders, miss."

"Miss McKissic," she said.

"Yes, Miss McKissic."

"And did you get a nice juicy little earful?"

"The juiciest, Miss McKissic. Quite satisfactory."

"All nicely recorded, I'm sure. So that Daddy can get his jollies listening to what a poor bitch his little girl is?"

"All nicely recorded, Miss McKissic."

"Hmmmm." She uncrossed her legs and looked into the driver's compartment, controlling the pickup with a gesture of her finger. She passed over the empty seat adjacent to him and focused on the car's recorder and directional zoom pickup. She knew it was all in perfect working condition; Phil was very good about such things.

She returned to the craggy features of the man. "I don't suppose you'd care to erase that tape . . . ?" she inquired.

"No, Miss McKissic."

"Even for, shall we say, consideration?"

"No, Miss McKissic."

"Pamela."

"No, Pamela."

"You don't know what kind I'd offer," she said. "It just might be money."

"The odds are long."

She let her knees spread toward the pickup. "What's the matter, Philly, don't you think you're man enough for the payoff? Don't you think you might enjoy it—once? Daddy didn't have you cas—made technically impotent, did he?" The spread increased. "Philly, don't you think—"

"No, Pamela."

"My little frilly panties, Phil? Much better than Vicinc."

"Looks more like a girdle to me." He was mocking her. He was the only employee who dared.

She controlled her explosive anger and smiled. "No girdle, Phil. Nice, smooth, warm—"

"Miss McKissic, if I had the proverbial three-meter glastic extension, I assure you that I would hardly be tempted to touch you with it—anywhere."

"Then you *are* a eunuch!" She cut off the contact and threw herself back against the seat, no longer concealing the fury she felt.

After a moment she put on the cameo expression and touched the control again.

The chauffeur's face in the screen had not changed expression. "If it is any consolation, miss, I found the floor show quite stirring. There is something appealing about 'technical virginity.' If you had a gyro to match your chassis—"

"Then—?"

"By no means."

"Why? What are you afraid of?"

"Why do you assume that it's fear that motivates me? The offer was neither sincere nor attractive."

He had her there. "Can't fool you, can I, Philly? But you can't fool me either. You wouldn't play the game if it didn't interest you. What *is* bothering you?"

"I've been your daddy's man for a long time—remember? I don't like to hear him maligned."

"You mean—what I said to that ringer?"

"Precisely."

"But Philly, that was only—only fun. Teasing. You know."

"Font didn't know."

She frowned. "I don't understand you, Phil. I really don't. What's that criminal to you? You know I don't give a damn about him."

"I know Mr. McKissic has his work cut out to protect your reputation from the truth, and his own from you. Why did you say he had leukemia?"

She shook her head. "That was a bad choice, wasn't it. He knew leukemia was curable."

"That isn't the point, Miss McKissic."

"Well, he was crowding me. I gave him something to think about. The ringer, I mean. Now he has something to hope for. I'll bet he'd give his innocent all to marry me."

"In a year and a half your lie will show."

"A year and a half is a long time. Philly, do you think he'd rather know the truth? That when his sentence is served Daddy will figure out some other way to bury him?"

"I think, Miss McKissic," and the voice shook, "that your father is one finer man than you realize. He has never tortured a man. He has never killed one to my knowledge. He has never performed a dishonorable deed."

"Not directly, no. Not so you could prove it. Not so

long as he stays clear of truthall, anyway. I've been his daughter, or a reasonable facsimile, longer than you've been his man, Philly; how naive do you think I am?''

''He is a decent man, Miss McKissic. Your suspicions do not become you.''

''Suspicions? Philly, have I ever told you what that fine man used to do with his little blonde secretary? The one with the pneumatic bottom? Right in his office? Right on the divan? With me, his darling little wet-panted baby girl, hiding under his desk, hearing it all?''

''You have told me many times, Miss McKissic. As many times as you have wanted something from me. You always neglect to mention that he was legally estranged from your mother at the time, and that the girl had a valid Vicinc license. The affair was legitimate.''

''He should have one with that ringer girl who took my place last week. She *has* to be good.''

''Your humor isn't even original.''

''Better yet, he could marry her. Ringers *can* marry nonringers, can't they?''

''Ringers generally refuse to marry nonringers. The proposition is too one-sided. I'm sure Font wouldn't marry *you*. You attract him physically, but he isn't stupid.''

The knowledgeable chauffeur had seen through her again. ''Who *is* stupid enough to marry me, Phil?'' she inquired, serious for the moment. ''Any man who learns what a bitch I am won't even touch your three-meter extension. How can I—''

''We're here, miss. Your father is waiting.'' The car slowed.

She straightened and touched the window. The glastic became transparent. Her eyes widened at the open field and the waiting helihopper. ''My, this *is* different, Philly.''

''Quite different, miss.''

She heard him get out and come around to open the door for her. She tried, unsuccessfully, to stamp his toe as she stepped down. Experience had taught him how to handle her. "Your father is waiting, Miss McKissic."

"Isn't that nice!" She mounted the ramp and entered the passenger compartment. Inside she found a grayhaired man with very wide shoulders and mechanic's hands.

"I hardly recognize you outside of your business cloak," she said.

"Sit down, Pamela." McKissic's voice was low, level, sad.

She let the door slide closed behind her and took her seat, watching him. The compartment was small, but there was room for massed electronic equipment behind his recliner. McKissic touched a stud and the hopper lifted with the smoothness of robot control.

He touched another stud and something began to crackle gently. She knew what it was: all-wave, shiplimited interference. No communication of any type was possible through that. He only used it when he had something to discuss in utmost secrecy.

McKissic looked at her, drumming his strong fingers on his kneecap. The great chest heaved.

Pamela swallowed. She did not like to admit it, but her father cowed her. "You—you got the full story, didn't you?" she said nervously. "Phil didn't record it—he relayed it here. The hospital and the ride."

He did not reply. She waited; there did not seem to be much else to do. From the port she could see the spires of the city, picturesque as a miniature reproduction. From this rising elevation it was beautiful: the tall buildings were rainbow in sun and glastic, like artificial flowers, and helihoppers in heterogeneous colors hovered like dragonflies beside them. The graceful ribbons of the elevated highways curled between and over, the traveling gyrocars like ladybugs. A whirlpool of hoppers descended into one of the monster hotels, sucked in from the surrounding sky as though there were a leak in the atmosphere. She could not make out the individual citizens on the pedestrian levels, but knew they were there, like social termites.

Over the river was Gunnartown, with its ugly, fascinating decay; the sun bathed this, too, and it was no more homely than any distant dungheap. Where was that tavern, the Easygo, where she had attended the sabbat? A dingy little place, which was part of its intrigue.

"Pamela," McKissic said, looking tired.

It was coming. The Lecture. She should have been more careful what she said—or at least have sabotaged the duocar equipment first. Well, this too would pass.

"Am I going to ring you, Pamela?" he asked.

She realized, horribly, that he was serious. And he could do it. He and Judge Crater were like shaft and counterweight. He would already have decided. Nothing she could say now would change his decision, one way or the other.

"If you want a ringer for a daughter," she said. "You know what will happen if I ever go under truthall. Be a little bit bad for business, wouldn't it?" But it was bravado. She knew he would bankrupt the business if he decided he had sufficient reason. He simply was not vulnerable to threats.

He did not move. "You believe that I framed my partner and had his son ringed, to protect my interest in the business?"

"Well, that's what the ringer believes, Daddykins. And you won't go under truthall to deny it. And I know the way you are about women. Maybe it wasn't just the business. I hear the ringer's mother, Ronda Font, was a handsome article. You knew her pretty well. Was that why she tried to throw that stuff in your face? Secretaries don't matter, I suppose, but your partner's wife—''

"You have a distorted view of the situation, Pamela."

She laughed, a shade hysterically. "Oh, Daddykins!"

McKissic would not be moved. She had never been able to make him angry. That was a trait he shared with the chauffeur. "The difficulty with truthall, Pamela, is that it is absolute. *All* the truth comes out. I have obligations that must remain private. What you believe you know about me could prove embarrassing if publicized, but I assure you G&G would survive it handily. What *I* know could destroy an industry and lead to wholesale economic anarchy. I must do as I find proper in the time remaining to me."

"In the time *remaining?*"

"It seems your little story about my demise was not so farfetched, daughter. I will not govern General Gyro very much longer."

"But leukemia is curable!"

"Leukemia, yes. This, no."

She looked out over the city again, but the too familiar buildings were repulsive now. The hoppers were like fruit flies lighting on festering stalks, the highways like festooned cobwebs. "Is that what you brought me here for?"

"In part, Pamela. To give you certain information and to put one stricture upon you. I have to do it now, while I am able."

"Not just to lecture me again about teasing people?"

"Most of those people can take care of themselves. I have confidence that in time you will discover that ethical behavior pays. If you don't, the ring will eventually assist you."

"So you aren't going to have me ringed by that domesticated judge of yours?"

"No."

"What were you going to tell me?"

"Two things, Pamela. First, that Geoffrey Font, Senior, was an innocent man."

"You admit it!"

"I have never denied it. Jeff, also, in a more devious manner, was framed. Since he is the survivor, I am doing what I can to help him."

"By making him a ringer!"

"That is true, strange enough."

She shook her head as though to clear it of cobwebs. "You have a funny way of helping people, Daddykins. What was the second thing?"

"That you are my daughter, and I know you for what you are—and I love you."

Pamela tried to laugh again, but it didn't come out. "You—"

"I wanted you to know."

Half a dozen clever remarks passed through her mind, but all collapsed before the realization that again he meant it. He knew about her, the obscene conversations, the lies, the teasing seductions, the general worthlessness concealed behind the cameo facade; he had it all on record—yet he loved her.

Perhaps he was the only man who ever had—or ever would. Few others saw beyond the cameo, and those who did were repelled by the selfishness and shallowness there. There was only one who neither worshipped her nor sought to use her. The most important one: her father.

She did not know how to comment, so she said nothing. Her eyes were blinded by unrehearsed tears. "What—whatever that stricture is, Daddy—I'll honor it."

McKissic sighed. "It will not be easy, Pamela. But it is most important."

"I'll *do* it! I'll obey, for once. Just tell me. Do you want me to marry the ringer, to make it up to him? I'll—"

"No, Pamela. Quite the opposite. I want you to stay away from him."

Her eyes opened. *"That's* it? *Not* to marry him?"

"Not even to talk to him again, Pamela. You must drop out of his life entirely. You may do anything else, but you may not associate with him."

She stared at him. "But you said he was framed. If you won't tell the court, and won't let me—"

"In time you will know the reason. Then you will know what to do. Until then, avoid him totally. This is all I ask of you."

"I don't know whether I can, now," she said. "You know the way I am about wanting what I can't have. That's why I was so jealous of those secretaries of yours. Can't you tell me *why?"*

"Not yet. Distract yourself in any way you wish, but do not see Jeff Font again. Believe me, this is the way it must be."

"I'll try," she said. "I don't know how I'll do it, but I'll try."

Ed Bladderwart looked out the window of his shack and lifted another bottle of beer. He drank an ironic toast to the skyway and its flashing lights—none of them on the nearer span.

He wondered whether *it* was running along the deserted section, sniffing out edible refuse. The years had passed, and his sister had long since gotten over the shock of the annulment and her sterilization, and she had moved to another section of the country. She had had a breakdown

when the thing escaped, but nothing had come of it;
probably it had fallen under the wheel of a gyro or drowned
in a sewer.

Still it haunted his memories. Such a penalty—for one
night of reveling under the spray. That's what the medic
had said: the drug left its mark deep inside, in the pattern
of the genes, where it didn't show . . . immediately. The
cure could not undo that type of damage, no matter how
promptly administered. A person could usually get away
with little doses—a hand or a foot or part of the face—but
one all-over binge would cancel any family plans.

They had been trying to outlaw the stuff for years, but
Vicinc had a lobby blocking that, and a lot of people
didn't want children anyway. And Sensuals was *still* the
rage at the Easygo. . . .

"Ed," Annie said at his elbow, "don't you think you
had enough beer tonight?"

"Naw, Annie." He continued to stare. "I've got a real
reason tonight—real reason."

"But Ed, there's nothing really linking you. You never
did anything. Just because one of their men got nabbed
bringing in a gyro—"

"I was stupid, Annie, stupid." Ed guzzled at the bottle,
but the liquid tasted like water. "A stupid man deserves
what he gets. They'll follow the trail, they will. Truthall.
They'll find me out. They'll ring me, sure."

"But Ed, all you did was talk. I mean, if everyone who
talked to Sam was ringed—"

"Stupid, stupid, stupid," Ed said. "Should've known it
wouldn't work. Should've known it. Even if they hadn't
fouled up the shipment and if the guy hadn't probably
done what I would've—tossed the happy pills into the
garbage—the whole thing was stupid. 'Just run the cars
down the cutoff, and the driver jumps out!' " he mimicked

Sam's high voice. "Sure, so naturally the engineers decide to do more than just lift the topping; they tear the whole pavement up, leaving just the bare girders, nothing else. Then for good measure they drop a beam across the ramp and build another barricade just before the junkyard. And they start working in the middle, not the end they were supposed to. Impossible to drive a thing like that, even if some punk wanted to cream himself for kicks. As for running down empty cars—"

"Poor Ed. Poor, poor Eddie," Annie said.

"Damn Sam," Ed said, feeling a headache through the beer. "Damn him! Lousy bastard should have the pill rammed down *his* throat!"

VI. Drive to Destruction

1

JEFF lay and looked at the ceiling, unable to relax after all. It *must* have been a dream, however real it seemed. To imagine that sweet, unspoiled Pamela would actually come to his bed and attempt to lure him into a drugged seduction . . .

Could George McKissic have leukemia? An incurable variant? That would change the whole picture.

No, it was all the product of the fevers of illness. He had imagined, dreamed, hallucinated, dredging up wish fulfillments from his unpenitent subconscious, and none of it had happened. What was the last thing he was certain of?

Alice. Alice Lang, proposing marriage and telling him of her past. That must have thrown him into an emotional spin. Her proposition had been logical: male ringer matches female ringer. She would make him a good wife. But how many deserving women had been damned by that uninspired praise?

Pamela, on the other hand, had—sex appeal.

His finger twinged. So now the ring was dictating his social life!

Or was it? Did he really believe Pam was innocent? His

158

dreams of her, the ones he had spilled out so horribly under truthall, had been exaggerated, but still based on fact. She had been precocious as a child. She had talked about playing "secretary," a game whose implications he had never quite grasped. She had liked to experiment, to take off her clothing, to do the things she knew she shouldn't, apparently *because* they were forbidden. There had been a sexual tone to all of it, he saw in retrospect. Unless her basic character had changed, she should have grown up to be an aggressive, offbeat nymph. Just about the type who would sneak into a man's bed and then repulse him with a degraded suggestion.

Assume it had happened as he remembered it, then. What were the implications? First, that McKissic was dying—which meant that Jeff's whole program had been pointless. No—it made things more urgent, since once McKissic died there would be no way to unravel the truth. It was justice he wanted, not revenge.

On the other hand, his memory could be accurate, but the information false. Pamela wasn't ringed. She had the privilege of lying. She—

The door opened. Alice entered. "You couldn't have done this," she said, holding up the sign that had been on the outside of the door. It was not a hospital sign, and it said: OPEN FOR BUSINESS.

"Why that little—" But he stopped before the ring acted. So Pamela *had* visited him—and lied about the sign. She hadn't cared whether they were discovered. She had even invited exposure. Any nurse who read the sign . . .

And how much else had she lied about?

The ring spoke this time. Correction: there could have been a misunderstanding. Pamela might have been a co-victim of a third party's practical joke. "Do you believe that, Ring?" he inquired of his finger.

Alice glanced at him. "Believe what, Jeff?"

He flushed. "A private joke. Forget it."

"The doctor said you were healing nicely," she said. "You can leave at any time, provided you're careful. That's what I came to tell you. Would you like to come with me?"

Gentle Alice, former call-girl and murderess, who wanted him for a husband. Yet it seemed the ring made her a better woman than Pamela. . . ,

"I don't know. Where did they hide my clothing?"

She rummaged in the closet. "Your old cloak was beyond repair, but I arranged for a fresh one." She brought out a handsome new outfit.

"You seem to be taking good care of me." He took the clothing into the minuscule lavatory. Yes, she was taking care of him—but she had been right when she warned him that he wouldn't like her history. No matter where he looked, Earth seemed to be ugly, underneath. His own motives had looked bad enough, under truthall—but he was coming to see that they were only average, for this festering culture. Did he want to become a permanent part of such a mess? Or would it be better to go to space again, where at least things were direct?

He stepped into the room. "My," Alice said appreciatively, "don't we look handsome."

"*My* mirror tells me I look corpse-pale. How can Ultra Conscience let you lie like that?"

"Opinions can differ," she said, taking his arm. He walked down the hall with her and through a reception room and out into the street. There was no checkout procedure for a ringer; the management knew the bill would be covered.

The sun was shining and the city was beautiful. Multicolored helihoppers glinted in the bright sky. A good many were that same tasteless pink of the one that had scared the park punks away, that first time. He had assumed that Pamela had done him that favor, but it was obvious now that she hardly cared enough. He had read meaning into coincidence, making his adjustment that much more complicated. It could also have been his own anxiety that had read a frightened expression as she left the ballet stage.

Well, she *had* done him the favor of showing him what she was. He took a deep breath of the fresh air and imagined his color improving.

"My car's around back, Jeff," Alice said. "I'll take you home—or anywhere you want to go. You don't have to report to work until you feel up to it. They—we—appreciate the brave thing you did, trying to help Dave."

"I had a visitor, after you left," he said, not paying attention.

"Oh? That's nice. Who was it?"

"Pamela McKissic."

"Oh!" He heard her short intake of breath.

"How well do you know her, Alice?"

She considered. "Not very well, really. She's the boss's daughter, after all. I've seen her at the annual parties and then when I—you know."

"But you have an opinion about her? Her character?"

"Of course. Why?"

"Anything bad?"

"Bad? Jeff, are you trying to make me into a gossip? If I knew anything bad, I'd have reported it to the police long ago."

"I need to know about her, Alice. Her motivations. A—a great many things." He walked beside her, his face turned downward. Alice wanted to marry him—so he talked to her about Pamela. Ironic . . . yet who else was there to ask?

"As far as I know, she's a very nice girl. Spoiled, of course, but no worse than usual. And her father—I know you don't agree with this, Jeff—Mr. McKissic is a very good employer. I don't think either of them would do anything wrong."

"Pamela wouldn't climb into bed with a man she hardly knew and make . . . suggestions, then?"

She looked at him. "What a strange question! Of course she would, if she liked him. There's nothing wrong with byplay between consenting adults."

Jeff saw himself as a country hick from Alpha IV. Except that his ring *had* protested that drug notion of Pamela's. Alice had naturally assumed that he referred to normal heterosexual activity. "But of course," he said, "if a McKissic *did* err, he or she would not advertise the fact to a ringer." Except that Pamela had told him some very dangerous things. What was her game?

"What did she say to you, Jeff? You're all upset."

He looked up from the pastel pavement as they approached the downslant into the parking lot. Earth buried its cars when they weren't moving; why couldn't he bury his thoughts?

Alice's sporter stood near the ramp. He turned to her, noting with embarrassment that she was very nicely dressed. She had made herself pretty for him.

"Alice, could I drive you straight to your hotel?"

"Certainly, Jeff." She handed him the key. "Do you want me or the car?" She wasn't being coy; it was a direct question, a ringer question. Ask a ringer whether she will or she won't, he thought, and she will tell you—whether she will or she won't.

"I don't know. If I were smart, I'd want you—but things aren't that settled. I have to do some serious thinking."

"She certainly is pretty. But—"

"So are you, Alice. That isn't the problem."

She did not question him further, and he drove on to her hotel. She got out without comment at her apartment and smiled bravely back at him. "Don't break any laws!"

He laughed, a trifle bitterly, and waved as he pulled away. It hurt him to leave her like that, but it would have been worse to build up her hopes before he was sure. He knew that she was right, and right for him, even apart from the ring factor; and he knew that Pamela was a dream of sensuality that could never be realized because it was phony. He knew—but what man willingly gives up the irrational adventure without at least exploring its potential?

He was uncertain what his destination was, whether or not it was in any sense physical, or what he expected to gain from so silly a thing as an unorganized drive. He couldn't even go very far, since he was not supposed to exert himself unduly during his recuperation, and the ring would see that he obeyed.

He passed a Vicinc outlet, gaudily lighted day and night. Strange, he thought, the way Vicinc was supposed to have abolished repression, just as technology had abolished need and the ring had wiped out crime. Civilization was utopia, in theory—but the theory was badly flawed. Crime was in fact rampant on every level, with thugs in the park and corruption among top executives. Need—well, inflation—had simply kept pace with technology, so that the fancy little gyrocars still cost more than the average man could afford without extended payments and prolonged debt. Repressions, sexual and otherwise, instead of being relieved, had discovered more and more morbid expressions.

He was approaching the skyway. Well, why not? He had never driven its length, having lacked sufficient leisure when he'd had a car before. Somewhere along this road was that junkyard, just off one of the turnoffs—Big Ed's place. How had Ed made out, after learning about that stolen car?

Jeff slowed, shifting his body to zero the vertical indicator, and steered the vehicle onto the elevated track. The thing about gyros was that they did not tilt with the landscape; they maintained their attitude whatever came, in the short run, which made possible the economy of the single tire. Of course, that whirling balance could make things inconvenient at times, and the driver always had to be alert—but overall, the gyro provided a compactness and stability that had never been available in the automotive field before. It was a real pleasure to be swinging out alone like this.

Afternoon thunderheads enclosed the highway ahead in a darkening canopy. That was right—Weathinc had scheduled rain for 1630, according to the morning fax. The law required a ten percent reduction in velocity during inclement driving conditions, but that was no problem. He slid into the high speed lane and applied power.

The little car shot up the incline at fifty miles per hour, its single tire singing against the dark firm plastop. The sporter was beautifully responsive.

Rain would not affect the driving surface, he thought, and wondered why the law had not been revised to allow for this. There were so many laws that an intelligent person could question. Regulations were not intended to endure past their time; they needed to be updated periodically. Maybe there should be a ringer on the highway board.

The hi-vee lane rose above the others, and Jeff could see beyond the sturdy guard-rails to the winking early lights of the city. The overcast had brought premature dusk, making the metropolitan structures stand out uniquely in the half-light. Overcrowded and dangerous it might be—but from above the lighted city was a splendor.

Perhaps that was what he needed to remember about the law: despite its defects, the great legal structure was—when viewed from above—a splendor. Man struggled in the darkness of his inner world to generate the light called ethics. Only a united ethical framework, formalized as law, could cast brightness and beauty where black anarchy had been.

As though that law benefited *him*. . . .

The business district fell behind. Below him, on the slower lanes, he saw staid sedans and larger duocars. Strange vehicle, the duo—its gyro had to be fixed into place with respect to sidewise motion, but free to swing along the forward axis. Otherwise the tilt of the highway, transmitted by the front and rear wheels, would set up a precession that would shove the car out of control.

The limit here was a minimum seventy. It occurred to him that he was not in a state of complete driving alertness and should not be driving at this speed. He would have to look for a shunt to a lower lane before the weather deadline.

He found one. He slowed.

No—it was a detour to the left. The skyway stretched before him, a mighty steel and plastic rainbow arching over twelve million citizens. He could see the tiered exit ramp drawing from the eastbound lanes, his included, right where he needed it. They merged into the handle of the fan, far ahead, forming the lane leading into Gunnartown.

But this section had been closed off for repairs. He could see the line of smoking flare-bombs (inert colored mist, technically) and the piles of dismantled and rusty guard-rails. The pavement seemed intact. Probably just rail replacement.

The car vibrated against its gyro as Jeff hesitated. The detour would keep him on the high-speed strip during the rainfall, which was the situation he was trying to avoid. What he needed was the normal exit further ahead, not a crowded temporary ramp. He continued to slow.

Other cars braked, blinked, and spun around him angrily, funneling into the detour ramp. The ring warned him; he had to match speed and get back in the line of traffic.

BLAAARRRRE!

A monster duo was bearing down on him. From this angle it loomed as large as a multi-wheel transport, though he knew this was a gross exaggeration of perspective. He had hesitated too long. This was not lawbreaking, but certainly poor judgment. And he fancied himself a good driver!

Now he was in trouble. He was trapped out of the direct flow of traffic, with the barricade ahead and no safe way to reenter.

Seconds to spare, no time to debate with Ultra Conscience and its version of right and wrong. To swerve back into the detour lane would be to risk his own demise as well as injury to other parties. There was now no break in the swiftly moving traffic, jammed together by the detour. He would have to run the barricade—a misdemeanor, but the only sensible course.

Shock!

The ring forbade it. He could not deliberately break a law.

But the alternative—

Shock! Shock! Shock!

No time. No choice.

SHOCK!

And he was driving over the unskirted ribbon, hand an

inferno, the nominal barricade toppled behind. He remembered making no decision; evidently the paradox of conflicting ethics had enabled him, in the explosion of pain, to do what he knew was best in the situation. What *he* knew, not Ultra Conscience. There was no substitute, in an emergency, for human judgment.

Paradox: this was the fatal weakness of the ring. He had heard that many ringers had died, apparently unable to adapt to a rigorously law-abiding life. But more likely they had adapted—while their rings hadn't. Seldom were human affairs so simple that there were merely two alternatives, one right, one wrong. Put a two-valued governor on a multi-valued man . . .

Still, the ring was tied to the wearer's own values matched against standard ones. It did differentiate. It gave a small shock for a small offense, a large one for the large. The eye-for-eye, tooth-for-tooth justice might fail at times, but it *was* consistent. His ring hadn't completely frustrated his attempt to save old Dave Paxton. A man was expected to help another in need, and not by simply adding his own death to that of the victim. A certain limited compromise was possible.

Could there, similarly, be some partial solution to the McKissic problem? Why *couldn't* he at least try talking with the man? There just might be factors he didn't know about.

But the immediate danger was not over. He had been slowing the car, his thoughts compressed into adrenalic seconds. The lane ahead where he had thought to turn was narrow. He had been doing over seventy when danger threatened, and had apparently speeded up to pass the barrier. Now he saw that they were repairing more than the guard-rails. The topping had been lifted to expose the corroded struts beneath. Only that portion of the surface required for the workmen's footing remained—hardly six feet wide. The other lanes, below and to the side, were similarly stripped. No wonder the section had been closed off.

Well, six feet was a full lane for a small car. Now that he was committed, it would be better to go on, rather than attempt a perilous turnabout and reentry into the speeding traffic of the detour.

The ring nudged him, but again he had to select the lesser of evils. He knew how to control a forward-moving monocar; his reflexes were geared for the automatic corrections for drift and precession, and by going on he endangered no one but himself. He could take that Gunnartown leadoff and be safely out of it.

It was eerie, driving over the suddenly narrow ribbon with open air below and no protective rails. He kept the tire centered, preserving as much clearance on each side as he could. This was not precisely analogous to the mountain driving he had done on Alpha. . . .

Perhaps it would be better after all to stop the vehicle. He could park it, get out, and spin it about by hand. That way he wouldn't have to maneuver across the narrowness of the pavement.

The storm broke. Huge drops splattered against his windshield and changed the color of the strip from frictive white to slippery gray. Danger! This pale underlayer had never been intended for wet driving.

A gust of wind from the side pushed the tire a few inches over. This was a hazard the gyro could not ease. What good was a faithful upright position, if the entire vehicle was hurtling through air toward destruction below?

Now he could neither stop nor slow. He had to keep the car under power, to fight the erratic gusts. He accelerated gently, feeling for the grip of the tire and peering through the murk ahead for the pathway.

Suddenly the pavement stopped.

Jeff braked instinctively, but as he had feared, the wheel skidded on the slippery surface. There was no road before him! They had taken up everything. Only the naked supporting girder remained. He was going over the edge!

No! He accelerated once more, feeling the tread grip again. The car jumped forward, skewed, straightened. The gap rushed up at forty miles per hour.

The bottom dropped out.

And he was on the bare girder, its eight-inch width matching the tread of his tire exactly. The gyro held him level as the lights of the city passed dizzily beneath the car. The periodic supporting struts flashed by like vintage railroad ties, glistening with treacherous moisture.

He had done it! The death of all his hopes yawned in the gulf below, but all he had to do now was maintain speed and steer.

All?

This was a straight-and-narrow that put the ring to shame. He'd be lucky to last more than a few seconds. Even if he could bring the vehicle to a safe halt, he would still be stranded on the girder, forced to walk or crawl along it to safety. Assuming that the wet wheel would grip well enough to brake at all, if he dared try it.

He didn't. Loss of traction now would—

There was a jolt. Some imperfection in the metal, some protruding bolt—he felt it like a stab in his own body, inordinately sensitive now to the contact between wheel and beam. His own nerves extended to that tire.

The car swerved—inches, but inches were too much. He held the steering bar, thankful that this was a finely machined pleasure model, not so much controlling it as willing it back to center. He could no longer afford those adrenalic reactions. A drift of inches either way would catapult him off the beam. Half the tire must have overlapped the abyss for a moment.

Too close. Only the stability lent by the gyro had prevented a suicidal tilt. He knew intellectually that he could not hold course very long, but emotionally he had to keep on fighting.

He thought of Alice, in her safe, snug apartment, asking no more of him than that he join her there.

He was still moving. His real speed through the ambient drizzle was twenty miles per hour, according to the indicator, but he felt as though he were in a rocket on a track. The bare metal strip plunged on into misty space, impossibly narrow. A knife-edge over nothing. Any twitch, any obstruction—

Then the skeleton of the exit ramp was at hand, curving off to the right. The pavement returned within a few hundred yards—if he could get to it.

He made the turn. He played it by feel, guiding the tire onto the diverging beam, still afraid to use the brake. The corrosion on the girders provided some essential friction, at least. He was coming around—

Too much. He was off to the right, and the continuing right curve made it even more chancy to counteract. He had to hold his position and hope that the strip would move under him again.

Three quarters of the wheel might be over the edge! The gyro whined as it resisted the powerful tilt. Precession angled the entire body forward.

The exits from their other lanes were converging; he saw the scant metal beams. He had to ease the pressure before they connected with his, or the chassis would scrape. That would spin the wheel around, since the gyro would also shift the car's attempted flipover into a force at right angles, and the vehicle would steer grandly off into space.

He could disconnect the gyro—this was supposed to be impossible while a car was in motion, but he knew enough to do it anyway—but it would be no solution. Without that remaining stability the car would immediately complete its fall to the right, since the tire was riding the rim and clinging there only by some miracle.

Jeff threw himself forward, *directly into the tilt.*

And the gyro began precession to the left, once more acting at right angles.

Jeff shifted to the left, following it, jamming his body hard against the inner curve of the bubble—and the car lifted its nose. Now he was in balance—his weight to the left as far as possible, counteracting to some extent the lack of support on the right. His hand still held the steering bar, braced against the panel to prevent any deviation. It was impossible to correct gyro distortion by steering—but he could easily have nudged the wheel off the beam by trying.

Now, and only now, did he tighten his grip, edging the bar over microscopically to steer the car back to center. As he did so, he leaned slowly back toward the middle, keeping it balanced.

The pavement resumed.

Jeff relaxed, abruptly weary. Probably few men on Earth could have gotten through, for normal reactions would have been disastrous. Right-angle response had to be immediate when a gyro was in trouble, and only a person raised with gyro technology and theory and used to rough driving possessed those reactions. Even so, he had been lucky—exceedingly lucky. He would not try a drive like that again, ever.

A second barrier loomed ahead of him—a sturdy one.

Beyond it he saw the curve of the exit, to the left—and the dropoff into the junkyard. Big Ed's place. His relief had betrayed him; he could not possibly brake in time.

There was no stopping, no turning off, no neat little trick with the gyro. He jammed on the brake, but the wheel skidded and skewed once more. It was the end.

At the last moment before the crash he threw up his arms to protect his face. His right hand was forward, as though the ring could somehow protect him from this. The car struck and went into a crazy, toplike spin; the lights of the city spun around him like an animate cocoon. He was in the air, and dropping. He was—

2

"Eddie," Annie said. "There's a car on the cutoff!"

"Ridiculous!" Ed said, gazing into his bottle as though there were a cockroach in it. "You're just humoring me because I'm drunk." He wasn't, though, and she knew it.

"No, Ed, really! Look, why don't you."

"I don't have time to look, woman. More important things on my fat mind. Things like money."

"It's where that single girder should be. It's raining; I can't see. If— Ed! There *is* a car. On the construction!"

"Impossible."

"It's coming, Eddie. Just like you planned it. Down here to get wrecked—only no road for it. It—if only I could *see!* It's driving without lights."

Ed stood up and walked to the window. "Holy ringer! There *is* a car out there! Why didn't you say so, woman?"

"Oh, Eddie—he made it! Over that—did you ever see such driving? Did you?"

"Naw. Must be a circus daredevil, practicing." He reached out a big hand and tried to wipe away the drops of water on the pane, though they were on the outside. "In the *rain?*"

"Ed, that must be the best driver in the world out there. The best! But he's still going to smash . . . he's—oh!"

"Poor bastard," Ed said. "What's he want to do that for?" Then, as though to convince himself: "Maybe he jumped out first, like they planned." And finally almost as an afterthought: "Hey—he landed in *my* yard!"

Annie caught the tone. "Ed! Wait a minute! How do you know—"

"The powerpak, Annie—it's mine! Got to get out there fast. Before the cops—"

Annie followed him out, still protesting. "But what if he *didn't* jump out, Eddie?"

"Get away from me, woman. Stay in the house. You know those things are booby-trapped."

"Ed! You can't—"

"Move!"

Frightened, Annie retreated. Ed approached the wreck. The car had landed on its side and skidded a number of feet. The barricade must really have bopped it, he thought, because the car had almost flipped over. And the gyro was intact; he could hear the characteristic hum. He could cut it out entire and—

Let's see. He'd have to substitute one of the old broken gyros, so the police wouldn't know . . . no, that wouldn't work. They'd compare numbers. Best just to hide the entire wreck for a few days, and if no one asked, then he could take it apart. And they might not ask, because how could they know for sure where the accident happened?

If that fallen barricade didn't give it away. He could say punks had done it, maybe.

He started up his power tripod and maneuvered it over the twisted mass. He swung the mechanical tackle—magnetic was no good for handling a live gyro—and anchored it to the solid chassis. But his mind kept working too.

Sam had fouled up the plan; the word was out. If the cops were on to him, they might be watching for something like this. They might even have set it up to trap him. Maybe they suspected he was in on it but needed evidence. So they—well, something like this would be a good pretext to haul him before the ringing judge and put him under truthall and tie a band on him. Sure, that was it—the car couldn't have crashed in his yard by accident.

The more he thought about it, the more certain he became that honesty was the most expedient policy. He would have to report the "accident" exactly the way a good citizen would. That would bollix their trap! It might even exonerate him from suspicion in the other affair.

Ed put away his gear, skirted the wreck, and returned to the house. At the door he cursed and turned back. He had to take down the car's registration so he could report it properly.

Annie opened the door, but he waved her back. If this was a trap, all the more reason to keep her out of it. He knew she'd be poking around the thing the moment he left it, but at least he could make his report properly.

He walked up and circled to peer at the tag behind the crushed bubble-top. That was when he saw the water-thinned blood dripping down.

Alice Lang sat in her hotel suite and stared forlornly at her phone. She might as well face it, she thought: her days as a voluptuous lady of desire were over. Even if she could be freed of the ring, she no longer had the temperament for it. No longer the flair to entice a man. Yet she hoped Jeff would phone, if he didn't actually come back. It was, at least, her car he was using.

No, she thought as she looked at her blonde hair in the three-quarter view mirror. She was not the only woman in Jeff Font's life, and Pamela McKissic was hardly a matter a virile male would take lightly. Jeff had yet to realize what a difference the ring made.

Suppose the McKissic girl *were* to marry him—and in view of her visit to the hospital, and Jeff's question about her climbing into bed, this was a distinct possibility—she would soon tire of the arrangement. No free woman relished being constantly subject to report for minor violations. Jeff would stop Pamela from joyriding at illegal speeds, from shopping for illicit delicacies in Gunnartown stores, from using G&G money for private parties. All children of wealth took such things as a matter of course, and even Pamela must indulge in some.

Her friends would tease her about her law-abiding sex life. The ringer would never strike his wife or swear at her or even criticize her unfairly—and a rich girl needed those things now and then, and wanted them. She had to have a masterful husband. Alice had seen too many rich girls; those who found strong, even unscrupulous husbands flourished, while those who did not, did not.

How could a woman be a woman, unless she had a man who was a man? The ring made a man into a law-abiding citizen, which was another matter. Except to another ringer.

And when Pamela tired of the novelty, she would divorce him. The mere fact of being a ringer was grounds for divorce by the other party. She could be free twenty-four hours after making the decision. He, on the other hand, could not divorce *her*. He had to have grounds, and unless she grew exceedingly careless or blatant, he would have nothing but suspicion, and be punished by the ring for *that*.

A ringer was prisoner to his unringed spouse, and very few such miscegenous marriages endured. Those few occurred almost invariably when the wife was the ringer, not the husband.

But when a ringer married a ringer, the terms were even. There was a very special mutual understanding, and absolutely no conflict over the letter of the law. The man had no need to concern himself about the fidelity of his wife, since adultery was still technically against the law; the woman was assured that her husband would never become involved in anything shady. Both were *sure*—because they were ringers. There were few ringer nuptials because there were few marriageable ringers—but there had yet to be a ringer divorce.

Alice took a strand of her hair and thought about the glory she had once evoked in it. Today it was short and rather straight. She had cut it, believing that men were no longer a part of her life, after the ring—until she met Jeff. There had been something almost-familiar about him that compelled her. A woman didn't have to be juvenile or rich, to desire a powerful man.

This somber, disciplined existence—she had told herself she was satisfied with it, but now she knew how lonely it had made her. She felt as though she were aging rapidly, and it was not a kind sensation. If only—

Her image in the mirror blurred. Tears—as though weeping would somehow—

The phone lighted. The call!

She dabbed at her eyes ineffectively, not wanting to show herself this way. The whistle cut in after the requisite interval, and she had to answer.

She slapped the "receive" button, trembling with dismay and eagerness.

The blue metal dome of a police robot formed in the screen. "Miss Alicia Lang?" the cop inquired.

"Yes," she said, suddenly apprehensive.

"A sport-model monocar registered in your name has been wrecked. Consolations," it said, as though the word of comfort, coming from a machine, could mean anything. "Was the vehicle stolen?"

"No-no," she said, tilting the pickup momentarily so that the robot could see her ringed toe. The police would not have to verify her statements. "It was driven with my permission." *What had happened?*

"Was the vehicle destroyed with your connivance or consent?"

Destroyed! "No!" she cried. "What about Jeff—the driver?"

"Please provide full identification."

"Geoffrey Font Junior, an employee of General Gyromotors, a qualified driver and—ringed," she said rapidly. "I loaned him my car. Is he all right?"

"We have no information on the present status of this man. The accident report was called in from a junkyard near the edge of Gunnartown. A service crew has been dispatched. Do you wish to receive a routine report at a later hour?"

"Just give me the address!" she said, too loudly. "Please. I'll go there myself."

This was one advantage to being a ringer. The cop did not question her reason for going; it knew that she would not interfere with due procedure, or attempt to molest the wreck. It gave her the address.

Alice rushed to the door. Then, prompted by the ring, she hurried back. She touched the "call" stud on the phone, and nervously combed her hair as she waited for the connection.

Pamela McKissic paced the floor of her bedroom restlessly. She was ashamed of herself, and it was not a familiar emotion. Here she had been blaming her father for his neglect of her, and all the time he had been watching her activities carefully. He had known about the trifling complaints she made to her supposed friends, her teasing of the ringer, her visits to cult activities. He had known it all—and never spoken.

In fact, he had probably been protecting her, for she knew best of all that her reputation as a "sweet unspoiled girl" was richly undeserved. She had a sweet shape and an unspoiled countenance, and she was a girl—but that was about as far as it went. Never before had she felt remorse for her actions.

For the first time, she wished she *were* innocent. If only she could be a genuinely fine person, such as that ringed woman, what was her name, Alice. The one who had agreed to sleep in this bedroom for a few nights, just in case, when they turned off the house defenses. Alice never spoke a harsh word, and was a loyal G&G employee. Of course she must have done *something* to get her ring, but it probably had nothing to do with sex or violence. She was a nice girl in the proper sense, the kind a good man would like to settle down with.

Pamela remembered her own exploits, and shuddered. To think that her father had *known!* That was the real cause of her sudden guilt. Yet she knew she'd be doing something similar again; as soon as she figured out some way to get around his bugging network. Why did she have this uncontrollable urge to get into trouble?

Those dreams Jeff had had of her, brought out by the

truthall—they *had* excited her, if only he had known. He had remembered a solitary session with her, in a closet, eight years old. She could not remember that episode at all—because it was lost among so many similar happenings, with so many other children. She had wanted even then to do with a boy what she had seen that secretary doing with her father—but somehow it didn't work, with little boys.

Later she had discovered the difference between little boys and big boys, but by that time she had also learned caution. She had explored what could be had at the fringe outlets of Vicinc, vicariously, for those of any age or station who had money and inclination. She had watched from behind a screen, so close she could have touched the participants, activities that even the liberalized broadcasting policies of the day forbade. The sensual, the morbid—these fascinated her.

How much had her father really known? "Truthall, where is now thy sting?" she inquired of her mirror. Her father always quoted Tennyson when he got upset. She'd have to find some poet of her own to quote. Not a man, and not British, not that it really mattered. Maybe a contemporary of Tennyson, however. Emily Dickinson might do. Wasn't she the one who heard a fly buzz when she died?

Her phone blinked.

Pamela squinted at the screen, afraid for the moment to answer. Could it be her father, calling to tell her he had changed his mind and was having her ringed after all? Or worse, had the terminal fit come upon him, and this was a medic summoning her to—

She decided not to answer. But she was already reaching for the button, unable to deny herself anything, even unpleasant information. She had to know!

"Emily Dickinson here," she said.

A woman's face formed. "I must have the wrong—oh, it's you, Miss McKissic. My name is Alice Lang. I'm trying to reach Mr. McKissic, and his office referred me here—"

The ringer-woman! What was *she* doing calling here? Had her father decided to follow up that facetious suggestion that he take this creature as a mistress? Pamela's face flushed with instant and righteous anger. "I'll take the message," she snapped.

The woman looked uncertain. "It is a business matter, Miss McKissic."

"I'll take the message!"

"Yes, Miss McKissic. An employee has had an—an accident, and I thought Mr. McKissic should know. The car was wrecked at—"

"Oh." Pamela was irrationally disappointed. It was only a routine report. Some ringer had killed himself stupidly, and her father would have to cover the liabilities and burial. It had happened before. "What's his name? Or *her* name?"

Another hesitation. "Geoffrey Font Junior."

"All right. I'll tell . . . ." Pamela paused as the name registered. "Jeff Font?"

"Yes. I'm going down to Gunnartown now to—"

Pamela severed the connection. Jeff—Jeff Font was the one! The dreamer of bliss. The ringer she had been forbidden to see again—and now he was dead.

She had not cared for Jeff particularly. She would never have noticed him at all if it had not been for that business with his criminal father. Except that now it turned out that her own father had somehow framed the man. And of course the kidnapping . . . if she had known about *that* in advance, she might have insisted on staying for it. Fabulous adventure! As it was, Jeff had become an intrigue of the moment, an itch to be scratched, a male to be teased along for a while.

But first her father had forbidden her to see Jeff again, as though she were not fit company even for a ringer, and now the man was gone. Had her father known this was going to happen? Had he planned it, just to make sure she *did* stay clear? Why?

Frustration and fury rose in her as she thought about it. This had all been part of a plan to keep her in line! Well, she'd see about that! She'd put on a show *nobody* could cover up! And if the cops ringed her for it, it would serve Daddykins right!

She reached for the chauffeur's signal, but changed her mind. If she had Philip take her anywhere, her father would find out too soon, and prevent it. And she couldn't break Phil himself. Not in the time she had. The man seemed to be made of iron, and his first loyalty was to the senior employer.

She reached for the phone. Something had suggested Gunnartown to her . . . what was the identity of that fake Vicinc outlet? The one with the sabbat. . . .

Sam Selmik faced Slim Jackson in the Easygo Tavern's private business office. Junk was piled everywhere, ranging from a lady's purse to a fragment of a G&G gyro, but Sam paid no attention to it. His eyes were fixed on the long sharp knife held expertly in Slim's brown fingers— the knife whose blade carried the unique electrochemical charge that parted flesh as though it were narcosmoke. That blade was advancing slowly upon him, its point glinting. He retreated clockwise around the cluttered desk at the same rate.

"You fool! You money-hungry fool!"

Sam held up his hands as though the diamond rings encrusting the digits could turn aside that experienced attack. "I told you how it was!" he pleaded, reverting to his natural dialect under pressure. "This dame called up, just like I said. A real rich bitch. Fancy furniture and everything in her room. Anyway, I think I saw her around once or twice, at the devil-meeting. She told me 'I want to be in that act—the sabbat.' I told her she was crazy, but she punched a fistful of bear'cash at me, you know, the kind the rich kids use so nobody can trace them down—"

"The kind I gave you to buy off Bladderwart!" Slim said disdainfully. He banged his free hand against the phone adapter: a machine that printed notes of thousand dollar denomination or less, when duly activated by a signal conforming to a coded, untraceable account with the city investment computer. Wealthy families had their codes built into their phones, so that they could settle their credit deficits, legal and surreptitious, without delay or complication. "You fool—it's a plant! A trick to get us all ringed. They've caught on that the tavern is just a front for the gyrofence business!"

"But didn't you have that driver blasted before he could—"

Slim scowled. "Sure, I took care of that. But they're suspicious now. I'll bet they're shooting agents into Goontown all over, trying to nab someone who knows something. All they need is a pretext to put one of us under truthall—"

"But this was a *girl*, Slim. An Uptown—"

"You idiot! You moron! It's got to be a plant. All that money just to be—be—"

"But lots of Goontown girls do it."

"They have nothing better to live for. We have them so hooked in debt they have no choice, and they're mostly

morons to begin with. They're so dumb they figure one
night of it and the cure next day makes it okay." Slim
took another step, twitching the knife suggestively. "First
you blab too much to Bladderwart, and now you—"

"That's what she wants, Slim! She paid for it; let her
have it!"

"Bonehead! Didn't you tell her about the demons? What
they do? How she would just about have to bathe in the
stuff, with them all watching, laughing, goosing her—"
But he stopped his advance.

"Sure, Slim, sure! She's seen the act. These rich bitches
are all crazy. The pretty ones most of all. She—"

"All right," Slim said, putting away the blade. "But
we're going to play it safe. She knows your face, so you
stay out of sight until she's committed. *I'll* bring her in.
She'll be showing up in half an hour, for the evening act,
since she says that's what she wants. Only I won't give her
a chance to snoop around and back out. She won't spring
any trap on *me*. I'll mug her with sleepnol before she
catches on and put a hood on her. By the time she comes
to, it'll be time for the spray. She won't turn *anybody* in,
after that."

He rubbed his hands together, enjoying it now. "Oh,
she'll get what she asked for, all right—double dose of
Confusion and a packed house! Anybody even *breathes* on
her, she'll climb the wall. We'll bill her nice and legal:
the Hooded Horror. Got a shape on her, you say? A sabbat
really goes for that, specially when the clothes come off."

"Yeah," Slim agreed, relieved. "She won't even remember her name for a week, after that."

"What's she look like? I don't want to make any
mistake."

"Long black hair and a figure like you wouldn't believe," Sam said reminiscently. "It's all real, though, or

I've lost my eye. But I figure she'll come in disguise, like they usually do, the rich buyers.''

"How will we know her, then? We can't wait for her to walk up and say 'I'm the spy from cop-puter-central, show me your unregistered gyros.' I don't want her to suspect we're on to her until she's nailed. I'm going to put the chain on her, too. Didn't she give you some sign?''

"Yeah," Sam said, brightening. "I remember now. She said she'd come as a ringer. You know, with a big fake band on her toe. So you look for a real hourglass doll with a ring, and it won't matter if she's wearing a wig or something. A mask. Ringers don't come *here*.''

"Now that's what I call a smart gimmick," Slim said, his humor restored. "You're damn right ringers don't come here. Not alive, they don't. Take over. I'm going down and set things up." He turned to the door, then remembered something. His swift left hand made a sweep, and the wad of bearercash notes was his. "*I* pay you—not the clients.''

Sam sat down at the desk without a word.

"Maybe that black hair was the wig," Slim murmured as he left. "She'll most likely come as she is, to lull our suspicions. Yes. . . .'' The door slammed.

George McKissic tramped into the house, leaving Philip to put away the duocar. He was tired, but he felt he had done the right thing. The business was doing well—so long as he ran it himself. But he could not run it much longer; the excitement and drive of twenty-five years ago had gradually faded into a race of endurance against the years.

" 'Forward' rang the voices then, and of the many mine was one," he said, quoting from one of his favorite poems by Tennyson. "Let us hush this cry of 'Forward' till ten thousand years have gone.'' The great poet made more and more sense to him as the years went by. Or perhaps it was the magic of the old Victorian period that entranced him—a period of such vigor and discovery, yet of such frustration too.

He had had vigor and frustration, but now the former was being mastered by the latter. He had built a mighty industry—but who was there to follow him? Certainly not his daughter—she was hardly reclaimable as a woman, let alone as management material. Perhaps he had succeeded in impressing upon her the need to reform. Probably the effect would be temporary, however. If only he'd had the courage to ring her, as he had Jeff—but he wasn't sure she could survive that discipline.

He had done his best, but there was so little time. His mind was under continuing stress, and he knew his medic had not been exaggerating. He could feel it: one more shock, one more overload, and he would be unable to hold on any longer. He would have to relinquish this ugly world and seek a better one. At least he had brought his will up to the moment, and made provision for his approaching loss of competence.

If only modern techniques had been able to—but that lament was futile. He was heir to the sins of his ancestors, as so many of his generation were. There was no possible explanation there.

He required every bit of his mind to hold the business together, since he had to do it alone and the gyrotheft syndicate was a perpetual annoyance. The one operation that might have extended his competence would certainly have reduced his effectiveness. Lobotomy had never been a genuine solution to madness, and microtopectomy could hardly compensate for so total a—

"I will drink life to the lees," he said aloud, remembering another poem. He, like the wanderer Ulysses described by Tennyson, had finally grown old, and had to endure the inevitable decay of once-renowned abilities. The Greek monarch had suffered physical decline, after physical adventures—but today there were other struggles as important and as fraught with peril.

He hoped Pamela had worked things out and settled down, in the hour she had been home before him. He had made his gesture by telling her as much of the truth as he could; if that failed, there seemed to be nothing but the ring. Certainly he could not continue to let her run wild— not any more. Samuel Crater had told him years ago that it would come inevitably to the ring, unless someone was found who could and would undertake the thankless task of taming her. He hadn't wanted to believe it, despite the mountainous evidence of her unruliness. But for sheer perversity, that incident at the hospital . . .

The house was empty. Well, it would be simple enough to catch up. Pamela was convinced now that he had an extensive spying network, as though she warranted such attention, and he had not seen fit to disillusion her. Sensible use of standard devices had always been sufficient.

He punched the phone playback. There were two recordings, both from her bedroom extension: an incoming call and an outgoing one. Also a sizable debit on the bearercash account. She was up to something. McKissic eased himself into the massage chair and listened to the first.

It was a routine accident report from an employee. He regretted the too-frequent mishaps, but he could not police the workers' private lives. He'd have the matter taken care of.

". . . Geoffrey Font Junior."

McKissic leaped up wildly. Not Jeff—not Jeff!

Then he forced himself to relax. He played the recording again. No—there was nothing about death, and the medics could repair virtually anything short of that. An accident, yes; but the details had not been given. Alice Lang had promised to investigate. He remembered her: one of his few female ringers, and a good worker. She had a level head. He had rewarded her cooperation in the kidnapping matter by putting Jeff in her section, just as she requested. She had taken an immediate interest in the lad, and McKissic liked to think he knew why, even if the girl did not. But that was a matter he schooled himself not to think about. At any rate, the association between these two was serendipitous, and could do no harm at all. It was essential that his daughter be kept away, and how better than by the interposition of another woman?

But this hadn't really been effective, and so he had had to forbid Pamela directly. He had never forbidden her anything before, and now he was not at all certain it would work. Yet the alternatives were—

He had lost his thread. There had been something urgent—

McKissic looked around. He was standing in his living room, beside the lighted phone, and the playback signal was holding. He must have been listening to a call.

He remembered. Jeff had been in an accident.

Loss of concentration: the major signal, for him, of incipient breakdown. He had taken a severe shock, and he was in trouble. If he could just hold on a few minutes, the fit would pass—for the time being. His medic had warned him, and told him how to fight it. He had to keep calm and act to relieve the tension immediately.

He recited the prologue to *In Memoriam A.H.H.*: "Strong Son of God, immortal Love . . ." Caught up in the powerful, somber mood of it, he felt his distress dissipate. He would be all right, this time.

What had he been—oh, yes. Jeff had had an accident, but perhaps it had been minor. Gyrocars were designed to protect the occupants even when totally smashed; that had been one of the features his erstwhile partner had worked on so carefully. What spectacular advances there might have been, had tragedy not removed Font Senior from participation!

He punched the playback for the second call.

Pamela's voice: "Easygo Tavern? The manager, please."

McKissic frowned. So she had decided to attend that repulsive sabbat again, drawing vicarious thrills from handling doped girls. Homosexuality was socially acceptable now, as was overt masochism, but this particular program disturbed him. Perhaps it was because he knew first-hand the insidious mechanisms of hallucinogenic drugs. Generations suffered for the pleasures of the moment.

A man appeared in the screen, an obvious Gunnartown entrepreneur. His fingers were tastelessly crusted with rings. Even looking at the diminished picture, McKissic could discern the inferior design of this gaudy merchandise. "He isn't here right now, miss. But I'm his assistant."

"All right. Here's what I want." She spelled it out.

McKissic leaped to his feet again. "Philip!" he bellowed.

The chauffeur's face appeared immediately on the servant's communicator. "Sir?"

"Take me to the Easygo Tavern in the slum and—"

He had lost his thread again. "And—"

If only he could keep *track!* "And find out why I'm going there!" he finished angrily.

Philip was imperturbable. "Certainly, sir." He was a very good chauffeur.

The stench of sweat and ammonia brought Alice gasping to consciousness. It was hot and dark, and somewhere

tribal bongo drums throbbed, too loud, too near. She sat
up—and discovered that she was chained and blind. A
hood of some fine netting covered her head. She touched
it, but the thing was knotted closely around her neck and
would not come free. She felt her ankle, finding the
plastoid band that encircled it, and the flexible links leading to the floor. She yanked, but the light chain was
strong. She was a prisoner.

She stopped struggling with the chain and concentrated.
What was the last thing she remembered? Her apartment—
she had been waiting for Jeff to return or to call in,
hoping—

It came back. The call about the accident, her decision
to investigate, only pausing to leave a message for Mr.
McKissic. The ride on the duobus to the stop nearest the
scene of the accident, praying that Jeff was not badly hurt.
The brief walk to—

Memory ended there. She could recall the street, glistening in the wake of the afternoon rain, and the garish
lights of an alley Vicinc tavern. She had passed a tall,
dark, sinister man idling there. He had stared at her ring,
taken a step toward her—

Sleepnol! She had been drugged and abducted—again!
She should have thought of the danger, walking alone
through Gunnartown in the evening. It was not a safe
section of the city for a ringer of either sex. If she hadn't
been so preoccupied by the accident—

Had Jeff died in the crash? Alice forgot her own dis-
comfort in her anxiety for him. She had to get to the
junkyard where the wreck had happened! She fumbled for
the chain again, caught it in both hands, and yanked until
her fingers smarted. It refused to give way.

The tempo of the bongo beat increased, and a low
suggestive chanting began, reminiscent of mummers in-

voking the supernatural. There was a shuffling somewhere—
then, abruptly, a curtain lifted. Light stabbed into her
compartment, blinding her through the hood. Someone
laughed.

Alice shielded her eyes with one hand, thankful that at
least she could see now. The material, stretched thin across
her eyes, only screened her vision.

She saw—faces! Painted, crowded faces, peering at her
eagerly. Juvenile faces, mouths open, tongues licking stained
lips, teeth clamping on narcos, eyes glittering through
enlargement lenses. The foreheads had horns, the ears
were hairy and pointed—

She was chained to an elevated stage. Curtains swept
back, leaving her alone in the open.

Still she did not cry out. The ring was punishing her for
her situation, since she was obviously involved in something untoward, but she refused to satisfy this gluttonous
audience by reacting foolishly. At least the hood gave her
anonymity. Only by rational behavior could she hope to
escape.

She thought about twisting her ring, to set off the automatic police alarm, but couldn't do it. She didn't *know* she
was in personal danger, and the ring would shock her into
apathy before she succeeded. No ringer was allowed to
tamper with the mechanism for any reason. It was like
committing suicide by holding one's breath: not feasible.

Shock and shame were useless; she was displayed on a
stage and could not physically escape the cynosure of the
eager, demoniac faces. Why? Surely she was not bound
here simply as an exhibit.

The bongos rose to crescendo, and explosions outside
shook the building. A man walked across the stage and
stood before her. He wore elbow-length hermetic gloves
and a sealed glastic helmet; she could see the air re-

circulation valves, the glassy tubing. Pointed horns perched atop the helmet, and a long tail trailed behind him, ending in a flat arrowhead. He held in his satanic gauntlets a tremendous pressure-cannister of—

Then she understood. She had said something, a figure of speech, to Jeff, at their first importunate encounter, and he had been terribly angry. Something about dosing himself with Confusion . . . something like that.

She had become naive, as a ringer; she had wondered at his offworld sensitivities. Now she remembered: the drug trademarked "Instant Confusion" was of offworld origin, and crude natural variants were found on the prison colony planet. Jeff would have known about these, not as a packaged game but as a deadly mind-destroying narcotic.

Now she faced it in context. The effect of dilute doses of limited application was bad enough, but this was to be a full-strength, all-over inundation. She was to be the victim of one of the nefarious thrill-parties . . . and it would cost her, at the minimum, her future as a mother.

Alice screamed and tore at the chain, unable to control herself any longer. The ring hurt her, savagely, not distinguishing between voluntary and involuntary wrong. The crowd laughed; they liked this.

The man lifted the can and broke the seal.

The drums kept pounding, impossibly loud.

VII. The Bad Samaritans

1

IT came to Jeff slowly that wherever he was this time, it was not a hospital. The ceiling was much too grimy and the sheets next to his bare skin were far too rough.

"How do you feel, Ringee?"

And that was no trim, decorative, efficient nurse supervising the aseptic medical robots! He turned his head and saw a coarse woman's face. The voice matched it. "Ringee?" he inquired.

"You were wearing one. Big Ed got it off you, and I bandaged up your hand."

He lifted his right arm, staring at the cumbersome cloth wrappings which concealed the hand entirely. "You took off the ring?"

"No," she said. "Ed did. You were pinned in the car. I pried you out while Ed phoned. But your hand was caught somehow. I think the gyro blew."

"Gyros don't 'blow,' " he said, probing the bandage with his other hand.

"Well, your finger was ripped half off. Ed put on his gloves and cut through the rest of it, soon's he got back. 'Cause we couldn't get you out without getting shocked,

192

otherwise. Then he put the ring in the press and pulped it, so it wouldn't hurt anybody any more. He doesn't like rings. You're lucky it was that finger that got it."

"You mean that's the only injury I had? That one finger? That's an incredible coincidence!"

"No, it's plain lucky," she said. "You ain't a ringer any more."

"Damn!" he said, and there was no shock. The ring was gone. He probably would never know for certain whether it had been an astonishing play of fate or deliberate sabotage by the lower class husband of this woman.

"And you're pretty lucky to get off without more'n that," she said. "Your car was so bashed in Ed never even looked inside, until he saw the blood. So he phoned in the wreck, and pretty soon the G&G crew came and lifted out the gyro, what was left of it, and gave him the fee to junk the rest of it. The cops asked where you were, but Ed said the car was empty when he found it, maybe you'd fallen out somewhere. That's why he had to get the ring off, so you wouldn't turn him in." She was unaware of what she had let slip. "But we got you out, and they never even searched the place. Those cops are pretty stupid."

Then it hit him emotionally: he was free of Ultra Conscience! He could decide for himself now what was good and bad and beautiful and reprehensible. He could make plans to attack McKissic, marry McKissic's daughter or look up Alice. Do any damned thing he felt like, *when* he felt like, whatever it was. He was a free agent again—one hundred percent free—and that meant that his battle for justice against injustice and a rigged system could be renewed in earnest.

But why had these people bothered to save him? He was certain they liked neither ringers nor folk from the wealthier sections of the city.

"You're a strong 'un, mister," the woman rattled on. "Goodness if you're not! Muscle on you like a weight-lifter. We saw you coming across the gap last night and I guess for you that was lucky. Ed got there just after you crashed. Didn't know it was some ringee. He thought there'd be—" Here she broke off, as though changing her mind about something. "Well, loot maybe, in the pileup. I guess he was right, but we didn't take anything. Ed got the rest of it anyway, so that's something. He and Flat-head—that's Flathead Looey, the simple kid who works for him . . ."

Jeff's mind wandered as she talked, since much of it seemed redundant. He felt over his body and found other bandages: he had not escaped without other injuries after all. His left arm was covered, and his ribs and his left shoulder. His gut was sore in a wide band where the safety harness had jerked it; he must have taken it off and put it on again automatically, during the crisis on the beam, because he didn't remember it at all. These injuries, on top of the ones he had been hospitalized for so recently, left him quite weak. But the loss of the ring gave him a compensating exhilaration; apart from a headache, he was ready to get up and begin planning.

There was no point in worrying about the ring. If he obeyed the law and reported immediately for re-ringing, he would never have another chance like this. The penalties were severe for failure to report—but he had to act freely while he could. If he proved his charge against McKissic this time—

". . . so that's why we saved you from the cops," she finished. Jeff tried to remember what he had been ig-noring, but it was too confused.

"What's this about 'loot'?" he asked. "You said you thought there'd be some, but you didn't take it. All I had was the car—which isn't mine—and part of a factory voucher. That what you meant?''

"Naw, I *told* you," she said without rancor. "Ed, he's got this big thing in his head about finding someone who's smart. Someone who knows how to get away with things. He says maybe the ring wasn't working right, or you never would've drove that way. Or it was a phony.''

"It was no phony," Jeff assured her. As he had hoped, she hadn't really listened to his question, but had repeated what she had said before. So they wanted something from him.

He saw her lip tremble nervously. There *was* something— something she wasn't supposed to talk about. "No, it wasn't any plant," he said. "I crashed through from the skyway by accident and had to keep going. The ring stung me all the way over, but it couldn't do much because I wasn't trying to commit suicide and there was no practical way out except straight ahead.''

"So you cracked up and got rid of the ring!" she exclaimed. "Ringee, you must be some kind of a genius. Ed, he said you were a smart one first time I washed the blood off. No, even before that. 'This here's a big 'un, Annie!' he said. 'He's our passport out—if that thing of Sam's don't get us all ringed first.' You know Sam?''

"No." He knew the type, though. Sam was probably a mobster with grandiose ideas and an appetite for money.

"He and Slim Jackson went partners on the sabbat,'' she said, as though Jeff should know the details already. "And he set up something for Ed, but it fell through. I don't like him—him and those rings. Gem-rings, I mean, not finger-rings, but he wears 'em on his fingers.''

Jeff tried to figure that out, couldn't, and put it from his mind. He realized that she could go on indefinitely informing him about items of no consequence. "My name's Jeff," he said. "Jeff Font."

"That's what your papers said," she agreed. Naturally they would have gone through his pockets. "Ed says you were real smart to come here like that. A man can beat the ring, he says, can do damned near anything. But you sure did it the hard way!"

Jeff's mind abruptly made an obvious connection it had somehow staved off until now. The Ed she was talking about was Big Ed the car junker. The man he had rented the first mono from, and who had come to inform him it was stolen. The yard was right at the turn the elevated ramp made, and off course he had dropped right into it.

Ed would have recognized him—and assumed that he had wrecked himself deliberately! No wonder the man talked of "beating the ring"! What better way than to knock yourself unconscious on the premises of someone in trouble with the law, and who knows you know it! Ed had read the implied message, and had acted accordingly.

And now that it had happened—was it necessary for Jeff still to tell himself that it had all been a phenomenal coincidence, that he had planned nothing of the kind? When he had so conveniently forgotten about the advertised construction on the skyway, then driven so ineptly as to force himself onto that construction in spite of the ring, then headed unerringly for this very place that he knew about? He had never consciously thought it out—the ring prevented that—but he had accomplished it.

He struggled to sit up and look out the grimy window. He could hear a hammering somewhere. He got his good elbow under him and peered out at a ramshackle collection of old car bodies. Yes, this was the place he had visited before.

"Ed should be around quick," Annie said. "He wants

to talk to you real bad. He said to call him when you woke up.''

Jeff squinted. He had thought it was day, but now he saw that there was a floodlight outside. It was night—probably only an hour or two after his crash. Probably it was his disorientation, and the fact that he had not thought of Ed as a family man, that had confused him about his whereabouts. "What's the time?"

"Twenty," she said, gesturing to the ancient clock on the wall. It was so old it still had the twelve hour scale. The hour hand pointed to the figure eight. "You can tell anyway, because that's when the lights dim at the Easygo up the street, for the sabbat. But I guess you can't see it from that window."

Jeff refrained from informing her of his extreme disinterest in anything that might happen at the Easygo. Right now he needed to know relevant things. He could make out a big man with wide shoulders, a bulging belly and a red face—Bladderwart, all right. The meaty arm was going up and down as the man hammered at a monowheel that had been bent almost double.

"Tell Ed I'm awake," Jeff said, deciding that the woman was not going to think of it for herself.

She went to the door. "Ed! Flathead!"

He saw a smaller and somewhat wizened-faced man with spidery arms and legs emerge from a car body and join Bladderwart in a dash toward the house. He heard them thump up some steps and onto a porch; then they were inside and staring at him.

Jeff studied the dent in Flathead's forehead, and the ferrety face; then he concentrated on the more animate features of Big Ed. There was no doubt about who was employer and who employee.

"Flont's awake," Annie said unnecessarily.

"Font," Jeff corrected her, aware of his hitherto unconscious feeling of superiority over these slum dwellers. "We've met. I rented a car from Ed once."

"I knew you was the one," Ed agreed. He plodded to the wreck of a refrigerator and yanked the front open. "You want a beer, Flont?"

"Not yet," Jeff said, giving up on his name.

"Annie, she talks a lot," Ed said, opening his beer at the sink, "but she doesn't say much. Me, I'm a man believes in doing things." He brought the opened bottle to Jeff and shoved it in his hand.

Jeff started to protest, but the wide back was already retreating. He shrugged and tasted it—and discovered that he was pretty thirsty for something like this after all. Folk medicine: sometimes it had a legitimate basis. At any rate, the stuff might ease his headache.

Ed opened a second beer and sat down in a rickety chair he dragged from the table. "Looey, you get yourself a pop," he said. He half-turned to the man and waited until he shambled out the door before speaking again.

Ed turned his face back and directed eyes like bloodstreaked walnuts at him. "It's like this, Flont. I'm a little king rat of the junkyard, here." He took a pull on his beer, and Jeff politely imitated the motion. He discovered it to be pretty heady stuff—cold and strong.

Bladderwart was working up to something. There must have been a loss on that gyro, the stolen one. Did Ed expect payment now?

"Yeah," Ed said. "Shrewd. Like a rat. Until now the biggest thing I ever pulled off was stealing a few bottles of beer. As Goontowners go, that makes me smart."

Jeff was becoming fascinated with the man, seeing an entirely different personality than the one he had imagined before. It hadn't occurred to him that Gunnartowners had

ambitions too. "And you know I'm not a 'Goontowner,' is
that it? You read through my papers and learned I was in
the Space Service. That I started from—"

"Alpha IV, yeah. You were there and I figure you
must've been a kid and then you were in the navy and now
you're here. I got to thinkin' why. Why does a man go
from space to the ring, and then fix things to get out of
that? Because he's stupid? Uh-uh, I saw the way you drove
tonight. I know you came to Earth for a reason—probably
money. I know you got the training and the plans. And
now you come to cut me in on it, right?"

"You deduced all that, Mr. Bladderwart?" Jeff said with
gentle irony. He drove well, ergo he was smart. He was
here, therefore he would share his plans. Simple.

Flathead returned, his pale lips applied to a pop-tube.
"Come here and show Flont," Ed said to him.

Flathead came, skinned up his T-shirt and revealed the
crude holster/sheath he carried below his armpit. He did all
this without removing his mouth from the refreshment. He
took hold of the handle protruding from the sheath and
brought out nearly six inches of finely polished, tapering
steel.

Jeff inspected the blade. "Very nice," he said, and
Flathead gaped with pleasure, missing the tone.

"You see how it is then, Flont?" Ed said. "We're like
all one family here. Rise or fall, space or sink, that's about
the way of it."

"I see the way of it," Jeff said. He was sure he could
handle the moronic Flathead. They seemed to think the
ringer had dropped to the bottom of the totem, and was
amenable to unsubtle threats.

Ed gestured with the bottle. "We're in this together, all
four of us. Just the right number, wouldn't you say?"

"For what?"

"You, me, Annie, Flathead—that's four, ain't it? Four for fortune."

"Four-four-four!" Flathead repeated happily.

"Fortune?"

"Come on now, Flont." Ed upended his bottle and worked his mouth at it. He set it down and contemplated its arid state regretfully. "Even an offworlder like you knows the code of Goontowners. Someone does you dirt, you get him. He does you a favor, you pay him. And nobody yells cop."

"And you assume that I owe you something? That I have the ability to 'pay'?"

Ed got up from the chair, slouched to the sink and dropped the empty bottle into an overflowing carton of trash. He drew another quart, opened it, and came back sucking noisily on it. He emptied it in several long pulls while Jeff tried to conceal his amazement, and flopped into the chair again.

Jeff was halfway through his first bottle and already his head felt light. He judged the stuff to contain a good eight to ten percent alcohol: exceedingly strong, for commercial "beer." Yet Ed seemed unaffected.

"We Goontowners remember things that smell like money. Years ago, when I was just a punk hauling trash, I used a four-wheeled truck, only thing I could afford. Then the classy one-wheelers got cheap enough, and I really went for 'em. I studied up, everything I could find. That's how I got in the salvage business—ain't just anybody can take apart a live gyro and live. Not that I do it without getting permission from the company, of course."

"Of course," Jeff agreed dryly. Such permission was never given to an individual.

"You got to know your way 'round all the booby-traps. That's how I remember back when the company wasn't

G&G, it was Flont & McKissic. Then Flont cheated on his partner and got booted to Alpha. Thought I knew the name before; this time I checked it.''

''He was framed,'' Jeff said.

''Of course,'' Ed said, using the exact tone Jeff had a moment before. ''Seems to me he had a boy, be about your age now.''

Jeff said nothing. Big Ed seemed to know what he was doing after all.

''Flathead, go out and do some work. I'll be there pretty soon.''

Flathead took his empty tube and went out. When nearly at the door he blew it full of air, pinched the top and bashed it against his fist. It popped. He looked back with a fleshless skull grin. He went out, banging the door.

''Pop tube,'' Ed explained. ''Flathead—well, his grandma was one of the old-time hippies. LSD, that stuff. Didn't show up until he was born—you know how it is.'' Jeff knew, though he hadn't recognized Flathead as a victim. There had been innumerable cases of deformed births following the use of the psychedelic drugs, and recessive genetic damage still showed up regularly after one or two generations. The drugs had been employed so extensively before this latent danger was recognized that no effective control was feasible.

''I heard your old man got killed,'' Ed was saying. ''Now you come back to Earth and got ringed. McKissic ain't dead, so that means you didn't settle your score before you got caught. Right? Now I can help you, and that's worth something to you, right? And if it works out, you just might get your mitts on some of that G&G loot, right?''

The man had worked it out very nicely, in spite of his general ignorance, Jeff realized. Obviously Big Ed Bladderwart knew how to take advantage of his opportunities, and had the courage to grasp what offered. He must have looked at the papers, realized Jeff's identity, formed his plan and done what was necessary—within minutes after getting him out of the wreck. He would have known he was placing his own freedom in Jeff's hands—but he had also assessed the motivations of a man who had a serious grudge against a powerful company. Ed was so desperate to get out of his Goontown rut that he was willing to risk everything—and he hadn't hesitated.

What he said made sense. Jeff had tried it on his own, and failed. Now he had been given a second chance—and he *could* use some help.

He felt a surge of optimism. His headache was gone, and his body was fit, despite bruises and some loss of blood. It could be the effect of the beer—or of the release from the ring. He would have to be on guard against a letdown. Yet—why not? Why not show the same decision Ed had, and settle with McKissic immediately, before the police knew what was afoot? Failure could not hurt him more than inaction, and success would recover his share of General Gyro, not to mention the reputation of his father. There would be more than enough financially to reward Ed's assistance; a tiny fragment of G&G interest would set Ed and all his friends up for life.

But this had been an individual project. He had shared his intent with nobody, until the truthall interrogation forced it out. Could he trust others now, particularly a bunch of Gunnartown denizens? A feeble-minded junkyard handyman; a coarse slum woman; Ed.

Ed: big belly, big gut, self-seeking, dissipated—yet a man of courage and action and some perception, however meager his social graces. If Ed had been willing to gamble on a stranger—shouldn't that stranger be willing to gamble on Ed?

Annie had disappeared some time ago. Now she returned, carrying a tray. "Guess you're hungry," she said. "Can you eat with your left?"

It was a bowl of thick soup and a chunk of dry bread. Jeff looked at the meal and realized that this medieval diet was probably the best they had to offer. He had protested too much about the rigors of life on Alpha IV: he had never gone hungry.

"Let me see that hand," Annie said, setting down the tray and picking up the bandaged extremity. "We got some paste to make it stop hurting, if you want it." She unwrapped the long gauze, evidently torn from a bedsheet. It did hurt, but Jeff kept silent.

The finger was gone, the compress on the stump soaked with blood. Annie placed fresh material and rewrapped it with fair competence. Her touch was surprisingly gentle. Jeff studied her face again, seeing now the compassionate lines of it. The skin was rough, the features overdrawn—but the personality was, he realized, a handsome one. Annie gave of herself, without affectation, whatever was required. What more could anyone demand?

Jeff remembered one other woman like that, now that he thought about it in such terms.

He could hear a drumbeat in the distance, as though the sabbat Annie had mentioned were reaching a climax. This was the real Gunnartown life: a man with ambition, a woman with compassion, grime everywhere and a background drumbeat signaling the onset of the tasteless pleasures of the Uptown slummers.

He wondered what Alice was doing now.

"All right," Jeff said. "I'll tell you what my position is and what I want to do, and you tell me what to watch out for. If we succeed, I'll have my settlement and you—all of you—will have the money you want. You won't have to worry about stealing beer—you'll buy the store. Perhaps we should draw up some sort of contract—an agreement, so nobody gets cheated."

"Naw," Ed said. "All I need is enough to buy me a little dealership in Uptown, and maybe some stock. I'll take care of Flathead and Annie."

"So we can get married," Annie said.

Jeff started, but they didn't notice. "Yeah," Ed agreed.

"You don't want a contract?"

"Ain't no contract as safe as a man's good will," Ed said. "And the cops can't use that as evidence."

Suddenly Jeff knew that things were going to work out.

2

The rain was long since over, but an evening fog remained, blurring the headlamps of the other vehicles. George McKissic sat in the back seat of the big duo and watched the colored lights of the city flash by. They were entering the skyway, and the glow seemed to be sinking as the car lifted. The effect made him uneasy.

"Where are you taking me, Philip?" he inquired.

"To the Easygo Tavern to rescue your daughter, sir," Philip said, his face in the screen serious.

McKissic remembered, though he did not recall giving the instructions. Philip must have listened to the recordings and taken appropriate action. It was this kind of subordinate competence that had kept him in McKissic's employ so long. The steady loyalty of people like Philip and that ringed girl who had called in was a sorely needed bulwark against . . . what was coming.

"Philip, I'd like you to give a personal opinion."

The eyes stayed on the road ahead. "Sir, in my capacity as—"

"I know, Philip, I know. But *you* know as well as I do that our association is very near the end. Don't worry— you will be well provided for, as will all my employees— but you have been close to me for a number of years and are in a unique position to develop a competent opinion. Please, I ask you as a man, speak without inhibition."

"Certainly, Mr. McKissic." The car swung left, following a posted detour, and temporary scaffolding obscured the nocturnal view.

"What do you think of my daughter?"

"She is certainly a lovely girl, sir, but almost totally irresponsible. She desperately needs guidance. Very firm guidance."

McKissic closed his eyes. "The ring?"

"No, sir. The ring would not guide her, it would destroy her. She needs human attention, flexible control."

"The kind I never gave her."

"You tried, sir—but you were unable to chastise her, and so she was unable in turn to respect you. A child needs discipline as well as affection, when it is strong-willed, or it loses the meaning of both."

His chauffeur was making a good deal of sense. Tennyson could have hardly said it better. "And a woman-child requires a strong man."

"Yes, Mr. McKissic."

He gazed at the patterned lights that now came into view below and considered. "Are you in love with Pamela, Philip?"

"I can't say, sir."

McKissic smiled. "Put it this way. Were she subject to your influence for a suitable period, would you be inclined to marry her, with the expectation that the experience would be worthwhile in the long view?"

"Yes, sir."

"In spite of the things she has already—that is, if it should materialize that she could bear no normal issue?"

"Yes, sir."

"Even if no inheritance went with her?"

"Yes, sir."

McKissic smiled again. This was the type of interplay he knew himself to be master of. "I will do this: I will settle one-quarter of the income from G&G general stock upon her for life, commencing from the date of her marriage. I will give you the formal first option on that nuptial, to be implemented within five years from this moment or forfeited in favor of a second option to be determined by the G&G personnel board. Her entire inheritance will be contingent upon conformance to the option. Do you accede?"

"Yes, sir." But Philip could not control the catch in his voice.

"Is the car recorder on?"

"Yes, sir."

"I so declare it." McKissic looked out the window again. "Bluntly: she's yours or no dough. We have just about time to seal that tape before we arrive. You'd better deposit it in a private vault as soon as we stop. Most of them close at twenty-one, and it's after twenty now." He glanced at his watch. "Just after."

"Gunnartown Trust is near our destination, sir."

"Good. You can park the car and walk over. You know how long that document would last if my daughter got her hands on it prematurely."

"But Mr. McKissic—"

"I'll handle the business at the Tavern myself, Philip. This is a private matter. I *am* her father."

"Yes, sir." The car drew up before the Easygo Tavern. "Sir—" the chauffeur began as McKissic got out, "thank you. I—"

This time McKissic did not smile. "It is the welfare of my daughter I am thinking of," he said. He walked briskly into the tavern, twirling the decorative cane he sometimes affected.

A man with tastelessly jeweled fingers met him at the entrance. "You have a reservation?"

"My card," McKissic said impatiently, handing him a glowing ticket in the shape of a gyro assembly. A reservation—in Gunnartown? Ludicrous. And those rings . . .

The man gaped. "President of General Gyromotors!" He looked appalled, then recovered himself somewhat.

"Sir, are you sure you—I mean, not even a costume?"

Then McKissic placed him: the man Pamela had talked to on the phone. The one who had agreed to arrange it, and who had accepted the money. "I'm here to recover my daughter."

"She—oh, you mean she's watching the show?" The relief on the man's face was almost comical. "That's all?"

There was more here than met the eye. Well, Crater and his truthall would clear it up in due course. McKissic prodded him in the belly with the cane. "She *is* the show." He marched on.

The man ran after him. "Sir, I don't understand—"

McKissic handed him a thousand dollar note and the man shut up. McKissic smiled briefly; from the reactions here, one would think they were stealing G&G gyros!

The lighted stage was ahead. A packed audience strained to see through the seemingly physical blare of drums, men and women garbed like devils. On the right side of the stage was a suited man holding an object. On the left was a young woman in conventional dress, a black hood over her head.

Pamela! She had gone through with it!

He had doubted that her nerve would hold up. Pamela's exploits had almost invariably been private, before; at least she had protected her reputation to that extent. She had never liked to make herself ridiculous in public.

But he had come, knowing that this time it might not be a bluff. He had told himself that it was probably a needless trip, and thus protected himself against the full shock. He had tried to make a permanent arrangement for her, so that there could be no more trouble—but she had done it. This time she had really done it.

He was striding down the center aisle toward the stage as these thoughts came to him. He had to keep moving now, or he would lose the thread—lose all of it.

The suited man walked toward the girl. She tried to stand up, and McKissic saw her foot was chained. She could not run—assuming that she wanted to.

Crescendo on the drums. Pamela screamed and struggled, but the chain was firm. Now, too late, she had changed her mind; she had gotten herself into trouble she couldn't hide from. The man lifted a pressure can and broke its seal.

For a moment her hooded face turned toward McKissic, and he knew she saw him through the fine mesh. "Help me!" she cried. Not "Help me, Father," or even "Daddy-kins!"—just a blunt summons as though he were a distant acquaintance whose interest might be presumed to be incidental. So far apart had he grown from his daughter, despite his efforts!

The man on stage depressed the nozzle. A fine mist columned out.

McKissic needed no more. He jammed the tip of the cane against the floor and vaulted to the stage as though he were still a young athlete.

"Hey! You can't—!" someone cried amid the angry yells from the satanic audience.

McKissic paid no attention. The man was standing over the hooded form—over his daughter!—aiming that terrible spray at her head while she leaned desperately away. McKissic charged into the man and caught him with a body-block.

The contact jarred him violently. The man was solid; the protective suit gave him weight and rigidity. But he stumbled aside, off balance, the can spraying upward. McKissic squatted at the girl's feet, took hold of the chain and pulled, but it was solidly anchored.

The man came back, aiming the can's nozzle at him. Realizing his own peril, McKissic struck at the hand. He missed, and the mist enveloped his sleeve as the other backed away.

He stalked the enemy, striking again, and this time rapped the bubble helmet ringingly. The man put his hands to it to still the vibration, and dropped the can.

The audience cheered, now taking this as part of the act. A mortal rescuing the succubus, perhaps to claim her for his own pleasures.

A tall dark man stood in the wings, out of sight of the audience. He was not cheering. He lifted a knife as though to throw it.

McKissic was panting, unused to such strenuous exertion—but discovering that he did not dislike it. "To strive, to seek, to find, and not to yield," he said, quoting his poet. He lunged at the dusky demon, rapping the knife-hand with his cane.

But this demon was swift. The knife did not wait for the cane; it flashed under and up, slicing along his arm so neatly that the cut was at first painless. No streetpunk, this, and no ordinary blade.

McKissic concentrated on the immediate matter at hand. No ordinary cane, his, either; he lifted it again, feinting at the knife-hand but this time driving for a more stationary target: the face. He did it with his wrist, quickly, so there was no warning, and scored. The demon fell back, clapping his free hand to his broken nose.

His cane was genuine white-ash wood, an expensive rarity—but a stout, effective weapon when properly applied. It stood him in the same stead as the big old pistol stood Judge Crater. He struck the demon again, across the eyes, and a third time, across the Adam's-apple. At the final blow the demon dropped his blade.

McKissic shoved the creature away and picked up the knife. He turned in time to see the helmeted man once more lifting the can he had recovered. He flung the knife, this technique too coming to him from his youth. His aim was sure.

The man clutched at his side, scraping ineffectively at the point buried in his loose-fitting suit. He half-turned, his bright-red blood flowing over the uniform. He threw the hissing can at the girl and stumbled off the stage, the knife clattering to the floor.

McKissic dived for the can and caught it in midair. Vapor washed over his face, choking him and filling his lungs. The mechanism was locked open and he could not concentrate enough to cut it off. He hurled the can, still spraying, into the cheering audience.

Pandemonium erupted.

McKissic ignored it and fumbled for the bloody knife still lying on the floor. He picked it up and kneeled to slide it under the band on Pamela's ankle, sawing crudely to free her. In such fashion might a knight of Arthur's table-round have rescued a chained damsel from distress.

"Get up!" he directed her, but she had swooned.

Alice woke to crazy lurching. Her foot was still numb from the punishment of the ring. It had stunned her when she saw McKissic kneel to cut it off with the bloody knife. Now, after the fact, she realized that he had severed not the ring but the chain that bound her.

A face of horror appeared: dark, with blood smeared over the mouth and dripping from the chin. It loomed, a gaping ghoul, then faded, and she saw another apparition: a large man with teeth bared in a snarl, carrying a headless woman with blood speckling her skin. More blood dripped to the floor.

It was a mirror. McKissic was carrying her, and it was the gore of the helmeted man she saw, and the blankness where the black hood covered her head. McKissic had come and saved her from . . . what had almost happened. He had driven back the man with the spray and perhaps killed him, and smashed the face of her captor and hurled devastation into the sabbat. Why?

How had he known that she was in danger, and why had he come to save her himself? She had always rather admired him—but he had several hundred employees scattered through the mechanized factories, most more important than she. Of course, she had helped him in that matter of the kidnapping—but he had repaid her by giving Jeff to her, in effect. He owed her nothing more—and if he thought he did, there was no point in indulging in personal physical heroics.

Yet here she was, being carried by her boss through the back rooms of some private pit of vice, after horrible adventures and bloodshed. And still she had no idea what had happened to Jeff.

McKissic saw that she had recovered, and set her down. She was amazed at his strength, but he seemed to be in a daze. He had been hit in the face by the spray—and had inhaled the stuff! It was due to take effect—but what would it do to him?

The knife was still in his hand; she had been lucky she hadn't been sliced by it as he carried her. She took it from his limp hand—and saw more blood running down his arm from a shallow cut.

There was renewed uproar behind. The sabbat crowd had finally reorganized. "Come *on*, Mr. McKissic!" she cried, realizing that he was no longer acting under his own initiative. Something had certainly happened to him.

Several men burst into the room, shouting angrily. Alice looked around, inhibited by the hood, saw a door and wrenched it open. An alley stood outside.

The cold air hit her with a shock as she drew McKissic outside, but pursuit stopped there. Apparently the men did not want to be seen outside wearing their devil-costumes. Or maybe someone had finally summoned the police. Alice didn't know, but didn't want to wait long enough to find out. "Mr. McKissic—where is your car?"

"Car?" The word as he repeated it had an alien flavor, but he led her down the alley toward the street. It was as though he were blindly following a directive that made no sense to him. But the car was there, the private G&G duo, parked directly in front of the building.

McKissic climbed into the chauffeur's compartment, awkwardly, as though unfamiliar with the vehicle. His hand fumbled over the panel. Alice didn't like the idea of him driving in this condition, but liked even less the prospect of recapture by the demons of the tavern. Her ring was prodding her into action. She ran around the car and climbed into the seat adjacent.

McKissic was still shifting about uncertainly. There was no sign of pursuit, but she was certain their head start was marginal. "Mr. McKissic—we have to get out of here!"

His hand reached into his clothing and came out with a key, but he did not seem to know what to do with it. Alice took it from him—and remembered that she still wore the hood.

The key was in the shape of the G&G symbol: not a perfect disk. She stretched her chin up so that the fabric of the hood was taut and sawed at it with the key. A point caught and the material tore. She jammed her fingers into the hole and ripped the hood apart.

She sighed relief as her head emerged. Then, quickly, she slapped the key against the magnetic panel so that the car could operate. McKissic did nothing.

Now men boiled out of the tavern, no longer costumed. "Mr. McKissic!" she cried, knowing that unless she could stimulate him into action immediately they were lost. "Go!"

The running men showed in the rear-vision screen. As though just becoming aware of the danger, McKissic started the drive motor and oriented the vehicle, which had been listing slightly. He gazed straight ahead.

The men drew up short, seeing their quarry escape. It would have been suicidal to attack a moving gyro. The car slid past them and on into traffic just as though nothing out of the ordinary were happening. The climactic moment had dissipated harmlessly.

Now that the car was moving, McKissic seemed to have no further difficulty. Had the hallucinogen worn off already?

"Pamela, there is something I have to mention to you," McKissic said. "I talked with Philip and—"

"Mr. McKissic—don't you know me?" But his eyes were fixed on the street.

"I wish I didn't," he said. Though he drove with confidence, she didn't like the way he maneuvered the car. She wondered how many years it had been since he had handled a duo himself. "But it is because I *do* know you, and love you, Pamela, that I am turning you over to—"

"Mr. McKissic! I'm *not* Pamela!"

He glanced at her as though irritated at the interruption. "Oh, hello, Miss—Lang, isn't it? Where did my daughter go?"

Alice tried to speak, but nothing came out at first. She coughed and tried again. "Mr. McKissic, I haven't seen your daughter since I talked to her on the phone yesterday—I mean today—to tell her about the—"

She remembered her original mission, so devastatingly interrupted, and became intense. "Mr. McKissic, do you know what happened to Jeff? Jeff Font? He was in an . . ." She tapered off, unable to finish. Too much had happened with too little explanation.

"Oh yes. Jeff." He considered the matter. He was speaking coherently but seemed to have difficulty formulating his thoughts. "Wasn't he in some kind of accident?"

"Yes, Mr. McKissic. He—"

The ramp to the skyway was blocked off, and Alice watched nervously as the car careened around the detour and back onto the ground-level street. This was dangerous driving. Where was his usual chauffeur?

"Are you in love with him, Miss Lang?"

"I—" This was getting worse! What was the matter with him? This was not a typical reaction to the drug, she was certain. He hadn't had that much.

He smiled knowingly. "Put it this way: were he subject

to your care for a suitable period, would you be inclined to marry him, with the expectation that the experience would be worthwhile in the long view?''

''Mr. McKissic, I don't understand!''

''In spite of the—the things he had done?''

''Mr. McKissic, are you all right?''

''Even if no inheritance went with him?''

She stared at him. ''Jeff?'' Then, irresolutely: ''Yes, Mr. McKissic.''

He smiled again. ''I will do this. I will settle three-quarters of the income from G&G general stock upon him for life, commencing from the date of his marriage. I will give you the formal first option on that—''

Alice shook his arm. ''Mr. McKissic! Please—are you all right?''

They were near the city park. He turned into it and stopped. ''Miss Lang, do not interrupt me. This is a matter of some concern and there is very little time.'' He paused, making sure she understood. ''Now where was I?''

Alice stopped trying to fight it. ''You were saying something about settling three-quarters of your income on Jeff Font. When he got married. Please, Mr. McKissic, I think you were—hurt. You should—''

But he was looking out the window. ''What are we doing here?''

''You just parked here, Mr. McKissic.''

''Oh—was I making love to you? I'm sorry, Miss Lang, I'm no longer in the mood. I'm afraid my daughter doesn't approve either. She saw me once, you know, and ever since she's been trying to compensate, not realizing—'' He broke off again. *''Where is Pamela?''*

''Mr. McKissic, I don't know. I was just asking you where Jeff was.''

He whirled on her, pain in his face. "Are they together? I cannot permit that. Where are they?"

"Mr. McKissic, please listen to me. I don't know where they are, but I don't think they're together. Your daughter was at home when I called this afternoon. Jeff's been in an accident. I think he's dead. You just rescued me from—from the tavern. I don't know how I got there or how you knew about it, but I'm deeply grateful. I think you were hurt in the fighting and I'd like to get you to a hospital, or at least your home where you can have the attention of a medic. Then I can look for Jeff. Please, I think we'd better go right away."

"Jeff dead?" he said. "But I thought he was with Pamela. I can't permit that. I can't—are you in love with him? I will do this. The second option will be determined by the G&G pesonnel board. I will drink life to the lees: all times have I enjoyed greatly, have suffered greatly, both with those that love me, and alone, on shore. I am part of all that I have met—"

"Mr. McKissic!"

"I am Ulysses," he said. "I follow knowledge like a sinking star, beyond the utmost bound of human thought."

"Mr. McKissic! Please, let me drive you to the hospital!"

He got out and stood beside the car, allowing her to move into the driver's seat. She was not familiar with the duocar controls, but knew she could handle the big vehicle in this emergency. There was no other choice.

McKissic remained outside. "This is my son, mine own Telemachus, to whom I leave the scepter and the isle—well-loved of me—"

"Please, Mr. McKissic!" She got out herself and tried to lead him around to the seat she had occupied. "Please get in. I don't know what you're saying."

He put his heavy arm around her. "You and I are old. Old age hath yet his honor and his toil."

Alice pulled at him, but he strode instead into the park, away from the lighted lot. "Come, my friends. 'Tis not too late to seek a newer world."

She tripped as she tried to follow him. The ring warned her against exposing herself to the danger she knew existed in the dark. McKissic marched on, looking for sea adventure.

In the bushes she saw sharklike faces appear. They were new faces, but their expressions were familiar. More muggers—violent youths like the ones who had attacked Jeff in this same park, not so very long ago.

There was the glint of a weapon. Cruel eyes followed McKissic's progress, eager hands came up, while Alice retreated to the car, unable to help or even to make him comprehend the danger.

VIII. Just and Unjust

1

JEFF climbed the wall of the McKissic estate a second
time—but now he was not alone, nor was he searching for
Pamela. It was dark and rather cold in the early morning
stillness, but company and confidence alleviated this.

Behind him came Flathead, that brainless animation of
flesh, loyal only to the knife, but *loyal*, who was to guard
the retreat.

After Flathead came the woman Annie. Jeff helped her
roll onto the flat top, inhaling her fragrance and marveling
again that this product of the slums was at once so clean
and so womanly. She was in fact a concubine, a common-
law wife of a brutal semi-alcoholic, and ignorant of the
so-called niceties of twenty-first century civilization—yet
she remained a gentle, understanding human being. She
too was loyal—to her man, Ed Bladderwart, for better or
worse, without complaint.

Seeing her, unpretty and unclever but capable within her
chosen areas—seeing her even for a few hours of an
eventful night, and knowing her—this had educated him.
He was aware of no decision, but now he knew what kind
of woman he wanted for his own.

Big Ed ascended last, puffing loudly. Barrel-bellied, crude in manner, slow in thought and perpetually unlucky in endeavor, he was still every pound a man. There was nothing devious about him, no self-centered froth. His yes was yes, his no, no, and that was all. So far as his context permitted, Big Ed was an honest man.

Jeff did not delude himself that human values were to be found exclusively in Gunnartown, or that genuine people predominated there or anywhere; but now he knew, beyond mere intellectual conjecture, that they did exist. Alice had told him as much, but all he had seen then was the cruelty: overt in the park, insidious at the middle class party, lawful for the rich and powerful. He had seen what he had been ready to see; now, with his enforced comprehension of the better side of lower class nature, he was ready to see other things. It was a circumstance that was worth the pain and trouble entailed in its achievement.

Jeff pointed the way and Ed nodded. This time they had come metallically armed, for the robotic scanners had been discommoded by what they hoped would be mistaken for a freak surge of power. Ed had taken care of that detail, having quite a practical knowledge of junkyard machines of all types.

Jeff dropped down and waited for Ed and Annie to lower themselves on the rope. He checked the bootleg vial of truthall sealed in a pocket, and the tiny 2V—voice and vision only—recorder strapped to his middle.

The plan was elemental, simplified to its essence by the Gunnartown minds which took no pleasure in superfluous artistry: break in, drug George McKissic, fire relevant questions at him, escape with the recording. Two witnesses, to keep watch and to testify later in court (not Judge Crater's!), in case McKissic still didn't elect to confess openly. The recording to be released by noon, barely eight hours away, to prevent effective legal maneuvering by huge G&G. There would be frantic maneuvering anyway, of course, to prevent the publication of the recording—but all that was needed was grounds for authoritative investigation, which would force McKissic under truthall again, legally, while Jeff himself disappeared and waited for vindication.

Inevitably the truth would appear: that Jeff's father had been cheated and maligned and sent to his death, an innocent man. That there had been no legal way to correct the original wrong, because the law had been corrupted too: the judge presently concerned was the puppet of the usurper. That the ring, far from promoting truth, had prevented effective protest.

Would it work this time? Jeff suppressed his uncertainties. Big Ed had confidence in it, and at times the crude, direct ways *were* the most effective. It was not a plan Jeff could have contemplated while he wore the ring— which might be its strength. This mainstay of the McKissic conspiracy had been unexpectedly nullified, and he was free to tear the lid off. He could, for a few hours only, do what needed to be done.

Afterwards—well, he would wear the ring again, if that was the way the decision went after complete evidence had been presented for a fair appraisal. He knew he was right— but *if* he was wrong, and they could *prove* that Geoffrey Font had been guilty as originally charged, Jeff would have to see it through and take the penalty. He was breaking the law this once, but never again; the law *was* good, if properly applied. He wanted it applied. He did not like playing the part of a criminal.

The ring—he was not certain it was the perfect answer to crime, but it *was* an answer. It had serious limitations—

yet now that he no longer wore it, he missed it, and not just because of the awkwardness of the bandaged hand.

Annie had given him a pep pill to tide him through the present excursion. Was that the reason his mind, if not his body, was vacillating during this cautious approach? Now the plan seemed incredibly clumsy and unethical.

An honest man should not be hampered by the ring. He should be able to wear it and hardly be aware of the difference. Only the criminal felt restricted—as Jeff had felt restricted. If he was ever to convince himself of his own integrity, he would have to conquer the ring by wearing it, not by avoiding it.

Yet that ring had allowed Dave Paxton to die. How could it represent a superior ethic?

They were crossing the somber garden. The great house was lighted, the beams of radiance refracted amidst the beams of glastic. Did they ever close it down for the evening, now, or was the owner expecting company?

It surprised him that a man like McKissic could display such artistic taste; everything about the estate, from the contours of the mansion to the placement of the minor shrubs, represented the touch of an esthetic sensitivity. Odd too, Jeff thought, that he should react so differently this time to a garden arrangement whose slant had struck him as entirely erotic, before. Had he misjudged McKissic?

Or did the wealthy criminal show his material beauty to offset the spiritual beauties he lacked?

Ed and Annie were beside him, silent outlines. Together they moved across the garden, watching for the caninedroids. Ed had a stunner tuned to their neural system; there would be no concern about attack.

The hounds did not appear. Ahead the large windows were translucent, letting out diffused light but admitting no inquisitive inspection of the interior. Jeff paused, uncertain how to proceed now that the crucial decision was at hand. McKissic should be asleep by this time in an interior room; he was known to be a man of orderly habits. Then why were all the downstairs illuminants going?

Ed looked at him, considered momentarily, and lunged at the ornate door.

Jeff leaped to stop him, but it was too late. The man had acted with rash haste, in a manner impossible to Jeff. That was another difference between them. If Jeff had opportunity to consider, he *had* to consider, and it took time.

Annie followed without hesitation, trusting in her man. They stood together in the doorway, outlined by the blast of light within. Neither moved or spoke.

Jeff shielded his eyes with one hand and peered between the frozen figures into the room. He knew something was wrong—but still could not bring himself either to join the two or to retreat.

The decision was made for him. "Come in, Geoffrey Font Junior, before I blast your accomplice in half!" a voice called stridently.

It was Judge Crater.

So much for the element of surprise. Ed had seen nothing wrong with the direct approach—and had charged into a trap. Hesitancy would have been better.

Jeff came to the door, almost relieved that it had come to nothing. Somehow he had begun losing enthusiasm for this venture from the moment of its inception.

The judge was seated with legs crossed, wearing an elegant black cloak, an enormous revolver resting upon his knee. It was an antique weapon, long since rendered obsolete by modern devices—and terrifying in much the way a medieval thumb-screw or choking-pear was. The old-time instruments were so unsubtle.

"Divest yourselves of your armament," the judge said.

"I was at one time a competent marksman with this particular field-piece. I have several bullets, and the range is close, but I can no longer guarantee to disable without killing, should I be required to fire. I would much prefer not to shoot at all. Will you give me your word to stay in place if I set this weapon aside?"

Ed looked at Jeff. "We could charge him—all three of us at once," he said.

"You will observe, Gunnartowner," Judge Crater said, "that Font is the one I have covered."

"Hey!" Ed said, catching on. "If he kills *you* nobody gets anything!"

Would Crater actually shoot? Jeff thought he would. Obviously the judge had not arranged this little confrontation and stayed up this late, alone, at another person's residence, merely for a bluff. It was strange that he was here at all, instead of the police; strange and significant. Why *advertise* his personal collusion with McKissic? Something extraordinary was afoot.

Or had they been afraid to call the police, who might demand to know *why?* Not only why protection was necessary, but why an unringed ringer should risk everything to get at the head of General Gyro? McKissic must really fear an inquiry of that nature, Jeff thought—and the judge knew why.

"All right," he said. "But you know you're taking the wrong side. You should be upholding justice, not hiding behind technicalities. All I intended was—"

"Was to make George McKissic confess to having framed Geoffrey Font. For three reasons, young man, your plan had no possibility of success." The judge set his revolver down upon the table beside him as the three visitors finished stripping themselves of stunners and other weapons.

Jeff felt the heaviness of defeat upon him. The judge

was so determined not to see! He must have been bought off so thoroughly that he no longer thought in terms of his oath of office. All was lost.

Not quite! Jeff still wore the recorder. The chance was slim, but if he could get away later, or even hide it somewhere, he might have his evidence.

"Why?" he asked, turning on the 2V as he sat down and facing the judge squarely so that the pickup was trained on him. If Crater spilled the story . . .

Ed and Annie also found seats, letting him carry it now. Subtlety was not Ed's way, but even he should have realized that their capture by this man could spell success.

Jeff had meant "Why are you doing this?" but the judge took it as a reply to his own statement. "First," Crater said, "because the medical robot in the accident squad detected your traces and determined that you had survived the crash. Since you were a ringer, I was notified. I arranged to locate you and monitor your conversation with Mr. Bladderwart."

None of the three found any suitable remark to make. Jeff knew that it was child's play to focus a directional pickup on a given building, and the special-frequency ones could penetrate the walls easily for picture and audio. A helihopper with damped rotor could have hovered silently above the yard in the night. . . .

Probably Flathead had already been picked up.

"Second, because George McKissic is in no conditon to confess anything at this time or in the future, as you will shortly see for yourself."

Jeff sat up, alarmed. If McKissic were taken out of the picture prematurely, this evidence might have no bearing. Could he have died prematurely? Leukemia? "What happened?"

The judge ignored the question. "Third—because George McKissic is in fact innocent of the charge."

"Sure," Jeff said tiredly, knowing that nothing he could say now would open a sealed mind. "That's why he never went near truthall."

The judge did not react. "I think it best that your compatriots be excluded from the information I am about to impart. If you will—"

"Oh no you don't! They're here as witnesses. I want them to hear it all."

Crater frowned. "This is a rather personal matter, Jeff. I am aware that your perspective is limited. Still it is unwise to—"

"*My* perspective limited!" Jeff was amazed. Just how much hypocrisy was he expected to stomach? "No. They stay. No private deals."

Annie smiled at him, and Ed grunted.

The judge sighed. "I fear you will regret this."

"I've regretted it for fourteen years. Since you aren't interested in the truth, I'm not interested in privacy. *I'm* not the one with anything to hide. I'll listen—that's all— and so will they. They have a share in this."

"We'd better go," Annie said, standing up suddenly. "We trust Mr. Flont."

"But not that bastard!" Ed exclaimed, gesturing at the judge. "He's the ringin' judge! The one who ringed BettySue—"

"Ed," Annie said, not loudly.

Bladderwart hesitated this time, surprised. There was a silence. "All right, Annie," he said at last, awkwardly. He got up and preceded her into the garden.

The judge watched them go. "I underestimated that woman," he murmured.

Jeff was also impressed. He had seen no evidence of such control on her part before. There was evidently more to Annie's relationship with Ed than acquiescence. But he refused to give the judge the satisfaction of agreement. "All right—what's the big secret?"

Crater rested his head against the back of his chair and closed his eyes. Jeff could see the folds of fat under his chin, unfolding. It would be easy, now, to overcome the man—but he had given his word and he valued it, ring or no ring. He waited.

"If Wordsworth the naturalist and Coleridge the supernaturalist were the principle figures of the English Romantic Period in literature," Judge Crater said, "so Alfred, Lord Tennyson and Robert Browning were the leading apostles of the more didactic Victorian Period which followed. Tennyson was born three years before Browning, and he died three years after him, but that is not to imply that he led a more tranquil life or accomplished less."

Crater stopped, but did not open his eyes or move. He seemed to have drifted off to sleep.

Jeff shook his head, perplexed. Was that the message? This astonishing lecture in English literature? So secret that no witnesses were allowed?

Was the judge simply stalling, for some reason known only to himself? That made no sense; Crater had captured the invading party and had no need to wait for help. Either he was losing his grip on reality, preferring some incredible practical joke—or there was special meaning in the words he spoke.

Crater had accused him of having a limited perspective. Probably that was a euphemism covering his attempted exposure of Crater's own laxity. A dishonest man's horizons were as wide as the world; he refused to limit himself by other people's rights.

Yet—the judge was not acting like a man with a guilty conscience. He could have shot them all. He could easily have gotten away with it, the way things were. Instead—

Jeff strained to remember. Wordsworth, Tennyson—he had encountered such names in the course of his education on Alpha IV. Dull poets, having little relevance to the world he had fought to survive in. He hardly recalled them, and retained nothing of their poetry. So Tennyson was born three years before Whatshisname; what could that have to do with current events?

A bizarre joke—or insanity? Had the judge really gone over the brink, mixing sense with nonsense?

Jeff studied the relaxed features. Would a paranoid sleep in the presence of his enemy? More likely he would remain suspicious and alert even in the company of friends. In any event, the assumption that the judge had lost his equilibrium was as negative as the belief that he had been bought off. Neither situation offered any prospect for justice. Jeff had to assume otherwise, or give up hope.

Crater had told him that McKissic was unable to confess, and was also not guilty of framing his partner. Crater had said that he had more personal information to give— then begun some kind of literary discourse. What possible motive could he have? Unless he was speaking metaphorically. . . .

Metaphor! That was the key, if any existed. To substitute one name or thing for another, in order to make a devious concept easier to understand. Or was that allegory? Suddenly Jeff wished he had paid more attention to the gentler aspects of his training. But he could still work it out. Tennyson might stand for someone else, likewise the other man. Tennyson was older—that was a clue. But who was he? What about the reference to "natural" and "supernatural"?

He didn't know enough—but he had the feeling he was on the right track. "Go on," he said.

Crater resumed as though there had been no extended

pause. Judges were never as sleepy as they appeared!
"Browning was born to wealth and was basically happy in
childhood. After some false starts, he found his niche in
poetry: the dramatic monologue. He portrayed novel characters, both good and bad, *as they were,* without attempting to moralize. The poet suspended judgment and in
effect allowed the characters to judge themselves. I have
always admired this principle, and sought whenever possible to apply it."

So Judge Crater identified himself with Browning. He
thought the ring allowed the criminal to judge himself. No
doubt it was a comforting notion. And truthall certainly
showed people as they were, convicted by their own
unstoppered mouths. But what was the point to such a
parallel, valid or invalid?

"I don't suppose you are familiar with *Fra Lippo Lippi*
. . . ?" Crater inquired, opening his eyes and glancing at
Jeff momentarily. His expression was disturbingly keen.
" 'I drew men's faces on my copy-books . . .' "

"No. I don't know any poetry." Except, he remembered, for stray bits that came to him at odd moments.

"You will have to follow me very closely, then." The
judge reclined and closed his eyes again. "Tennyson, on
the other hand, was subject to melancholia. Though not
born to poverty, he suffered from pecuniary insufficiency
for a number of years, and his social life was problemati-
cal. He was lonely and depressed, and even as a child he
sometimes felt the desire for death. He lost his money by
investing in an insecure enterprise—"

"My father!" Jeff exclaimed, catching the parallel.

"Please do not leap to conclusions," Crater said sternly.
"Tennyson had a close and very talented friend, Arthur
Henry Hallam, the 'A.H.H.' of some of his most impor-

tant expressions. He had great faith in Hallam, who seemed destined for greatness. . . ."

As Geoffrey Font had had great faith in George Mc-Kissic, Jeff thought bitterly. And now the judge was trying in some devious fashion to justify what had happened between them. No amount of metaphoric veiling could make right that misplaced trust, however.

"And Hallam's early and tragic death shocked him terribly. For many years his poetry was colored by this—"

"What?"

"I said Hallam's death affected Tennyson's entire framework, and was perhaps the most profound influence upon his later work," Crater said. "Tennyson was to become Poet Laureate of England in 1850, yet—"

"Hallam died?"

Judge Crater frowned at him. "You are not an attentive listener, young man. If—"

"Don't move, Judge!" Ed cried from the doorway. "I got you covered."

Jeff whirled in the chair. Big Ed was standing with a projectile weapon in his hand, one almost as venerable as the judge's own. He must have gone all the way back to the car to fetch it, Jeff thought, or sent Annie on that mission. *Was* the area patrolled?

"Put it away, Ed. I gave my word."

"Yeah," Ed agreed respectfully. "You were real smart. Annie caught on before I did. You stayed to talk so we could get out and get a gun. And now we got the ringin' judge in our sights, as well as your McKissic. This's going to be great!"

A double-feature, Jeff thought, rebelling against the memory this brought up. "You don't understand. I gave my word for *all* of us. That was implied."

"But you ain't a ringer anymore," Ed pointed out.

"And he's going to break up the whole plan, and ring you again, and us too, likely. Everything'll be twice as bad as it was!"

He was right. Jeff *was* free of the ring. Because he had deliberately failed to turn himself in immediately, he had made himself subject to a far stiffer penalty. He would never get another chance; only a freak combination of circumstances and willpower had allowed him to get this far. He could not afford to let one scruple about an agreement made under duress interfere with the plan.

"Put it away," he said, surprising himself.

Ed's face clouded in sudden suspicion. "You make a deal with him while we were—?"

Annie spoke behind him. "No, Ed!"

But Bladderwart's formidable temper had taken control. The pistol swung in a quarter-circle toward Jeff.

Jeff was out of the chair and hurtling in Ed's direction before he knew what he was doing, but he was too slow. The pep pill was letting down at last, slowing his reactions. The muzzle centered on his body in the moment it took him to cover the distance separating them.

Another shape came between them before Ed could fire. It was Annie, flinging herself against Ed's arm.

There was no time to stop. Jeff crashed into the pair of them, hard, and all three tumbled to the floor. Jeff rolled away and flipped to his feet, watching the gun, but Ed did not try to lift it.

"Ed!" Annie cried.

Then Jeff saw it: Ed's arm, the focal point of the action, had been caught under the descending weight of all three bodies. A dark stain appeared on his long sleeve. The arm was broken.

Annie gripped the cheap cloth with both hands and tore the sleeve open.

It was not a pretty sight, but Jeff had dealt with such things commonly on Alpha. "That's a compound fracture," he said. "I could set it, but it's better to leave it alone until we can get help."

Ed grinned painfully. "I couldn't shoot," he said. "I had time, but—I'm getting as bad as a ringer. Soft. And I'm glad—" He winced as Annie tightened the tourniquet she had fashioned from the torn shirt sleeve and the barrel of Ed's pistol. "Because I would've hit my wife." He looked at his arm. "It don't hurt, you know?" he said, and fainted.

Jeff looked around to find Judge Crater still seated, judicially immobile. "A medic is on the way," the judge said.

Several minutes later the medical robot appeared. It picked up Ed's arm, sprayed anesthetic over it, washed away the dirt and blood, clamped off the torn flesh, set the bone, inserted an interior bonite splint, filled in with pseudoflesh, applied an expert external bandage and sprayed on a slim, firm cast. "To whom should this service be charged?" it inquired, funneling antishock plasma into Ed's other arm while it incinerated the sodden shirt-fragments in its abdominal burner.

Ed recovered and stared uncomprehendingly at his arm, while the med fastened next on Jeff's hand, slicing away that bandage.

"To the McKissic estate," the judge replied. "Both services." The machine operated so quickly that this qualification was necessary.

"Who was responsible for these injuries?" it demanded as it assembled bone-segments and shaped them to match Jeff's opposite finger.

"Accidents, both. There will be no police report," the judge said.

"This patient has worn a ring recently."

"I am cognizant. Just do your job and be on your way."

The medic fitted the new finger to Jeff's stump, closed the joints, vulcanized the connecting tendons and sealed the whole thing together, its multiple surgical tools resembling the legs of a great spider. It applied a small individual cast and closed up shop. "Thank you, Judge Crater," it said, and rolled away.

Jeff looked at the new finger, bemused. Under the stiff transparent covering, it looked natural and healthy. He squeezed the cast and saw the skin beneath whiten. The sensation of pressure was normal.

"Mrs. Bladderwart, if you will take your husband into the garden," the judge said dryly, "Mr. Font and I will finish our discussion."

"We aren't really married," she protested. "That's just—"

"In a few minutes a JP clerical robot will join you. Provide it with the necessary information and it will issue the certificate. Fee and waiting period have been waived."

"Yes, Your Honor," she said, cowed. She guided Ed out.

Judge Crater returned to Jeff. "I am glad to see that you are now independent of the ring," he said, and Jeff knew he meant emotionally, not physically. "Yes, of course Hallam died. Tennyson outlived him by more than fifty years. Perhaps he blamed himself for his friend's demise, though in fact he had no part at all in that."

Jeff contemplated Crater with new respect. This was hardly the pompous, wide-bottomed, narrow-minded snob he had imagined. The judge had known he would keep his word—or had been unafraid to take the risk. And the legal mind had returned unwaveringly to the topic, as though the interruption had been no more than a point of order.

Something else came clear. "Tennyson is not my father! Hallam—"

"I asked you not to jump to conclusions," the judge reproved him again. "But perhaps the analogy has served its purpose. Are you ready to accept the truth now?"

"Yes," Jeff said, and realized that until this hour his own mind had been as firmly closed as he had thought the judge's was.

"George McKissic founded G&G in partnership with Geoffrey Font some thirty years ago. Font had the original patent, while McKissic had the business acumen. Both were expert mechanics with ambitious ideas, but neither had any money to speak of. I happened to be the bright young lawyer who arranged the initial loan. The two men designed, constructed and tested the first commercially feasible gyroscopic unicar, and I saw to it that it was thoroughly protected by patent law. I also was vigilant in prosecuting infringements, otherwise the property would have been lost in much the way Elias Howe's sewing machine was lost to Isaac Singer.

"It was an immediate success. The internal-combustion motor had been outlawed for automotive use because of its pollutive properties, but the electric motor had not captivated the public taste and steam still frightened a sizable segment, though its unfortunate reputation was unwarranted. Our society was ready for a complete change, and the gyromobile provided it. It was demonstrably more efficient than the four-wheeled electrics and a lot more pleasant to drive.

"Instead of paying off the first loan, I arranged for an additional one ten times as large. In five years the company was on secure financial footing, and was, through certain legal stipulations too complex to go into now, a virtual monopoly. It was well on its way to becoming the foremost power in the automotive industry. The controlling interest that the original partners held was already worth a phenomenal fortune.

"When my opportunity came for service on the bench, I divested myself of G&G holdings and options which were also quite valuable, to avoid conflict-of-interest, but I remained close to both partners. Font elected to minimize the risk and stand pat, but McKissic mortgaged some of his holdings in order to purchase mine outright. Neither Font nor I had properly appreciated the potential of G&G; we had somehow thought that its then total assets of something less than a hundred million dollars—dollars were worth more in those days, of course—represented a peak or plateau. Only McKissic knew; or perhaps he gambled and won. At any rate, he wound up, by perfectly legitimate means, with controlling interest in the fastest-growing industrial company in the world. Had Font listened to him, he would have had an equal share; McKissic was always open about his own plans.

"Then Geoffrey Font married. Unfortunately, he did not marry wisely. His—"

"What?"

Crater looked at him inscrutably. "Do you want the truth, Jeff?"

Jeff sat down again, silenced.

"His wife Ronda was a beautiful, talented and very intelligent woman—but a gold-digger. That is, in case you're not familiar with outdated idiom, she married him only to gain wealth and power. Within a year she had dazzled him into giving her personal control over his holdings, and she managed them very well. But she quickly discovered that these now represented a minority share of the company. Ronda wanted more than that, and she set out to get it. McKissic was the obvious target.

"George, however, was fully alert to the danger. He knew that his partner, Font, was no longer master in his own home, and that any concessions made to him would only lead to control of the company by Ronda. This would be disastrous, for she had little interest in the welfare of either investors or employees. She wanted power for power's sake, like some emperor of old, but she did not use it graciously. Just as Font had been helpless before her intellect, McKissic was victimized by the weapon she brought to bear against him: her sex-appeal. He had always had a severe weakness for women, and she was more than ordinarily attractive and knowledgeable and . . . determined.

"He married, less from love than to protect himself from Ronda. He knew how deeply Font loved her, and sincerely wanted to avoid trouble of this nature. It was an almost useless gesture. His own wife was foolishly temperamental and Ronda irresistible. Without the knowledge of either spouse, they had a torrid affair enduring for several years. But George held on to one thing: he refused to part with any of his control over G&G, no matter what blandishments she offered. When she roused him and then withheld her favors, he had an affair with a Vicinc-certified secretary. It was Ronda, not McKissic's wife, who later maneuvered to have that girl fired.

"Ronda tried every inducement she could think of—and she was imaginative—including a particularly insidious form of blackmail, but he would not give in. Finally she attempted to steal a controlling interest by a complex semilegal and unethical device, believing that George would be unable to bring himself to expose it because of the damage such exposure would do to the company and the partnership. But he consulted with me, in his desperation, and we decided to call her bluff."

Crater paused, checking to see how Jeff was taking it. Jeff was sitting rigidly, listening to the words but holding his emotions at arm's length. The judge's story was contrary to everything he had believed in since childhood—but now he remembered his mother's indomitable will, and her frequent absences from their home on Earth. He had not come to know her well until the exile—and then he had thought it was the unfairness of the sentence and the savagery of the life on Alpha IV that made her so bitter and harsh. Crater was telling him that Ronda Font had always been that way—and he had to believe it, now. There were too many trifling hints, reactions and allusions, that the judge could have had no knowledge of, that confirmed the story.

"She had done it all in her husband's name," Crater continued. "He was the nominal partner, not she, and Font had long since ceased to concern himself with what she did with the legal and business aspects. He labored over improved gyro design and its applications to other fields. Believe me, that is a complex matter."

"I know," Jeff said. He remembered the early visits to the shop. At the age of six he had understood the basic theories of precession and the nuances of gyro design. His father spoke only of gyros, and models and fragments littered the laboratory. It had been a fascinating place. He remembered McKissic, too, from those days, bigger than Font and more hearty: "But is it commercially feasible, Geoff?" with reference to a particular process. And McKissic once had turned to him, Jeff, and given him a capsule lesson in economics. He had liked the big man, then.

By the time Jeff was eight he had visited the McKissic mansion many times, and not just to play closet games with little Pammie. McKissic had taught him that a good idea was valueless unless properly exploited and marketed, and that great industrial power brought concurrent responsibilities. Jeff had listened and learned, knowing that two-fifths of the business would eventually be his—and more, if he grew up to marry Pamela, though that was never mentioned.

Until his dreams crashed down with those of his father, and hardship and visions of revenge replaced pleasure and trust.

"And so it was Geoffrey Font who paid the penalty for his wife's intrigue," Crater finished. "McKissic knew Font was innocent—but also that he dearly loved his wife and family. It was better to let him be framed by circumstance, than to destroy the rest of his world. Ronda had been sure McKissic would retreat from these alternatives, but he did not. She was left to confess her own guilt—or to join her husband in exile. If she renounced Font, of course, then McKissic would be free to tell the truth, since Font could not be hurt more. She played her final card—"

"That's why she threw acid at McKissic?" Jeff asked, realizing that the question implied his own acceptance of what the judge had been telling him. More things were clicking into place.

Crater stood up. "Not exactly," he said. "But I think you'd better learn the rest from another source. The truth will not be easy for you, Jeff."

"You mean there's more? Worse than this?"

The judge nodded gravely. "Turn off your recorder and come into the next room," he said.

2

He stood before the window and watched the dawn diffuse. "A soft air fans the cloud apart," he said. "There comes a glimpse of that dark world where I was born."

"Please, Mr. McKissic—you've been up all night," the girl said. "You must try to rest."

The glow increased. He saw the great stallions on the horizon, snorting wisps of fire and casting off diamonds from their flashing hooves. Magnificent animals, coruscatingly harnessed, drawing the golden chariot of the sun. "And shake the darkness from their loosened manes, and beat the twilight into flakes of fire. Lo! ever thus thou growest beautiful in silence. . . ."

She drew on his arm, now sealed and mending, and he turned compliantly to face her. She was the one he had rescued from the evil castle and borne horseback to safety, thinking her Guinevere, though she was not. Guinevere was another man's wife, and that was over. This girl was young—but prisoned again within walls, isolated, pretty enough but unappreciated, though she had cleaned herself and taken new apparel. He felt sorry for her. "But who hath seen her wave her hand? Or at the casement seen her stand? Or is she known in all the land, the Lady of Shalott?"

He sat down, courteously avoiding the sight of her still somewhat common garb, but noticing the band about her great toe. Yes—this was in some way the token of her bondage. The magic ring, which laid a peculiar curse upon her. "There she weaves by night and day a magic web with colors gay. She has heard a whisper say, a curse is on her if she stay to look down on Camelot."

The Lady of Shalott plopped indelicately into a chair. "Oh, I'm tired," she said. "The judge said—but if only I knew for sure what happened to Jeff."

He smiled at her sympathetically. "She only said, 'My

life is dreary, he cometh not,' she said; she said 'I am
aweary, aweary, I would that I were dead!' ''

She laughed nervously. ''Are you making that up, Mr.
McKissic? I don't know whether to take you seriously or
not. Why can't you talk to me directly?''

Strange that she could not comprehend the language of
the master! ''The air is damp, and hushed, and close, as a
sick man's room when he taketh repose an hour before
death,'' he told her, feeling the room become a closing
coffin buried in a forest cemetery. ''My very heart faints
and my whole soul grieves at the moist rich smell of the
rotting leaves, and the breath of the fading edges of box
beneath, and the year's last rose.''

''I'm sorry,'' she said. ''You couldn't be inventing *that*.
I guess you're as worried as I am, in your way.''

At last she was beginning to understand! ''O me, why
have they not buried me deep enough? Is it kind to have
made me a grave so rough—me, that was never a quiet
sleeper? Maybe still I am but half dead; then I cannot be
wholly dumb. . . .''

The door opened. ''Jeff!'' the Lady cried, tripping across
the room to fling herself into the visitor's arms. ''You're
safe!''

He looked at the young man. Dressed in glowing armor
overlaid with a handsome tunic—''My good blade carves
the casques of men, my tough lance thrusteth sure, my
strength is as the strength of ten, because my heart is
pure.''

''You understand, every word he says is a direct quotation from Tennyson,'' the robed sage—Merlin—remarked.
''Identities are taken pretty much from *Idylls of the King*,
to the extent they fit, and individual quotes from almost
anything. But he's perfectly rational within that framework. That was the opening stanza to *Sir Galahad*, for

example. Galahad was the bastard son of Sir Lancelot, in King Arthur's court—but still a better man than his famous father. Do you understand?''

The young knight lifted his visor and looked at him. ''No, I don't. I know you drew an analogy to Tennyson, but—''

He approached and put his hands on Galahad's shoulders. The sun was ascending behind the young knight, illuminating his helmet with radiating beams. ''So pass I hostel, hall and grange; by bridge and ford, by park and pale, all-armed I ride, whate'er betide, until I find the holy Grail.''

''He is speaking for you,'' Merlin explained. ''You are Galahad, the only knight with the purity of power to fetch the Grail. This is the very highest Christian honor.''

''I don't even know what the Grail *is*,'' Galahad replied querulously. His right hand appeared to be stiff, as though injured in jousting.

''It was the cup in which the blood of Christ was caught, as it dripped from the cross where He was crucified,'' Merlin said. ''At least, that's the variation of the legend used for the Malory/Tennyson interpretations. There's more to it than that, of course—but the point is that only a knight completely pure in spirit could behold it. Even for Galahad, the search was not an easy one. Consider it the symbol of one final success, despite adversity; it is within your grasp, if you only persevere.''

''Is this—is this why you said he couldn't confess anything now, even if he—is this why you made me analyze the metaphor myself? So I'd know how to—?''

The Lady drew them both to divans. ''It was a miracle he survived at all. After he—'' She hesitated delicately. ''Well, I tried to get him to the hospital, but he said something about seeking a newer world—''

He jumped up. "To strive, to seek, to find, and not to yield!"

"That would be from Tennyson's *Ulysses*, one of his favorites," Merlin said. "The aging adventurer leaves his throne to his son Telemachus and goes back to the sea—or at least to some exciting world of his own. The old life had become too burdensome."

"But there were boys in the park, just like the ones that attacked us before," the Lady said. "They seem to appear faster than they can be ringed. And Mr. McKissic just walked on, as though he didn't see them, and they followed him. I couldn't do anything. The ring . . . and the car didn't have a police alarm. All I could do was watch. I couldn't even use the car to run them down. Those three had knives and things, and he had nothing, not even his reason—"

He smiled reminiscently. "Theirs not to make reply, theirs not to reason why, theirs but to do and die," he said.

"That's *The Charge of the Light Brigade*," Merlin explained. His magical arts revealed all things. "Through a confusion in orders, the English Light Calvary was thrown into the midst of the entire Russian army in 1854, during the Crimean War. They were outnumbered twenty to one, yet—"

He saw the Russian emplacements emerge from the smoke of the belching cannon, but now his men were too close for the enemy artillery to bear effectively. The black and gold defenders gaped beside their guns, hardly crediting what they saw, but already others were kneeling to fire their long rifles. Half his men had already fallen, but he could see the red breeches of the riders beside him, and the flash of their sabers as they sliced at the black plumes.

"Stormed at with shot and shell, boldly they rode and well, into the jaws of death, into the mouth of hell—"

"He's living it," the Lady said, wrinkling her nose at the burning stink of powder. "But he beat them. He didn't have a weapon, so he picked one of those boys up by the feet and swung him at the others—"

"He is still a powerful man," Merlin agreed. "Even allowing for hysterical strength."

"But he didn't kill them," she said. "One was unconscious and the other two dazed . . . and he just turned around and walked back to the car, and I drove him here. He didn't even seem angry. He had slashes all over—"

"Cast the poison from your bosom, oust the madness from your brain. Let the trampled serpent show you that you have not lived in vain," he told her gently.

"Yes, Mr. McKissic," she said, looking dubious.

"You see," Merlin said, "you *can* talk with him, but it has to be on his terms. I don't place that particular quotation, but you can be sure it is from Tennyson. George has gone to a more harmonious world, and if you had as comprehensive a familiarity with the poet as he does, you'd understand him very well. As it is, you'll miss much of the subtler purpose, but you can still pick up the superficial content, just as you would from a quick reading of the poet."

"But why can't he just—*talk* to us?" the Lady demanded.

"Because aphasia doesn't work that way. This isn't classical aphasia, of course; it's a schizoid variant that we see quite a bit of these days."

"Insanity?" Galahad inquired cautiously.

"Not exactly. My layman's understanding probably glosses over the fine points, but as I see it, this is part of the price we pay for what our society is. As the world has become more crowded and more pressured, the incidence of mental illness has steadily increased, in spite of the remarkable advances in medicine. We still don't know enough of the mechanisms of the brain. We don't have raving lunatics any more, but we do have an enormous amount of—compromise with sanity. I'd say that fifty percent of our population is technically incompetent at the time of termination.''

''Half die crazy? Just because it's *crowded?*''

Merlin looked at Galahad wisely. ''Haven't you seen the mouse demonstration? I thought that was standard even at offworld schools.'' The young knight shook his head negatively.

''Take a few pairs of mice, any breed. Put them in a controlled-environment cage with automatic feeders. Leave them alone. Do you know what happens?''

''They should do very well. A protected situation, no hunger or thirst—''

''They do. They multiply quite rapidly, as a matter of fact. Their population rises exponentially. The only thing that is limited is the size of the cage.''

Comprehension came. ''When they run out of room—''

''Fighting, turmoil, personality withdrawal, insanity. Babies trampled under foot. Some adults simply stop eating and die. Most animate creatures need territory as well as food and security. Take that away and they just can't function properly.''

''But *our* population is stable!''

''Stable at a pretty uncomfortable level. But it's more than that. Life is more complicated than ever before. The average person tries, but he just can't maintain the modern pace indefinitely. He loses ground, he can't cope, he turns to escapism, to drugs. And *that* pyramids, as you know. In George's case, the addictions of his parents and grandparents—''

"Flathead!"

"I beg your pardon?"

"Someone I—know. Recessive genetic damage—"

Merlin nodded. "Yes. That was why an operation couldn't do George much good. His mental infirmity was inherent; every cell of his nervous system was affected. It took some time for it to develop, and it probably won't show up in his offspring at all, but—"

The chamber door burst open and a flashing, angry young woman strode across the flagstones.

"On the other hand . . ." Merlin added grimly.

The woman ignored the others. "Daddykins, you have to fire the chauffeur! He tried to—"

He cast a reproving glance at her. "I have play'd with her when a child; she remembers it now we meet. Ah well, well, well, I may be beguiled by some coquettish deceit. Yet if she were not a cheat, if Maud were all that she seem'd, and her smile had all that I dream'd, then the world were not so bitter but a smile could make it sweet."

Maud stopped short. "What?"

"Pamela," said Merlin, "you are interrupting important business. Please wait in the other room until we are ready for you."

She turned on him in regal fury. "Who do you think you are, Crater? I'm not one of your court-ringers!" She paced about briskly. "Don't quote your stupid Tennyson at *me*, Daddykins! I tell you Philip came charging into my bedroom just now with some fantastic story about nuptial options and tried to make me—"

"Good for Philip!" the sage Merlin exclaimed, surprisingly.

"You mean you were home all the time?" the Lady demanded, as close to anger as her curse allowed. "Your father thought you were—"

"Certainly I was home. I went out for a while last night, but I . . . changed my mind and came back. What business is it of yours, ringer?" Then, as though abruptly seeing through the fog of her own indignation, she stared at Galahad. "What are *you* doing here? She said you were dead!"

He sighed, intercepting the young knight's bafflement. "Shall it not be scorn to me to harp on such a moldered string? I am shamed through all my nature to have loved so slight a thing."

Maud stamped her foot. "I want him fired. That chauffeur. I want him ringed. *Nobody* can come in like that and demand—"

"Weakness to be wroth with weakness! Woman's pleasure, woman's pain—Nature made them blinder motions bounded in a shallower brain."

Maud opened her mouth, but was cut off by another voice. "Exactly my sentiments, sir," Tristram said. And could this bold knight convert the faithless Maud into a loving Iseult, or was he doomed to fail again? "If you have no objections, I will convey her to the garage and finish at leisure the lesson I started." Tristram bounded across the room and caught the woman's arm.

If not yet Iseult, perhaps at least she was Amy. She had never fit a proper category. She stood, too surprised to resist. "You mean Daddy *knows?* Even this?"

"He arranged it. Now come and show me what you can do."

"Isn't the garage an unusual place to—?" Merlin inquired.

Tristram smiled confidently. "We could do it outside, but that would mean turning on the floodlights for proper visibility. As it is, all the paraphernalia is convenient.

"The—paraphernalia?" Everyone was listening now.

"The detergent, sponges, water-hose, wax—"

"He's making me polish the car!" Amy exclaimed indignantly. *"Me!* By *hand!"*

Galahad's cheeks puffed out with contained laughter. Even Merlin smiled.

Tristram turned to her. "You are going to marry me, little girl—but only when I'm satisfied. I would not have a woman who could not beautify a car."

Still she stood, staring at him for a long moment. "You really want to—to *marry* me?"

Tristram let her go without speaking again and walked to the door. After another pause, she yielded and followed him.

"On her pallid cheek and forehead came a color and a light," he said, accurately. "As I have seen the rosy red flushing in the northern night. And she turned—her bosom shaken with a sudden storm of sighs—all the spirit deeply dawning in the dark of hazel eyes—saying 'I have hid my feelings, fearing they should do me wrong'; saying 'Dost thou love me, cousin?' weeping 'I have loved thee long.' Love took up the glass of time, and turned it in his glowing hands; every moment, lightly shaken, ran itself in golden sands."

The door closed behind them. "Which summarizes *that* situation very nicely," Merlin said. "Remarkable memory—I think that's from *Locksley Hall*. Most people remember only one line from that piece: 'In the spring a young man's fancy lightly turns to thoughts of love,' or perhaps that vision-into-the-future excerpt. As I was saying, communication *is* possible—but obviously George can't run General Gyro by quoting Tennyson. He is now permanently confined to his poetic realm, and we should be thankful he was able to retain this one avenue to our own world. There's no telling what might have happened after he took that shot of drug-mist, if he hadn't had this niche to fall into; he was on the verge of breakdown anyway, and that hallucinogen toppled him over. Fortunately, he *did* have this syndrome arranged, and he had already made provision for his children and his business. George planned ahead, anticipating his present incapacity. Not many men are that realistic.''

"His *children?*" Galahad inquired.

"To his daughter goes one-quarter of the income from the business, but no control—provided she marries properly," Merlin said. "I rather think she will, now. To his son—three-quarters of the income, and, after a suitable interval, the controlling stock. This, too, is predicated upon a suitable marriage.''

"But he *has* no—"

The Lady suddenly came alive. "Three-quarters of the—Jeff! He means you!"

"Me!" Galahad faced the window. "He's giving *back* my father's share?''

"You don't want to admit it, the knowledge of that final weapon," Merlin said quietly. "The thing that Ronda Font thought would break George McKissic. She sent him copies of the test reports and showed him the boy, establishing paternity beyond question. That was the reason he could never submit to truthall—not while his partner lived, and not in a public hearing. That's why he paid anonymously for your education, and made it possible for you to return to Earth. That was why he had to act to keep you away from Pamela—"

"The son of Lancelot. . . ." the Lady said. "You *are* a lot like him, Jeff. I never realized that before, consciously.''"

"But I—" Galahad hesitated, looking from one face to another. "How could—I can't believe it.''

"Even there, you show your heritage," Merlin observed. "You are a man of decision and power, a leader, a conqueror—but when you have to make a really important moral decision, you become stranded. George could never bring himself to do what was necessary about Ronda, and so he let her keep his child—*their* child—and raise him under a false name. He allowed her to maintain her pretenses and to cuckold her lawful husband for the better portion of a decade. And even when she forced a confrontation in court, George was unable to hurt his partner more, by simply telling the truth. Even the Font exile did not solve the problem; George continued to torment himself with it, to drive himself inexorably to—this.''

"I've seen it in you too, Jeff," the Lady said. "You fought the savages in the park in spite of the ring, but you couldn't make up your mind about Pamela or—"

"I made up my mind," Galahad said. "And it hasn't changed. I'm going to put on the ring again."

"Jeff, the reasons for your trial were as much a matter of expediency as of legality," Merlin said. "As you suspected. We could not trust you immediately, because you had been raised on another planet and conditioned to hate your true father. Had the Fonts not died, you might never have been free to return to Earth . . . in time. Fate undid some of the damage Ronda did—yet it was essential that you be introduced to the inner mechanisms of the business rapidly. That's why we made it possible, even easy, for you to break the law, so that there was a suitable pretext to examine you and ring you. But now you know the truth, and you have demonstrated to me that you don't need the ring. You have a business to master; you are not a criminal.''

Galahad faced the old sage, and never had there been such radiance about him. "I *know* I'm not a criminal, Judge. But I *did* break the law. You can arrange a pardon if you want, but I'm going to wear the ring. Only not the usual kind. The problem with what you use now is that

Ultra Conscience is not a realistic morality. It enforces set standards even when common-sense proves them ridiculous, such as forbidding fighting to protect the life of another person. It isn't moral to accept *all* ridicule and attack; sometimes the other party *is* at fault and won't listen to reason. Those thugs in the park . . . The ring makes a man a pacifist when the world is a battlefield. While it may be best to *try* the gentle approach, a man must be free to change when it is obviously leading to disaster. Ultra Conscience has to be modified to allow for this; to yield to reality.''

"You may have a point there, Jeff," Merlin said. "But it can hardly be that simple. There'd have to be considerable research, development, testing—"

"I'll be the first subject. Just modify Ultra Conscience to say 'We don't want to fight, but by God if we do—' "

"You sound like a real knight in armor!" the Lady said.

"My armor will be the ring," Galahad told her. "A ring that knows when to restrain *itself* as well as the wearer. An impractical morality never did anyone much—"

"There will be time, Jeff," Merlin said. "Perhaps you *do* have the nucleus of a good idea here, but it can wait until a few immediate matters are cleared up. Your Gunnartown friends, for example, are still in the garden. There's been a little ceremony there—"

"That's right! I'll have to arrange for a G&G dealership for Ed. He can't take his bride to the slum."

"You mean I'm missing a wedding?" the Lady cried in anguish, true to the nature of the sex.

"That's another reason I need a ring," Galahad said. "This creature insists on a ringer husband, and—"

"Oh, Jeff!" the Lady exclaimed.

"And finally there is your father," Merlin said. "Are you able to accept him now?"

Galahad looked down thoughtfully, then approached. "I thought you were my enemy," he said. "There was a time when I thought about killing you. If you can forgive me that—"

He smiled and put his hands upon the young knight's shoulders again. "Have we grown at last beyond the passions of the primal clan? 'Kill your enemy, for you hate him,' still, 'your enemy' was a man."

"He was a man," Galahad agreed.